A Watch-Dog Of The North Sea
A Naval Story Of The Great War

By

PERCY F. WESTERMAN

A watch-dog of the north sea
A Naval Story of the Great War
by Percy F. Westerman

Copyright © 2024

All Rights reserved.

No part of this publication may be reproduced, stored in a retrieval system, or transmitted in any form or by any means, electronic, mechanical, photocopying or Otherwise, without the written permission of the publisher.
The author/editor asserts the moral right to be identified as the author/editor of this work.

ISBN: 978-93-63056-66-4

Published by

DOUBLE 9 BOOKS

2/13-B, Ansari Road
Daryaganj, New Delhi – 110002
info@double9books.com
www.double9books.com
Tel. 011-40042856

This book is under public domain

ABOUT THE AUTHOR

English author Percy Francis Westerman wrote a lot of children's books. He was born in 1876 and died on February 22, 1959. A lot of his books are action stories with military or naval themes. He was born in Portsmouth, England, in 1876 and went to Portsmouth Grammar School. When he was twenty, he got a job as a clerk at Portsmouth Dockyard. It was in 1900 that he married Florence Wager of Portsmouth. They loved sailing so much that they spent some of their vacation sailing in the Solent. John F.C. Westerman, their son who was born in 1901, also wrote boys' adventure books. He had to leave his houseboat for dry land because of a fall when he was 70 years old, but he kept writing quickly. He died at the age of 82, and his last book, Mistaken Identity, came out in 1959 after he had died. He is said to have started writing after he and his wife bet sixpence that he could write a better story than the one he was reading to their sick son at the time. He wrote his first book for boys called A Lad of Grit, which came out in 1908 with Blackie and Son Limited.

CONTENTS

CHAPTER I
H.M.S. "POMPEY" 9

CHAPTER II
THE RESULT OF THE LEADING STOKER'S CURIOSITY 15

CHAPTER III
GREENWOOD SENIOR'S DISCOVERY 21

CHAPTER IV
THE SECRET PETROL-DEPÔT 28

CHAPTER V
EXPLANATIONS 34

CHAPTER VI
AN EXCELLENT NIGHT'S WORK 39

CHAPTER VII
THE DAY FOLLOWING 47

CHAPTER VIII
SPY AND SUPER-SPY 55

CHAPTER IX
AN ADVENTURE ON THE HILLS 61

CHAPTER X
THE FOILED RAID 68

CHAPTER XI
ONE ZEPPELIN THE LESS 75

CHAPTER XII
AN OCEAN DUEL 82

CHAPTER XIII
ADRIFT 87

CHAPTER XIV
A BREACH OF NEUTRALITY 93

CHAPTER XV
A PRISONER OF WAR 99

CHAPTER XVI
THE FIRST DAY OF CAPTIVITY 106

CHAPTER XVII
A DASH FOR LIBERTY 111

CHAPTER XVIII
THE DERELICT OBSERVATION BALLOON 119

CHAPTER XIX
THE DESERTED HOUSE 124

CHAPTER XX
TRESSIDAR SOLVES A MYSTERY 130

CHAPTER XXI
CHECKMATE 138

CHAPTER XXII
THE SHELL-BATTERED HOSPITAL 144

CHAPTER XXIII
AT AULDHAIG ONCE MORE 152

CHAPTER XXIV
A FIGHT TO A FINISH 158

CHAPTER XXV
IN THE MOMENT OF TRIUMPH 164

CHAPTER XXVI
THE HOMECOMING OF THE S.S. "MEROPE" 170

CHAPTER XXVII
A DAY ON DARTMOOR 177

CHAPTER XXVIII
AND A NIGHT 183

CHAPTER XXIX
WHEN THE TRAWLERS SHOWED FIGHT 191

CHAPTER XXX
A NOVEL DUCK HUNT 200

CHAPTER XXXI
MONITORS IN ACTION 211

CHAPTER XXXII
 THE "ANZAC'S" DAY 216
CHAPTER XXXIII
 A SPLINTER OF SHELL 221
CHAPTER XXXIV
 EXIT OBERFURST 226
CHAPTER XXXV
 TRESSIDAR'S REWARD... 233

CHAPTER I
H.M.S. "POMPEY"

A bugle-call rang out shrill and clear in the wintry air.

"Thank goodness—at last," murmured Eric Greenwood. "That's an end to 'Action Stations' for the time being. Let me see. Tomorrow coal ship, next day make up the money. Payment on Friday, and ten to one there'll be half a gale of wind—and paper money is a strafed nuisance."

Thus musing, Assistant Paymaster Greenwood, R.N.R., completed his preparations for vacating the fore-top of H.M.S. "Pompey," where he had been acting as assistant to the lieutenant in charge of the fire-control arrangements.

The fore-top, a caged-in structure measuring roughly eight feet by eight, was situated ninety feet above the upper deck. In long-range actions it took the place of the conning-tower as "the brains of the ship," for in that limited aerial perch seven officers and men, all working with a common set purpose, were able to direct salvoes of death-dealing missiles with uncanny accuracy to a target invisible to the guns' crews at their stations behind six inches of Krupp steel.

"Carry on, old man," said Vickers, the lieutenant, indicating a small trap-hatch in the floor of the top. "Be careful; there's ice about."

Greenwood had already made up his mind to be careful. A man who, up to within fifteen months ago, had led an eminently sedate existence as a bank clerk does not take to work aloft with the same agility and confidence inspired by years of training at Osborne and Dartmouth.

At the outbreak of war Eric Greenwood was a ledger clerk at a bank in a quiet Devonshire country town. The notion of serving under the White Ensign had never occurred to him, even in his wildest dreams, until the Admiralty called for additional accountant officers for the Royal Naval Reserve. Eric promptly sent in his application. It was curtly acknowledged; and then followed weeks of tedious, sickening suspense, until, when hope seemed dead, the bank clerk received an envelope marked "O.H.M.S.," the contents of which transformed him into an acting assistant paymaster, R.N.R.

After a short term at the Naval Barracks at Devonport, Greenwood was sent to a small base on the east coast of Scotland. It seemed as if he were fated to remain ashore until the termination of the war, when, to his unbounded satisfaction, he was appointed to H.M.S. "Pompey."

The "Pompey" was an armoured cruiser of 14,000 tons, armed with two 9.2-in. and fourteen 6-in. guns, in addition to several weapons of lighter calibre. Although by no means a modern vessel, she was generally considered to be a "tough nut" and able to give a good account of herself on The Day—that long-expected and long-deferred event—when the Germans finally made up their minds to decide by ordeal of battle whether they could attempt to wrench the trident of sea-power from Britannia's grasp.

Lieutenant Vickers's caution was necessary, for as the A.P. lowered himself through the narrow opening, his feet came in contact with the ratlines of the wire-shrouds. They were slippery with ice, for it had been drizzling, as it almost always did in the North Sea when it was not blowing a gale, and the moisture settling on the rigging had frozen hard.

The ship was rolling considerably. At one moment the starboard shrouds were almost perpendicular, at another they inclined at such an angle that Greenwood was almost lying on his face at full length upon a gigantic wire net. Clouds of eddying, pungent smoke enveloped him, for the vessel had a following wind. The keen blast seemed to cut him like a knife in spite of his bulky, additional clothing.

The young officer descended rapidly. He was anxious to gain the deck for two reasons. He wanted to warm himself by the wardroom fire; he was also aware that a destroyer had a few hours previously sent on board a batch of mails—the first for nearly a fortnight. After thirteen days of patrol work without being in touch with land, the prospect of receiving letters from home was one that outweighed all others, unless, perhaps—harrowing thought!—the mail-bag was a blank so far as Eric was concerned.

"Hello, old bird! A trifle nippy up in your little perch!" exclaimed a voice as Greenwood stepped over the threshold of the wardroom door.

The speaker was a tall, broad-shouldered sub-lieutenant, Ronald Tressidar by name. Between these two there existed a friendship that was almost of lifelong duration, for their respective homes were in the same Devonshire town. Of recent years they had seen little of each other. Their careers were set upon totally different lines till by a pure coincidence they found themselves appointed to H.M.S. "Pompey."

"Beastly cold," agreed Greenwood as he made his way to the letter-rack. Thanks be! There was a goodly sheaf of envelopes bearing his name. Eagerly the A.P. possessed himself of his correspondence and sought a chair in the sadly depleted wardroom, for upon the outbreak of hostilities the cosy atmosphere of the place had given way to a state of almost Spartan simplicity.

Silence reigned. The rest of the officers off duty were literally devouring their greetings from home or else were burying their heads between the pages of newspapers that were at least three days old.

In the warm glow, with his mind fully occupied with thoughts of home and distant friends, Greenwood forgot completely the rigorous period of "Action Stations" in the fore-top. But all things come to an end. Reluctantly the A.P. folded his letters and placed them in his pocket. As he did so he caught Tressidar's eye.

"Anything startling?" asked the sub., taking a vacant place on the lounge within a couple of feet of Greenwood's chair.

"Heaps," replied the A.P. "For one thing, an aeroplane came down on the pater's greenhouse. No one hurt. I can imagine the governor cutting up rough about it. He never could see the humorous side of anything. The mater is still knitting for the troops. I pity the poor fellows who get hold of any of the gear she turns out. Once upon a time in the dire days of my youth she knitted me a pair of socks. I didn't forget to chip her about them, too."

"She makes awfully decent cakes," remarked Tressidar reminiscently.

"She does," agreed the A.P. "And I remember the time when we brought a hammer and a cold chisel to the tea-table and pretended to split the almond paste asunder."

"Wasn't that the cake your sister Doris made?"

"Might have been, now you mention it," said Greenwood. "Talking of Doris, she's now a probationer in the Reserve Nursing Service, and she's appointed to Auldhaig."

"Is that so?" asked Tressidar with ill-feigned disinterestedness. Nevertheless a deep flush overspread his tanned and weather-beaten features. The sub. had always been extremely partial to the girl, but Doris had been in the habit of keeping him severely in his place. That was long before the war.

"Strange that she should be sent to our base," continued Eric. "We may see something of her this Christmas, for I heard the fleet paymaster say that we are likely to remain in harbour until early in the New Year. He had the tip from the engineer-commander, who submitted a list of defects as long as your arm."

As a matter of fact Ronald Tressidar knew more about Doris Greenwood's plans than did her brother, for a letter from the girl was reposing in his pocket. Generally outspoken and communicative in most matters, Tressidar maintained a studious reticence in his chum's presence whenever the subject of Greenwood's nineteen-year-old sister was discussed.

"There's 'Action Stations' again!" exclaimed a lieutenant-commander as a bugle blared on deck.

Instantly there was a rush on the part of the occupants of the wardroom, to the accompaniment of the sharp cracks of the quick-firers.

But before Tressidar gained the deck the danger—at least for the time being—was over. The "Pompey" had ported helm, while at less than twenty yards on the port beam the surface of the water was marked by a pair of diverging lines that indicated the track of a torpedo. By a smart display of helmsmanship the cruiser had escaped destruction.

Already the skipper, who after an arduous night had turned in, was on the bridge, with his feet in carpet slippers and the legs of his pyjama suit showing below the bottom of his great-coat.

"See any signs of a periscope, Mr. Flanders?" he inquired of the officer of the watch.

"No, sir," was the reply. "We opened fire at what turns out to be a floating spar. The torpedo came from broad on our port beam before I ordered the helm to be put hard over."

"Good!" exclaimed Captain Raxworthy. "We'll see if we can't nab her."

In ordinary circumstances a battleship or cruiser that has the good luck to be missed by a hostile torpedo steams off at full speed from the dangerous locality. Should destroyers or patrol boats be in the vicinity, they are brought up at full speed to attempt to intercept the submarine. But on this occasion the "Pompey" was alone in this remote portion of the North Sea.

Contrary to precedent, Captain Raxworthy gave orders for the cruiser to slow down and come to a standstill. At the same time volumes of steam were allowed to hiss through the steam-pipes. All the six-inch and light quick-firers were manned, ready at the first glimpse of the hostile periscope to let fly such a weight of metal that the still submerged hull of the submarine would stand no chance of resisting the powerful shells.

The skipper of the "Pompey" was correct in his surmise. By slowing down and letting off steam the cruiser behaved in much the same way as if she had been actually torpedoed. The crew of the submarine heard the sounds that apparently betokened the cruiser in her death-agonies, and they could not resist the temptation to approach the surface and survey their work through the periscope.

Four hundred yards away on the "Pompey's" starboard quarter a pole-like object shot stealthily above the surface. It wanted the trained eyes of a seaman to discern the ripple of foam that denoted the position. Half a dozen or more of the "Pompey's" crew spotted the expected target.

[Illustration: "A MAELSTROM OF FOAM HID THE SPOT WHERE THE PERISCOPE HAD BEEN VISIBLE"]

A Watch-Dog Of The North Sea

The next instant twenty shells were shrieking through the air on their way towards the doomed submarine. A perfect maelstrom of foam, mingled with smoke and fragments of metal hid the spot where the periscope had been visible.

The columns of foam subsided; the smoke drifted rapidly away in the strong breeze; but ominous air-bubbles and an ever-increasing oily patch that had the effect of quieting the crested waves denoted the undisputed fact that yet another *unterseeboot* had shot her last bolt. Eight hours later H.M.S. "Pompey" entered Auldhaig Firth.

CHAPTER II
THE RESULT OF THE LEADING STOKER'S CURIOSITY

"Clear lower deck. Hands fall in to coal ship."

The hoarse orders following the shrill trills of the bos'n's mates' pipes rang from end to end of H.M.S. "Pompey". In the stokers' messes men arrayed in motley garbs, for the most part consisting of old canvas suits and coloured handkerchiefs tied tightly over their foreheads, cleared out at the double to fall in on the quarter-deck.

Stoker James Jorkler, otherwise known as Rhino Jorkler, heard the order not without emotion. He was a tall, sparely-built man of about twenty-four years of age. At first sight he lacked physique, until one noticed the ripple of supple muscles on his partly-bared arms. His face was long and pointed, his eyes blue and deeply set underneath a pair of thick and overhanging brows. His hair closely cropped, tended to exaggerate the elongation of his head. His features betrayed neither signs of good humour nor bad temper, but rather an intelligence bordering upon cunning.

Three months previously the Royal Navy in a somewhat excusable haste had accepted the services of James Jorkler. In war time, with a heavy drain upon personnel the authorities had to be a trifle less particular as to whom they enlisted for temporary service, and amongst a batch of stoker recruits was Jorkler.

His answers upon enlistment evidently satisfied the petty officer responsible for obtaining the necessary particulars. He was a Canadian, he declared, born at Woodstock, New Brunswick. Former occupation? Trimmer on board a White Star liner. His discharge papers confirmed that statement. Next of kin? James Jorkler rubbed his chin thoughtfully. He was on the point of replying that he did not possess such a luxury, but upon consideration he gave the name of Jonas Brocklebunk, his half-brother, of Leith.

Promptly the newly entered stoker was fired off to the R.N. Barracks at Portsmouth. His cap-ribbon, like those of the rest of the men borne on the books of that establishment, was embellished with the words "H.M.S. Victory," although his acquaintance with the time-honoured three-decker was limited to a distant glimpse of the ship as she swung to her moorings in Portsmouth Harbour.

The rest of the stokers' mess could not come to a unanimous decision concerning the tall recruit. His reserve puzzled them. Although he made no attempt to "choke off" any questions, he kept much to himself. He had no bosom pal. He showed no inclination to "split brass rags" with any of his messmates, who, for some unexplained reason, nicknamed him "Rhino."

When in due time he emerged from his course of preliminary training and was drafted to H.M.S. "Pompey," the name stuck. He showed neither appreciation nor resentment at it; it would have been useless to have done either. So he accepted the sobriquet without any outward and visible sign of interest in his messmates' solicitude for his need of a nickname.

The mess-deck was all but cleared. Jorkler, usually amongst the first to respond to orders, lingered until he was almost the last. Then, kneeling over his ditty-box, he unlocked and threw back the lid, delving amongst his belongings until he found what he required. "Wot the 'Ades 'ave you got there, mate?" broke in a deep voice.

Jorkler turned with a start to find that a leading stoker was standing behind him.

"Kind of souvenir," he replied weakly. "I guess is isn't of any interest to you."

"Thought as it might be a plug o' 'bacca," continued the man. "Fact is, I believes it is. 'Ow about it?"

"Reckon you're wrong," snapped Jorkler with returning confidence as he slammed and locked the box.

"Too jolly fishy to my liking," rejoined the petty officer bluntly. "You just wait till we've done coaling and I'll see for myself wot your little game is. Strikes me it ain't all jonnick."

At this threat Jorkler started to his feet Fortunately for the leading stoker there were others still in the mess, otherwise— —

Jorkler set his jaw tightly and followed his inquisitor on deck. At the first opportunity he would nip below and throw the object of discussion overboard rather than let the leading stoker see it.

It was still night, with a cold, drizzling rain. Overhead arc-lamps threw a pale gleam upon the serried lines of men—seamen, stokers, and marines—on the quarter-deck. Everything liable to be affected by coal-dust had been covered up. The huge 9.2-in. guns were swathed in sacking; canvas covers encased the closed hatchways; whips for hoisting inboard the sacks of coal, trollies for bearing them to the nearest shoots, and a medley of other gear were in readiness, while steam was already raised to operate the winches.

Skilfully a large "haulabout"—a hulk converted into a floating coal-depôt—was manoeuvred alongside to starboard. To port a couple of deeply laden lighters had already been made fast.

"Commence—carry on!" shouted the commander from the after-bridge.

Instantly it seemed as if pandemonium had broken loose. With a rush the men set to work, for, if possible, H.M.S. "Pompey" was to break her own record.

Winches clattered. Jets of steam drifted across the slippery deck. Men shouted, knocked one another and each other, and worked till, in spite of the chilliness of the morning, their faces, quickly blacked with coal-dust, ran with perspiration.

Most of the junior officers joined in the actual labour. They found that even handling sacks of coal was preferable to standing by and shivering in the damp air. Clad in garments that outvied the bizarre rig of the hands, sub-lieutenants and midshipmen were soon toiling like Trojans.

With an almost reckless disregard for life and limb, sacks in batches of half a dozen at the time were hoisted from the coaling craft and dumped with a dull crash upon the cruiser's deck. Woe-betide the luckless wight who failed to heed the warning cry of "Stand by, there!" Like a pack of wolves the energetic men threw themselves upon the bags and dragged them to the shoots, until the ship vibrated with the clatter of coal descending to the bunkers.

At eight bells the word was passed to "Stand easy." A hasty breakfast, consisting largely of coal-dust washed down with ship's cocoa, was served out. The mess-decks were seething with human beings resembling imps and satyrs in their grimy garbs and blackened faces.

Reluctantly Stoker Jorkler came to the conclusion that this was no time to go to his ditty-box. Up to the present no opportunity had occurred.

Again the ship's company resumed their labours. It was now daybreak. The rain still fell, unheeded by the enthusiastic toilers. The only people who minded the horrible climatic conditions were the band, who, to keep up the spirits of the coaling party, were discussing lively airs in which rag-time predominated.

Suddenly an engine-room artificer working the main derrick hoist gave vent to an oath. "Here, one of you; bear a hand," he claimed. "I've nipped my fingers."

Without a word Stoker Jorkler relieved the luckless man at the steam winch. The E.R.A., with two fingers crushed to a pulp, hurried away to the sick-bay; while Jorkler, whose knowledge of machinery and of winches in particular was far from perfect, remained in control of the hoisting gear. He, of the whole of the ship's company, didn't exactly see why he should break his back over sacks of coal when he could take on the comparatively light job of running the steam hoist.

"Avast heaving there on the main derrick!" shouted Sub-lieutenant Tressidar, whose quick eye had noticed that something had gone wrong aloft.

Jorkler obeyed promptly, shutting off steam and applying the band-brake. A hundred pairs of eyes followed the direction of the sub's outstretched hand. The wire hawser had "jumped" the sheave at the end of the derrick that, projecting at an angle of forty-five degrees, terminated fifty feet or more above the deck of the lighter.

"Up aloft, one of you," continued Tressidar, addressing the men whose operations had perforce to be suspended.

But before the order could be carried out a man working in the lighter gripped the wire rope, shouting for the winch to be put in motion.

Dangling at the end of the rope as he rose swiftly into the air was a burly figure rigged out in grimy canvas. With his teeth gleaming in contrast to his black face and with a dash of colour imparted by the scarlet handkerchief bound round his head, the volunteer for the dangerous service cut a picturesque figure.

Stoker Jorkler gave an involuntary start. He recognised the man as Leading Stoker Smith, the petty officer whose insistence had given him such a bad turn. For a few seconds he thought—and thought hard.

The winch was still in motion. Higher and higher rose the petty officer until his head was almost level with the huge metal block at the end of the derrick.

Sub-lieutenant Tressidar raised his hand as a signal for the winch to be stopped. Jorkler, his eyes fixed upon the man who had aroused his enmity, made no effort to obey.

Leading Stoker Smith realised his peril. The wire rope which he was grasping was being drawn completely through the sheave. He changed his grip from the rope to the metal block, but the latter afforded no adequate hold.

"Stop winding, you blithering idiot!" roared the commander, who from the after-bridge was a witness of all that occurred.

Still Jorkler, ostentatiously fumbling with the mechanism, allowed the winch to revolve. The end of the rope, including the eye-splice, pulled through the sheave and fell with a thud upon the deck, the men scattering right and left to avoid it in its descent.

In the midst of his peril Smith espied a short length of rope bent to the end of the derrick. Again he shifted his hold, and, grasping the rope's-end, strove to fling his legs athwart the steeply sloping spar.

As he did so the rope parted like pack-thread. Groans escaped the on-lookers as the doomed man, with arms and legs outstretched, hurtled through the air. To the spectators he seemed to fall slowly, but with a sickening crash his back came into contact with a beam in the hold of the lighter.

A dozen of his shipmates rushed to his assistance, but the man was beyond mortal aid.

"What the deuce have you been up to?" inquired the engineer-lieutenant of the man at the winch.

"Sorry, sir," replied Jorkler with well-feigned grief. "The engine got out of gear. Is he dead, sir?"

"As if he could be anything else!" retorted the irate officer. "Stand aside, you blithering idiot! There'll be something for you to answer." Five minutes later the interrupted work was resumed. The lifeless victim had been removed; only sheer hard work could dispel the gloom that had fallen on the ship's company.

Beneath the mask of regret Jorkler was smiling to himself; from which it was evident that the mysterious "thing" that had excited his victim's curiosity was something of great importance, since Jorkler put its value above that of the life of a shipmate.

He was a firm believer in the adage, "Dead men tell no tales."

On the following day the county coroner and twelve good men and true assembled, as the law directs, to inquire into the manner of Leading Stoker Smith's death.

Although not knowing the difference between a derrick and a hand spike, a whip or a tackle, they listened with an air of profound wisdom to the engineer-lieutenant's technical explanations. They heard Stoker Jorkler's account, although most of his sentences were Dutch to the Highlanders who formed the jury. They accepted the commander's statement that everything had been done to safeguard the interests of the crew, and, satisfied, returned a verdict of Accidental Death.

Leading Stoker Smith received the only salute to which a lower deck man is entitled—three volleys over his grave; *and the "thing" still remained locked away in Rhino Jorkler's ditty-box.*

CHAPTER III
GREENWOOD SENIOR'S DISCOVERY

Early on the following afternoon a train in connection with the night express for King's Cross arrived at Auldhaig station from Edinburgh.

Amongst the passengers were Mr. Theodore Greenwood and his daughter Doris. The former's object in making the long and tedious journey from Devonshire to the bleak north-east coast of Scotland was twofold. He wanted to hand his daughter over safely to the Naval Hospital—and this in spite of the nineteen-year-old young lady's assurances that she was quite capable of travelling alone. He also thought that there might be a possibility of seeing Eric, since he knew that the "Pompey's" base was at Auldhaig. Notwithstanding the fact that the Assistant Paymaster R.N.R. had studiously adhered to the regulations and had made no mention of where the ship was or what she was doing, that information had been forthcoming.

Nor was Mr. Greenwood alone in the possession of the supposed secret, for already several of the officers' wives and families had braved the rigours of the wintry climate and had taken either furnished houses or apartments in the town, which since the war had developed out of all knowledge.

Having duly rid himself of his responsibility of handing Doris over to the Head Nursing Sister, Mr. Greenwood set out on his quest for H.M.S. "Pompey." Being naturally of a somewhat nervous disposition, he hesitated to ask if the cruiser were in harbour, reflecting that such a question might lead to his arrest as a spy. In his imagination he fancied that everyone he met eyed him with suspicion.

At length he arrived at the shore of an arm of the intricate harbour. Lying at moorings in the channel were half a dozen destroyers, but there were no signs of any vessel approaching the armoured cruiser in tonnage.

For some moments he stopped to read a notice-board on which was set forth a list of things that the inhabitants of Auldhaig must or must not do, the document being signed by the senior naval officer of the port.

"There's nothing like taking every possible precaution," murmured Mr. Greenwood approvingly. "One cannot be too particular in wartime."

Just then an old fisherman sauntered by. To him the stranger addressed himself, inquiring if he knew whether the "Pompey" was in harbour.

The old Scot shook his head.

"I dinna ken what you say, mon," he said.

Mr. Greenwood repeated his question.

"Oh—ay. Weel, tak yon path——"

He gave his questioner lengthy and bewildering directions which not only left the Devon man completely tied up in knots, but with also a reply to a misunderstood question, for the old man had come to the conclusion that Mr. Greenwood was asking the way to Ponhaugh, a small fishing-village about four miles from Auldhaig by the cliff-path.

Gaining the outskirts of the town, Mr. Greenwood commenced the long climb to the edge of the rugged granite cliffs. From the moment he struck the open country he did not see another person of whom he might make further inquiries, but with complete reliance upon the old fisherman's directions he walked briskly along the narrow, winding path.

This he followed for nearly two miles without finding any signs of his quest. Instead, he made the disconcerting discovery that the track split into two parts, one branch trending inland, the other descending steeply to the beach.

Mr. Greenwood took the latter route. Upon gaining the shore he found that the track ended at the firm sands that fronted the base of the rugged and indented line of cliffs.

Undaunted, he proceeded, expecting as he rounded each projection to find the non-existent harbour in which he supposed H.M.S. "Pompey" to be lying; but headland after headland was passed without any satisfactory result.

Presently he arrived at a little bay. The distance between the two enclosing promontories was less than a hundred yards apart. The shore was of sand, but, unlike the rest of the beach, was interrupted by a series of low ledges of rock. Between the water's edge and the base of the cliffs the distance averaged twenty yards, although the waves were almost washing the wall of granite at either end of the bay.

Suddenly Mr. Greenwood caught sight of a cylindrical object lying on the shore. It was a little larger than a football and glistened in the dull light.

At every undulation it was flung upon the sand, whence it receded in the undertow until thrown back by the succeeding wave. Attached to it was a short length of frayed rope.

"That must be a mine," decided the alarmed man. "The authorities must be informed."

Although half inclined to retrace his steps, he walked cautiously past it, keeping as close to the cliffs as possible, until he gained the furthermost headland. Here, to his dismay, he found the distant aspect was a misleading one, for his progress was barred by a deep gulley through which the tide was surging right up to the wall of granite.

"I hope the tide is going down," thought Mr. Greenwood.

To satisfy his curiosity on that point he wasted ten precious minutes, only to be ocularly assured that the tide was on the flood, and that there was no possible chance of going further.

Again he passed the cylindrical object. By this time it was within a few feet of one of the ledges of rock.

"When the waves throw it against those rocks it will explode," commented Mr. Greenwood. "How dangerous! Thank goodness I have yet time to put a safe distance between me and that infernal machine."

Thirty seconds later he "brought up all standing." Where a short time previously had been an expanse of hard sand, the waves were lapping against the cliff. His retreat was cut off.

Even then, at the expense of wet feet, he might have negotiated the passage, since the water was only about a foot or eighteen inches in depth; but Mr. Greenwood hesitated and, figuratively, was lost.

Step by step he retreated before the rapidly rising tide, each step taking him nearer again to the object of his apprehension. A belt of seaweed rising six or seven feet from the sand marked the limit of mean high tides on the face of the cliffs. It was evident that nowhere within the arms of the bay was safety to be found except by scaling the frowning precipice.

Discarding his umbrella—he wedged it tightly into a crevice in the granite in the hope that he might be able to retrieve his trusty friend—Mr. Greenwood sought for a suitable spot at which to commence his hazardous feat. At the same time he kept an anxious watch upon the derelict mine, which, having escaped being cast upon the ledge, was now being carried close to the main wall of rock.

In his heated imagination he fancied himself fifty or a hundred feet up the cliff with the powerful explosive going off and hurling him to a terrible death upon the rocks beneath. He shouted, but only the echoes of his own voice mocked his appeal for aid. In vain he looked seaward, where the mists of evening were already creeping over the wild North Sea. Not a sail was visible.

Mr. Greenwood was one of those men who, by disposition timid and unassuming, possessed a great reserve of courage and determination when called upon to extricate themselves from a tight corner. And, having found himself in a tight corner, he acted accordingly.

After a brief search he discovered a rift in the cliff, which at this point was not so sheer as it appeared at first sight. In any case the footholds obtainable extended sufficiently high to enable him to climb above highwater mark. Here he could wait until the tide fell and take his chance with the mine.

The first six feet gave him great trouble, for the weed and kelp afforded little foothold, but beyond this height he was able to maintain a steady progress. Up and up he climbed, not daring to look down, although the attraction of that deadly cylinder was almost irresistible. He wanted to watch its progress towards the base of the solid rock.

At length, fifty feet above the sea, he gained a fairly broad ledge, the presence of which was invisible from the beach. Nor could it be seen from the top of the cliffs, for higher up they projected well beyond the ledge, the face being so smooth that further climbing was a matter of sheer impossibility.

"At any rate, I am safe for the time being," soliloquised Mr. Greenwood. "That is something to be thankful for, although I would infinitely prefer the comfort of a bed to the prospect of spending a winter's night less than halfway up a wall of rock. And even if that mine explodes I think this ledge will provide sufficient protection to minimise the force of the detonation."

Cautiously extending himself, he peered over the edge. In the fast-gathering gloom he could just discern the mine as it rolled to and fro on the shelving sand. The waves had almost borne it to the base of the rocks.

A new danger now confronted the stranded man. Perilous as the climb had been, the descent was doubly dangerous. When the time came, he could no more essay the feat of regaining the beach than he could hope to clamber up the remaining two hundred feet of beetling cliff. Unless aid were forthcoming, he was in danger of perishing of cold and hunger.

Mr. Greenwood's next step was to prepare for his approaching vigil while there was yet light enough for him to see. The ledge was almost twelve feet in length and five in its widest part, gradually diminishing to nothing at either end. One portion was covered by a withered bush, a circumstance that aroused the investigator's curiosity, since it seemed remarkable that vegetation could grow on the face of a granite cliff.

"Thank goodness I have pipe, matches, and tobacco," he thought philosophically. Now that the immediate danger was past, he determined to make the best of things.

He again directed his attention upon the bush. To use it as a seat would be preferable to sitting on the hard, cold rock.

As he sat the bush gave way. In vain he clutched wildly for support. Toppling backwards, he disappeared into what appeared to be the solid rock.

For some moments he lay helpless, too dazed to realise what had occurred. He was almost in darkness. A peculiar pungent smell assailed his nostrils. Could it be possible that he owed his present predicament to the explosion of the derelict mine?

After a while Mr. Greenwood raised himself. Grimly he reflected that his visit to Auldhaig had not been uneventful. Adventures were crowding upon each other's heels. His zest for excitement was increasing.

The bush had broken his fall. He found himself on a flat floor of what appeared to be a cavern. Where the foliage had been, appeared an irregular opening through which the dim twilight filtered without sufficient intensity to reveal his surroundings.

"One thing, I've a roof over my head," he soliloquised. "Now I am getting on. But I really cannot understand this peculiar odour. It reminds me very forcibly of a garage. Yes, petrol fumes. To be on the safe side I don't think I'll smoke just at present. In fact, I think it would be well to investigate."

Cautiously and on all-fours Mr. Greenwood commenced his tour of discovery, crawling lest there should be a hole in the floor.

Soon his head came in contact with a metallic object. It was a filled petrol tin, one of dozens, possibly hundreds, stacked in orderly manner against one wall of the cave.

"Now, that's strange," murmured Mr. Greenwood "It is pretty certain that that lot would not have been brought into this place from the cliff, so there must be an outlet besides the hole through which I tumbled. Why should a place like this be chosen to store petrol? And why was the hole so carefully hidden with a dead bush? It looks jolly fishy. Of course I've heard plenty of talk of German secret petrol-bases in Great Britain, but I never believed the tales. By smoke! I fancy I've stumbled upon one now. The first question is, how am I to find a way out without being seen?"

Resuming his cautious crawl, Mr. Greenwood penetrated into the recesses of the cave, keeping within touch of the rows of petrol-cans on his right. Contrary to his expectations, the floor was smooth, though tending to rise in the direction in which he was proceeding.

At about twenty yards from the hole through which he had tumbled, he remembered that he had left his tracks uncovered. No need to creep on all-fours now, for he had the irregular patch of light to guide him. Grasping the displaced bush, he replaced it in the opening, and chuckling to himself he again resumed his tour of exploration.

His spirits were rising rapidly. The love of adventure, that had lain dormant for years, was reasserting itself. Also he began to realise that he had now a chance of doing something definite for his country—a chance that hitherto had been denied him on account of his age.

He had quite forgotten the derelict mine. The fears that he had entertained on that score had been completely dispelled by the thought that he had lighted upon a discovery of real national importance—the existence of a secret base for hostile submarines.

For quite a hundred yards he groped his way. The darkness was so intense that it appeared to have weight—to press upon his eyes. The tunnel, too, had contracted, for by extending both his arms he could touch the enclosing walls. Once or twice he stood erect to relieve the aching muscles of his back. He could then just touch the roof, which, although of solid rock, was bone-dry.

Suddenly his forehead came in contact with a hard object. It was the bottommost step of a stout ladder. The steps extended from side to side, for the tunnel was still contracting. Further progress, except by the ladder, was impossible, since the wall of rock terminated a short distance beyond the base of the steps.

Mr. Greenwood examined his surroundings with great exactitude before attempting the ascent. Everything had to be performed by the sense of touch. The steps were of far greater thickness than the usual type of ladder, and were more apart. Apparently they had been constructed to bear very heavy weights, each one being strengthened by means of a circular iron bar on the underside.

"I'm half inclined to use a match," thought Mr. Greenwood. "It's risky, with all those petrol fumes about, but— — No, I won't; I'll make the best of it."

Slowly he ascended. It reminded him of an infant attempting to climb a staircase for the first time. The steps, in spite of their solidity, creaked under his weight. The sounds, intensified by the enclosed surroundings, added to the uncanniness of the mysterious cave.

At the eighth step he found a trap-door above his head. It was what he expected; but the question arose, what was on the other side? He had no desire to blunder into the presence of half a dozen desperadoes, who would doubtless have no scruples in knocking him over the head and toppling his corpse down the cliff.

Even as he was considering the best thing to be done, he heard footsteps overhead and a deep voice exclaiming, "Now, then, Max; let's get on with the business. It's quite time we showed the signal. Hand me yon crowbar and bear a hand to lift this trap. It's heavy."

CHAPTER IV
THE SECRET PETROL-DEPÔT

"No, I don't want to meet Max & Co.—at least, not just yet," soliloquised Mr. Greenwood as he hurriedly and silently descended to the floor of the tunnel. His first thought was to retrace his steps, scramble through the opening and lie at full length upon the outside ledge, until he realised that the mysterious frequenters of the cave would still be between him and freedom.

Then he remembered that there was a space between the foot of the ladder and the end of the tunnel. It was not at all likely that this would be examined.

With an agility that he did not think himself capable of, Mr. Greenwood crawled between two of the steps and crouched in his place of concealment.

Barely had he done so when the trap-door was raised. A flood of light streamed from above, although, fortunately, the flight of steps threw a strong shadow upon the recumbent form of Mr. Greenwood.

"You vos leave open der door?" inquired a guttural voice.

"Yes, Max," was the reply. "It's main heavy, and there's no call to exert ourselves to bustin'-point. No one'll come here after dark."

The speaker descended, holding an electric torch in his hand. He was a short, thick-set fellow, dressed in soiled velveteens. He looked a typical gamekeeper.

The person addressed as Max followed. He was a tall, fair-haired, broad-shouldered man of about thirty years of age. He wore a long overcoat and muffler, a hard felt hat, grey trousers and brown boots, the latter being almost hidden under a thick deposit of mud.

"I've got a rope further along," continued the short man. "When they answer our signals and send a boat, I'll lower you down. Only don't forget it's cash on the nail."

"Vot vos dat?" asked Max.

"The fifty pounds agreed upon. We'll signal at intervals, but don't be too jolly cocksure. They can't always be to time. If they show up afore four in the mornin', count yourself lucky."

The men, still talking, moved down the tunnel, until a bend, that Mr. Greenwood had passed without being aware of it, screened the light from the place where he lay concealed.

"Now or never," he thought.

Extricating himself from his cramped position, he scaled the ladder. Then, with his head almost level with the trap-door, he waited until his eyes grew accustomed to the blaze of light.

The opening was placed in the floor of a room — the kitchen of a small cottage, apparently. The two windows were heavily curtained. The door was secured, in addition to the massive lock, by a stout oaken beam resting in iron staples at either end. The furniture was scanty, consisting of a deal table, on which lay the remains of a meal and a large oil-lamp; three rush-bottomed chairs; a dresser, and a well-worn horse-hair couch. On one of the beams overhead were slung a couple of double-barrelled sporting guns. Opposite the door was another opening to a second room.

Mr. Greenwood's first impulse upon emerging from the tunnel was to slam the heavy trap-door and pile the furniture on top of it. But, he reflected, the men had a means of escape by the rope of which the short man had spoken. Moreover, they would raise the alarm and prevent the approach of the expected boat, which, more than likely, would put off from a German submarine.

No, he must make his escape without arousing suspicion. It would be an easy matter to unbar the door, but since he could not replace the cross-bar after he was outside, such a step would be unwise.

Throwing back the curtain he tried one of the windows. It was a latticed casement. With a little agility he could squeeze through, replace the curtain and trust to luck that the unsecured window might escape detection.

Two minutes later he was breathing the open air — a free man.

He looked about him. The night air blew cold. He had no idea of the direction of Auldhaig. For the time being his quest for the cruiser was out of the question.

Far away and at a considerably lower level two rows of lamps glimmered through the darkness. They were the anchor lights of the decoy boats of the fleet lying in Auldhaig Harbour. The town and the actual ships were shrouded in darkness, but every night numbers of small boats, each showing a white light, were moored at some distance from the fleet. At one time they might be placed half a dozen cables' lengths to the north'ard of the anchorage, at another a similar distance to the eastward, the idea being to mislead any Zeppelin that might attempt to drop bombs upon the harbour and shipping.

Setting his face towards the friendly lights, Mr. Greenwood began the descent of the rough hillside. Before he had gone a quarter of a mile the irresistible yearning for a pipe assailed him. Turning his back to the wind, he struck a match, and was soon puffing contentedly at his gratifying briar.

Suddenly half a dozen dark forms pounced upon him. Before he could utter a sound he was seized by a pair of muscular hands, and a hoarse voice exclaimed:

"Now, then, wot's your little game? Flashing lights at this time o' night, eh?"

Mr. Greenwood did not immediately reply. His dignity as a respectable British citizen had been outraged. He drew himself up with as much hauteur as the circumstances would permit.

"Allow me to inform you," he said stiffly, "that I will not be spoken to in this dictatorial manner."

"All right, old sport, don't bust yourself," rejoined his questioner. "Now, what are you doing here this time o' night? Wanderin' along the cliffs at ten o'clock wants a little explanation."

"As a matter of fact I was looking for H.M.S. 'Pompey,'" began Mr. Greenwood.

A roar of laughter greeted this announcement.

"D'ye expect to find her on top of a cliff?" asked the man when the merriment had subsided. "Look here, this is a serious matter. We're the Coast Patrol. We saw a light about a quarter of an hour ago and another just now."

"When I lit my pipe," added Mr. Greenwood, who, still ruffled by his reception, had decided not to impart the secret to the uncouth crowd that had waylaid him; "and what I said about the 'Pompey' is absolutely correct. I was directed along the cliffs, missed my way, and got cut off by the tide. My object was to visit my son, who is an officer on board the cruiser in question. If you have any reason to doubt my statement, inquiries on board will remove all suspicion."

"You came up over the cliffs, sir?" asked the man respectfully, for Mr. Greenwood's declaration that he was the father of a naval officer could not lightly be ignored.

"I did," replied Mr. Greenwood with studied pride. He did not think it necessary to explain how.

"Well, you're a game 'un, pardon my saying so. P'raps, sir, you won't mind if we sees you back to the town. Dooty is dooty, an' we must satisfy ourselves that you are what you says you are. Got any friends at Auldhaig?"

Mr Greenwood was adverse to causing his daughter anxiety at that time of night. At the hotel he was known only as a stranger putting up for a few days.

"I'm afraid I haven't," he replied. "But, if it is not too late, I suppose you could accompany me on board the cruiser?"

The men conferred amongst themselves; then the spokesman again addressed the object of his suspicion.

"All right, sir; that'll be the best way, I'm thinking. Best foot forward, sir. We may just catch the six-bell boat from the staith."

The speaker and another member of the patrol fell in on either side of their suspect, while the rest of the party disappeared in the opposite direction.

"We are members of the National Guard," explained the senior of the two men. "'Tain't exactly a soft job, but it's something. Not often do we come across strangers on the cliffs after dark. When we do, we generally run 'em in. My word, I'd like to know how you got up here from the beach, sir!"

Mr. Greenwood declined the bait. He was well satisfied with the way events were shaping themselves. In spite of his misadventures and the lateness of the hour, he stood a fair chance of seeing his son that night.

Half an hour's steady tramp brought him and his escort to the staith or quay. Answering the challenge of the armed seaman on sentry, the patrol men ascertained that the "Pompey's" boat had not yet put off to bring back a party of officers who had been ashore on leave.

Presently several great-coated forms appeared through the darkness. Amongst them was the commander.

"Beg pardon, sir," said the sentry. "Three civilians require passage to the 'Pompey.'"

"Eh, what?" queried the commander. "At this time of night? What for? Who are they?"

Mr. Greenwood seized the opportunity by explaining to the naval officer that he had urgent reasons for seeing his son—Assistant Paymaster Eric Greenwood, R.N.R.

"Personal reasons?" asked the commander. "I am afraid you will have to defer your visit till the morning. Sorry; but personal considerations have to stand aside in wartime. And who might your companions be?"

"My—er—my goalers, I suppose I must term them," explained Mr. Greenwood. "I am, I believe, under arrest. In addition to personal reasons I have a matter of national importance which I wish to bring to the notice of the authorities. Since I know only two people connected with the service, both of whom are officers on the 'Pompey,' I thought—— But I'd rather explain to you alone."

The commander hesitated. He was a genial man, ready to do anyone a good turn. If, however, he took the responsibility of introducing a civilian on board on the strength of what might prove to be a cock-and-bull story, he might be rapped over the knuckles by the Admiralty—and, he reflected, being rapped over the knuckles by My Lords generally resulted in the sting remaining for many a long day.

"Why not make your report to the flag captain?" suggested the commander suavely. "His shore office is open day and night, and that would save you a tedious boat journey on a cold night like this."

Mr. Greenwood could be very obstinate when occasion arose. Having gone thus far, he was determined to see the business through in the manner he had intended.

"No, sir," he replied. "I do not want to run about after flag captains at this hour of the night. If you cannot see your way clear to accede to my request, the important matter of which I hinted must wait. The responsibility which is no light one—will be transferred to other shoulders."

It was the turn of the commander to be taken aback. He was not used to be talked to like this by civilians. He tried to fix the middle-aged gentleman with his best quarter-deck glare, but the darkness foiled him. Had he been able to see the dishevelled individual in the light he would doubtless have come to the conclusion that he was being tackled by a person with an unhinged mind.

"Very well—carry on," he exclaimed. "Here's the boat. Coxswain! assist this gentleman into the stern-sheets."

"And us, sir?" began the National Guard, but the naval officer "choked him off."

"No, no," he interrupted hurriedly. "I'll be responsible for your—er—prisoner."

Guided by the coxswain, Mr. Greenwood stepped off the quay into the stern-sheets of the picquet-boat. In fifteen seconds he found himself sandwiched between two young officers, while another half a dozen completely crowded out the strictly limited space.

The coxswain sounded a bell in the engine-room. The engines were reversed and the long, lean boat backed from the quay. Then, at full speed ahead, she glided rapidly, without lights, through the pitch dark waters of Auldhaig Harbour.

CHAPTER V
EXPLANATIONS

"Pass the word for Mr. Greenwood," ordered the commander as Greenwood, Senior, found himself on the quarter-deck.

The voyage, short as it had been, was a revelation to him. It showed him how the navy men handle their boats on a winter's night, without a light to guide them, and unable themselves to show the orthodox red, white, and green steaming lights. He was in momentary dread of finding himself in the water owing to the picquet-boat either colliding with something or else being cut in twain by another marine race-horse. He marvelled at the sangfroid of his uniformed companions, who chatted and cut jokes with each other with the utmost unconcern. The hoarse challenge "Boat Ahoy!" from the sentry on the "Pompey's" fore-bridge and the seemingly inconsequent "Aye, aye" of the picquet-boat's coxswain gave him an insight into the ceaseless vigilance of Britain's first line of defence.

Almost in a whirl he found himself ascending the accommodation-ladder and gaining the spacious quarter-deck.

"Eric, my boy!" exclaimed Mr. Greenwood delightedly, as his son, arrayed in unfamiliar garb, ascended the companion.

"By Jove! pater, what on earth brings you here?" inquired the A.P., astonished at the identity of his visitor. Then he paused, having become aware of the presence of the commander, who stood like a guardian angel behind the benighted visitor.

"Your father has told me that he wishes to communicate a matter of urgent importance, Mr. Greenwood," said the commander. "I think it would be well if you saw him in your cabin. If, in your opinion, the business is urgent, you will please report to me."

He moved away to consult with the officer of the watch before going below. Father and son stood irresolute; Mr. Greenwood hardly knowing how to begin, while Eric was beginning to wonder how and by what possible means could his parent possess a certain knowledge that would require to be reported to the commander.

Down the ladder and the half-deck Mr. Greenwood followed his son. Here an alert sentry drew himself up as the young officer passed. Then the stolidity of his face gave place to an amused expression as he noticed the dishevelled appearance of the A.P.'s companion.

"This way," continued Eric. "My cabin's under repairs. Haven't got it quite ship-shape after that little affair off the Belgian coast. I'll take you into Tressidar's cabin. Of course you know he's shipmates with me?"

He knocked at the metal door. Receiving an invitation to enter, he opened the door and drew aside a curtain. The cabin was small and brilliantly lighted. Over the closed scuttle a curtain had been drawn to make doubly sure that no stray rays were visible from without.

Seated in an arm-chair drawn close to a very small and compact stove was Sub-lieutenant Ronald Tressidar.

"I say, old man——" began Eric; then, noticing the look of astonishment in the sub.'s eyes, he broke off and followed the direction of Tressidar's gaze. For the first time he became aware of his usually precise parent's appearance.

Mr. Greenwood wore his coat buttoned tightly round his throat. The coat was literally caked with mud and dust and in addition was rent across the right shoulder. His face was as dirty as the proverbial tinker's; on his left cheek was a line of dried blood, the result of an unheeded scratch received in his tumble in company with the dead bush. His hair, generally sleek and well brushed, was tousled and matted with wisps of grass.

"Pater!" exclaimed Eric in utter amazement.

"It's all right, my boy," declared Mr. Greenwood reassuringly. "I've had the night of my life—absolutely. No, don't go, Tressidar. Listen to what I've discovered."

"Have a stiff glass of grog, sir?" asked the sub., after Mr. Greenwood had washed his face and hands and had smoothed his ruffled hair.

"Thanks, I could do with one," replied Greenwood, Senior. "In fact, I was on the point of asking for a whisky, only I thought from your look of astonishment that you imagined I had already had one too many. No, thank Heaven, I've got off lightly, but I've left my best umbrella on the beach."

"Fire away, pater," said Eric. "We are all attention."

Mr. Greenwood "fired away." Uninterrupted he pursued his narrative until he came to the discovery of the supposed derelict mine.

"It wasn't glass by any chance?" asked Tressidar.

"Glass?" repeated Mr. Greenwood. "Well, now I come to think of it, perhaps it did resemble glass. But why do you ask?"

"Because, judging by your description of its size and buoyancy, I am inclined to think that your mine was one of the glass buoys we use for marking the position of our submarine obstructions. After on-shore gales the coastguards find hundreds of them."

The narrator mopped his forehead. A wave of horrible uncertainty swept over him. Perhaps, then, the second episode of his nocturnal. adventures would have similar harmless interpretation?

"Carry on, pater," said Eric encouragingly.

"By Jove, sir!" exclaimed Tressidar, when Mr. Greenwood arrived at his discovery of the petrol-depôt. "Cut it short, if you don't mind. Let's have the salient facts. Every minute is of extreme importance."

Five minutes later the sub. was reporting the matter to the commander, who, in turn, communicated the discovery to the captain.

In ordinary circumstances the captain of the cruiser ought to have submitted a written report to the senior naval officer at Auldhaig, but red tape had long since gone by the board so far as naval matters were concerned. Other Government departments were still tied hand and foot with fathoms of red tape. Well it was that at the Admiralty the Gordian knot had been severed on that memorable 4th of August, 1914.

In a very short space of time the skipper's plans were formed. A landing-party, under the orders of Sub-lieutenant Tressidar, was to proceed at once to the solitary cottage. Since Mr. Greenwood was very hazy as to its locality, the assistance of the National Guard forming the coast-patrol was to be requisitioned.

Two pulling-boats, in charge of the first lieutenant, were to proceed to the bay where the entrance to the cave was situated. Mr. Greenwood's description of the spot was sufficiently accurate for the place to be identified. Examination of the chart showed that for miles northward from the entrance to Auldhaig Firth there was only water deep enough for a submarine to approach within easy distance of the shore at this particular indentation, which bore the name of Sallach Dhu Bay.

Eric Greenwood asked and obtained permission to accompany the landing-party. He felt that as his father had been the means of locating the petrol-store, his son had a kind of interest in the proceedings.

Mr. Greenwood, who was now feeling the reaction of his unwonted exertions, asked to be put ashore. He was content to have a good night's rest at the hotel and learn developments in the morning.

"Bless my soul, Eric!" he exclaimed as his son, with a conspicuous revolver-holster strapped to his great-coat, appeared in the doorway of his cabin. "What are you doing with that weapon? I thought assistant paymasters were non-combatants?"

Eric grinned. He did not think fit to enlighten his parent on the matter. Mentally he recalled a certain forenoon off Ostend. For three hours he was on duty in the fore-top, with hostile shells flying thick and fast. One, he vividly remembered, hurtled a few feet from the mast, cutting away the shrouds on the starboard side, but fortunately without exploding. He and his comrades in that lofty perch had missed annihilation by almost a miracle.

"Get so much work in the ship's office that I'm glad of a breather," he remarked. "Oh, by the way, we're having a sort of informal reception on board to-morrow afternoon. Several of the officers' wives and families are turning up. You might bring Doris, and then you can sample naval hospitality in wartime. The boat will be at the staith at six bells—that's three o'clock."

"Come on, old man," called out Tressidar. "The boat's alongside. Are you ready, Mr. Greenwood?"

The cutter, in which about twenty armed seamen were already seated, had dropped back from the boom to the accommodation-ladder. Tressidar, the A.P. and a midshipman were Mr. Greenwood's companions in the stern-sheets.

At the landing-place Mr. Greenwood waited as the men silently "fell in," while a seaman hurried off to enlist the services of the National Guard to guide them to the scene of operations.

In a very short time the two coast-patrol men arrived. Briefly the situation was explained to them. Tressidar gave the order, and the landing-party moved forward and were soon lost in the darkness.

For some moments Mr. Greenwood stood still, hardly able to convince himself that he was not dreaming. Then he broke into a run in the direction of the armed men. Guided by the thud of their footfalls, he overtook them before they were clear of the market-place.

"I say, Eric," he exclaimed breathlessly. "If you've a chance there's my best umbrella on the beach. Don't forget it, if you can help it, there's a good lad."

And having eased his mind on that point, he wended his way to the Bantyre Hotel.

CHAPTER VI
AN EXCELLENT NIGHT'S WORK

"There's the cottage, sir," whispered one of the guides, pointing to a dark object silhouetted against the starlit sky.

The sub. halted his party and called them to attention. Six of them with the A.P., were to accompany him to the house; the others, under the command of the midshipman, were to form a cordon round the building and also to establish communication with the boats when the crucial time arrived.

Stealthily Tressidar approached the window through which Mr. Greenwood had effected his escape. The casement was ajar. He opened it and drew the curtain aside the fraction of an inch. The room, still lighted, was deserted. Signing to his men to remain, he stole quietly through the window and approached the trap-door leading to the tunnel. He could detect the fumes of petrol. With the burning lamp the cottage was in momentary peril of being blown up by the ignition of the air and volatile spirit with which it was so highly charged. Either the occupier was a madman or a fool, he argued.

Unbarring and unlocking the door, Tressidar brought his men into the room. Extinguishing the lamp, he switched on his electric torch and led the way down the ladder to the tunnel.

Contrary to his expectations, the descent was effected without any of the seamen stumbling, dropping their rifles, or making a noise that would betray their presence. In silence the men awaited their officer's next order, which was given by signs.

Tressidar weighed the matter over in his mind. To act quickly it was necessary to have light, since the darkness gave the miscreants an undoubted advantage. To attempt to stalk them in the pitch-black darkness would be running a risk of premature discovery. As far as he knew, there was about eighty yards of tunnel, including a fairly sharp bend between him and the seaward end of the cave.

Still keeping the torch switched on, Tressidar advanced swiftly and silently down the tunnel. He found not one but two turns in the passage. Upon rounding the second, the rays of his torch fell upon the two men of whom he was in search.

They were both lying across the sill of the natural opening communicating with the outside ledge. Both had night-glasses glued to their eyes, and so intent were they in keeping the expanse of dark water under observation that they failed to notice the illumination that flooded the cave.

There was no peremptory order of "Hands up!" No dramatic covering with revolvers. The British seamen simply grasped the recumbent men and dragged them back to the floor of the cave almost before they had time to utter a sound.

"Take that fellow back to the cottage," ordered the sub., indicating the man who had been addressed as Max. "Search him, question him, then report to me."

The German was hurried off. He offered no resistance.

Tressidar waited until unmistakable sounds told him that Max and his captors were ascending the ladder, then he turned to the second prisoner.

"You are expecting to communicate with a German submarine?" he began.

"No, sir, no," expostulated the man, his face contorted with fear. "I'll explain everything. I'll make a clean breast of it. That man"—and he pointed with his thumb along the tunnel—"is an escaped prisoner. He is a German officer. Some of my pals put him on to me, and, like a fool, I said I would hide him until a fishing-boat could take him across to Holland."

"You're a British subject," declared the sub. contemptuously.

"I am, sir. Never got into trouble before this. I've been led into it, sir, honest, I have."

"Honest you haven't," corrected Tressidar sternly. "Now, listen, you know the penalty—death.

"What, for harbouring a German prisoner, sir?" asked the man.

"No—for supplying hostile vessels with petrol. You have hundreds of gallons stored here, and I'll swear you cannot satisfactorily account for that quantity. Moreover, you were heard to say that a submarine was expected about three or four in the morning. Now, look here, what are the prearranged signals?"

"Curse you!—find out," muttered the man surlily.

"I mean to," rejoined the sub. suavely. "Let me put the facts before you. You're caught red-handed. There are no extenuating circumstances. You are deliberately betraying your country for the sake of a few hundred pounds, I suppose. If you give us all the assistance that lies in your power, that fact will be taken into consideration at your trial. I'll vouch for that. Now, I'll give you five minutes to think things over."

Leaving the prisoner in charge of a couple of seamen, the sub. approached the seaward entrance. Drawing his binoculars from their case, he focussed them on the water of the bay. The tide was now on the first of the ebb, with perhaps six feet of water close to the base of the cliffs.

By the aid of the powerful night-glasses he could just discern the grey forms of the "Pompey's" two boats. The first lieutenant had lost no time in proceeding to the spot, for his preparations were already complete, and the boats were even now withdrawing to a discreet distance to await developments.

With a grunt of satisfaction Tressidar replaced his binoculars and again confronted his prisoner.

"Time's up!" he exclaimed laconically.

"I'll tell you everything——" began the man.

"And mind you speak the truth," warned the sub. "Now, fire away."

"A submarine is expected," declared the prisoner. "At what hour I cannot say—it might be any hour between now and daybreak. She won't show any lights. She'll anchor in Half Way Deep and send a boat ashore. The men will imitate the curlew call three times, and I was to reply with a cry like the hoot of an owl. Then I had to lower petrol-cans as fast as I could."

"And your companion?" inquired Tressidar. "Who is he?"

"As I said before, sir, a German officer who broke out of one of the prison camps."

"His name?"

"I don't know, sir, except that it's Max."

The prisoner, who gave his name as Thomas Telder and was a gamekeeper in the employ of a large landowner in the vicinity, was removed under escort to the cottage, while the midshipman, having questioned the German, appeared to report to his superior officer.

"The fellow's a pretty cool customer," declared the midshipman. "Now that the game's up he doesn't appear to mind in the least. He says his name's Max Falkenheim, and that he's an unter-leutnant of the cruiser 'Mainz.' He was one of those fellows who were reported to have escaped from Donington Hall by digging a tunnel."

"Jolly rummy that he should fetch up here," commented the sub. "He's a long way out of his reckoning."

"Unless the east coast of England is too closely guarded," added the midshipman. "However, the fact remains that he was within an ace of getting clear. He swears he knows nothing about the unterseeboot, but that he had agreed with that skunk to put him on board a lugger."

"H'm; well, that's good enough for us. See anything, Parsons?" added Tressidar, addressing one of the seamen who had been told to keep a sharp look-out.

"No, sir; fancied I did, but it was a wash-out."

"Any of you men know how to hoot like an owl?" asked the sub.

"Yes, sir; I do," replied a tall able seaman, who in his youth had been a farm hand in the North Riding of Yorkshire.

"Very good; stand by, and when Parsons reports the submarine's signal—three cries of the curlew—do you hoot: once only, remember. The rest of you stand easy. I say, Greenwood, you might rummage up aloft and see if there's anything of an incriminating nature in the cottage. Make sure that all the blinds are drawn. I'll give you the word as soon as the strafed U-boat is sighted, if you don't finish before."

As a matter of fact the A.P. carried out his orders long before the submarine revealed her presence. It was within an hour and twenty minutes of sunrise—the tide being well on the flood—that the long-expected cry was faintly borne to the alert ears of the watchers.

Promptly the able seaman replied, and barely had the weird echoes died away when the sub. heard the muffled sound of oars being boated and the crunch of heavy boots on the dry kelp.

"Right you vos," exclaimed a guttural voice. "Lower der cans as fast as you vos like."

In reply Sub-lieutenant Tressidar whipped out his revolver and fired three shots in quick succession into the darkness. Then, with nerves a-tingle, he waited.

It will now be necessary to follow the movements of the two pulling-boats under the orders of the first lieutenant. On putting off from the cruiser, the boats made for the harbour's mouth. Outside the sea was fairly smooth, with a long, oily swell, for during the night the wind had backed to north-west and blew diagonally off shore.

Owing to the proximity of several dangerous ledges that extended seven or eight cables' length seaward the boats had to make a long detour before they arrived at Sallach Dhu Bay.

"We can't be so very far off now," remarked the first lieutenant to the midshipman in his boat. "It's that confoundedly black that goodness only knows where we are."

"Allowing for the tide, sir, I should think we're almost over Half Way Deep. Shall I have the lead heaved, sir?"

A cast gave the depth at two fathoms—certainly not enough to float a submarine, still less to enable her to submerge. The leadsman could feel the sinker trailing over the rocky bottom, as the boat drifted with the tidal current.

Again and again the lead-line gave approximately the same soundings. The first lieutenant began to have doubts as to whether he had already overshot the looked-for spot.

Suddenly the water increased in depth to fourteen and a half fathoms. That, allowing for the state of the tide, was the depth shown in the chart for Half Way Deep—a bottle-shaped depression extending well into the otherwise shallow waters of Sallach Dhu Bay.

The kedge was let go and, riding head to tide, the boat brought up, to enable the first lieutenant to confer with the officer in the second boat.

Carefully screening the light with a piece of painted canvas, the "No. 1" consulted the boat-compass.

"North one hundred and ten east, is your course," he announced to the officer in charge of his consort. "That'll be taking into consideration the cross set of the tide. I'll pay you out a hundred and twenty fathoms of grass warp, then you'll steer due north. When you've let go all the charge, make for the shore. We'll be on the look-out for you. Suppose you've tested circuits?"

"You bet," replied the other with a grin. "Between us there won't be a fish left alive in Half Way Deep, or a strafed U-boat either, I hope."

The second boat pushed off, her coxswain steering by means of a luminous compass. As soon as the strain of the connecting line grew taut, her kedge was dropped. Then both boats, approximately two hundred yards apart, allowing for the sag of the grass-rope under the influence of the tide, rowed on parallel courses, paying out lengths of sinister-looking objects that resembled strings of exaggerated sausages. This they continued to do until Half Way Deep was mined by a double chain of explosives.

The first lieutenant's boat was the first to reach the shore. Cautiously the crew scrambled out and drew her clear of the water, a petty officer handing the battery and firing-key ashore as carefully as if it were made of priceless metal.

Five minutes later the second boat loomed through the darkness.

"All correct, sir," reported her officer. "Suppose this is the bay? Wish to goodness I could smoke."

"And so do all of us, old boy," replied No. 1. "But curb your desires: you'll see plenty of smoke presently."

Huddled together under the lee side of the boats the two crews spent a tedious time, while their officers, treading softly, walked up and down the sands.

At intervals they exchanged curt sentences in whispers; otherwise the strictest silence was maintained. As the night wore on, the first lieutenant consulted the luminous dial of his watch with increasing frequency, until he began to wonder if the A.P.'s parent had been dreaming or was the victim of hallucinations. But throughout his monotonous patrol No. 1 took good care to keep within twenty yards of the firing-battery.

Presently he stopped dead and listened intently. Yes, he could just detect the faint sounds of muffled oars. The noise came from a spot considerably nearer than he anticipated: much too close to the drawn-up boats. What if the new-comers spotted the grey shapes as they lay on the sand?

The seamen heard the sounds, too, for several of them knelt up and peered over the gunwales. There was a concerted movement of the now alert men. The tedious vigil in the bitterly cold night was forgotten.

Then through the darkness came the curlew cry of the submarine's men, followed by the distant hoot of the British seaman who had been deputed to assume the rôle of an owl. What these meant the first lieutenant knew not. His pre-arranged signal had not yet been received. Bang! bang!! bang!!!

Fifty feet in the air the blackness was pierced by three vivid flashes, to the accompaniment of the sharp cracks of cordite-charged cartridges.

"Now!" shouted the first lieutenant.

The men in charge of the firing-batteries depressed the keys that completed the circuit.

Instantly the waters of Half Way Deep were lashed into two parallel columns of foam as a double chain of cascades leapt a hundred feet or so in the air. Then a terrific crash, mingled with the roar of the falling water and the thud of fragments of flying metal coming in contact with the granite cliff.

In the village of Auldhaig the concussion was severely felt. Windowpanes were shivered; solidly built houses literally rocked. People, aroused from sleep, dashed blindly for the streets or to their cellars, fully convinced that the Zeppelins had arrived. Only one individual slept through it all; Mr. Greenwood, dreaming of petrol-cans, floating mines, and his lost umbrella, and buried under the bed-clothes, knew nothing of the concussion until next morning. Barely had the echoes died away ere the first lieutenant and his party were doubling along the beach towards the place where the unterseeboot's dinghy had landed.

The canvas boat, with a long rent in her bilge, had been carried far up the shore by the rush of water following the tremendous upheaval. Her crew, consisting of a petty officer and two men, were too dazed to offer resistance, for upon the approach of the bluejackets they threw up their arms and yelled dismally for quarter. Almost at their feet was a large fragment of metal — one of the propeller blades of the shattered submarine.

"Are you all O.K., Mr. Tressidar?" sang out the first lieutenant.

"All correct, sir," replied Ronald. "We've nabbed the pair of them."

"Very good," rejoined No. 1. "Leave four men to guard the cottage and return to the ship. By the bye, have you a cigarette to spare? I left my case on board."

It did not occur to the speaker how he was to receive a cigarette from the sub., who was fifty feet above him, until he became aware of a dark object descending the cliffs by means of a rope.

Eric Greenwood, with a double purpose, had ordered two of the men to lower him to the beach.

"Here's my case, No. 1," he announced, as he fumbled under his pile of clothing. "Matches? You have? Would you mind giving me a passage back in the boat? I have a little commission to undertake."

[Illustration: "THEY THREW UP THEIR ARMS AND YELLED FOR QUARTER"]

Receiving permission, the A.P. made his way along the beach, the first lieutenant watching him curiously, for dawn was now breaking. Presently Eric returned with his parent's umbrella.

An hour later both boats ran alongside the "Pompey." Tressidar had already returned and had lost no time in making his report and retiring to his cabin to make up for arrears of sleep.

In spite of the early hour Captain Raxworthy was on desk, and as the first lieutenant came over the side he was waiting to congratulate him.

"An excellent night's work, Mr. Garboard!" he exclaimed delightedly — "a most excellent night's work!"

CHAPTER VII
THE DAY FOLLOWING

"Say, Snatcher, you're warned for D.B. party, ain't you?" inquired Stoker Jorkler. "D'ye mind if we change about?"

Stoker Flanaghan, commonly known as Snatcher, paused in the act of conveying a knifeblade well laden with peas to his capacious mouth. Such a request—for a man to voluntarily offer to undertake the disagreeable duty of cleaning and painting double bottoms—figuratively "took the wind out of his sails."

"Wot for?" he asked guardedly. "Wot's the bloomin' move?"

"Only there's leave for the starboard watch, and I'm some keen to nip ashore," replied Jorkler. "And you can have my tot of rum for a week if you do."

"Wants considerin', Rhino, old man," declared Snatcher. "Wot price the lootenant of the watch an' the jaunty?"

"They won't twig," said Jorkler. "I guess the bloke don't know the names of half the men in his watch-bill, and the master-at-arms won't care a brass farthing whether it's Snatcher Flanaghan or Rhino Jorkler who goes out of the ship so long as he comes back without being three sheets in the wind. And trust me for that, Snatcher. You've never seen me fresh?"

"True, that I ain't," replied the man reflectively, "or you wouldn't be so keen on chuckin' away your tot o' rum. Orl right, mate."

"Thanks," said Jorkler briefly, and without further delay he hurried off to change into his canvas suit for double bottom work.

Before he left the mess he had transferred a certain object from his ditty-box to his spacious jumper. Then, satisfying himself that there was no suspicious bulge to excite the curiosity of the officer of divisions, he fell in with the rest of the party.

Ten minutes later Stoker Jorkler, armed with a tin of red lead, a brush, some cotton waste, and a lighted candle, was surveying the oval-shaped aperture leading to a confined space between the outer and inner plating of the ship's hull. With him were a dozen others, similarly equipped, under the orders of a leading stoker.

It was not a pleasant occupation that Rhino had taken upon himself. In each of the cellular subdivisions of the hull a man had to crawl in as best he might, having first ascertained by means of the lighted candle that the air was sufficiently pure. Unless the candle burnt clearly, the place was dangerous to life. Stringent regulations were laid down to prevent accidents, fresh air being pumped into the double bottoms, while men were always on the watch to see that the workers were unaffected by the poisonous gases from the red lead.

"Right as ninepence," declared the leading stoker, referring to the light that gleamed in the space to which Jorkler had been detailed. "In you get, mate, and look slippy."

Jorkler obeyed. By dint of much writhing he succeeded in squeezing through the manhole. He found himself in a slightly curving space measuring about fifteen feet in length and twenty to twenty-four inches in height, and twenty feet or more below the level of the sea.

"Now, if the ship's torpedoed I'm a fair goner," thought Jorkler, but he knew that that possibility was very remote. The steps taken to guard Auldhaig Firth from submarine attack were so elaborate and efficient that no hostile craft could hope to get in. Moreover, the "Pompey" was well up the longest arm of the harbour. Between her and the entrance were at least half a dozen cruisers and twenty destroyers.

He worked with desperate energy, "scaling" off the rust, removing the metal flakes, and smothering the plating with liberal doses of red-lead. Then he paused and listened intently. He could hear the noise of the men at work in the adjoining compartments. It was now close on eight bells (noon). By that time the work would have to be completed.

"Guess I'm in luck," he soliloquised. "Unless I am much mistaken this part of the double bottom is right bang underneath the for'ard magazine. Pity it wasn't under the after one, but that can't be helped."

Turning on his side he extracted the "thing" from his jumper. It was a high-explosive charge, to which was attached a small but powerful battery. The charge he placed in the furthermost end of the compartment behind a tee-shaped flange. Here, unless deliberately sought for, it was safe from detection.

His next step was to produce his watch. To all outward appearances it was an ordinary silver timekeeper, but minute examination would reveal the presence of two small holes drilled through the back. Into these holes he inserted metal plugs attached to two insulated wires from the battery. One of the plugs projected beyond the face sufficiently to impede the progress of the hour hand, while the minute hand could clear it by a fraction of an inch. At four o'clock the hour hand would come in contact with the terminal, the circuit would be completed, and then— —

"Nearly finished there?" inquired the leading stoker, shouting through the oval aperture. "Just about done," replied Jorkler. "How goes it?"

"Close on eight bells," was the reply. "Buck up and don't keep me hanging about all the blessed day."

With the perspiration pouring off him and his clothes daubed with red lead and iron rust, Jorkler emerged from the compartment to find that the rest of the D.B. party had already completed their respective tasks.

Lowering an electric inspection lamp into the compartment, the leading stoker made a perfunctory examination of Jorkler's legitimate handiwork.

"You ain't half slapped it about," he remarked casually. "Guess you knew it was his Majesty's stores you were using and not your own gear."

After inspection by the ship's surgeon, who superintended the issue of a glass of lime-juice (in which sulphuric acid was a component part) to each man to ward off the injurious effect of the red lead, the men washed and changed. After dinner they were at liberty to do practically what they liked, it being Thursday, or "Make and Mend Day."

Just before five bells the liberty men fell in on the quarter-deck for critical inspection before going ashore. As Jorkler had expected, he had no difficulty in passing under the borrowed name of Flanaghan, for the M.A.A. took it without question.

Packed like sardines, the boat pushed off. Halfway to the staith they passed the "Pompey's" steam pinnace with a couple of officers and a small party of ladies and children in the stern-sheets.

"What's the game?" inquired the pseudo-Flanaghan, indicating with a jerk of his head the passing craft.

"Bloomin' at-'ome, I'll allow," replied one of the men. "They take jolly good care not to let our pals on board."

Jorkler nodded sympathetic assent.

"They're looking for trouble," he muttered to himself. "How was I to know? Anyway, that's their look-out, not mine."

On arriving at the quay the stoker slipped away from the rest of his shipmates. Out of sight he stepped out briskly, making in the direction of the hills at the back of the town.

"Where's Eric?" inquired Mr. Greenwood of Ronald Tressidar, as he gained the quarterdeck. The sub., engaged in animated conversation with Doris Greenwood, did not hear the question until it was repeated.

"Eric? Oh, I really don't know. I'll inquire."

Doris Greenwood was a golden-haired, blue-eyed girl possessed of a wealth of natural vivacity and an even-tempered disposition. Slightly above middle height, with a graceful bearing, she looked particularly attractive in her nurse's uniform.

Already she was the centre of attraction of a group of young officers, who, while envying Tressidar for his good luck, were inwardly reviling their comrade for his dog-in-the-manger policy.

"Seen Greenwood?" asked Ronald of an engineer sub-lieutenant.

"How about an intro?" inquired the officer addressed, ignoring the question.

"Go slow, old bird," rejoined Tressidar, laughing. "I'll introduce you all in good time. If you want to be in her good books, find young Greenwood. She's his sister."

"Brothers are generally in the way," retorted the engineer sub-lieutenant. "Greenwood isn't: he's gone ashore. The fleet pay sent him to the cashier's office."

Meanwhile, Doris had been unostentatiously taking stock of her brother's messmates. Life afloat, she reflected, does make a man. She compared Tressidar most favourably in his neat and serviceable uniform to the Ronald of her early days. Then, when he wasn't bashful, he was rude; now he was the personification of self-possession and mental and physical alertness.

As for Mr. Greenwood, he remained in wondrous meditation of the vastness of his surroundings. Apart from his nocturnal visit to the "Pompey," he had never before set foot on the deck of a British man-of-war. The tompioned muzzle of the after 9.2-in. gun, the towering superstructure with its array of quick-firers and searchlights, the lofty masts and enormous funnels—all in turn demanded his attention.

The vastness of his surroundings almost overpowered him. He had no idea that an armoured cruiser was so immense.

That afternoon there were nearly twenty adult visitors, mostly of the feminine sex, and a dozen or more children on board. It was not a usual procedure in wartime, but, giving due consideration to circumstances, the captain of the cruiser had good reasons to believe that there was no danger to be anticipated. In any case, the visitors would be clear of the ship before sunset.

The amusement of the children fell to the lot of the junior officers, and soon the gunroom resounded to the unusual sound of juvenile voices. Two little boys, rigged out in fencing helmets and padded coats, were mounted on the backs of a couple of midshipmen and were engaged in a realistic encounter with single-sticks—most realistic in the opinion of the human steeds, who had to bear the brunt of the warriors' energetic and ill-directed blows.

Another pair of youngsters were belabouring each other with boxing-gloves, amidst the plaudits of the junior sub. and the assistant clerk; while a tug-of-war, boys versus girls, afforded vast amusement for the rest of the small guests and their hosts.

In order to make sure that the engineer sub-lieutenant was not "pulling his leg," Tressidar went below to the ship's office. Here he found that the information concerning Eric was correct. He had been sent ashore with a party of marines to bring back sacks of coin for the ship's safe.

Upon returning to the quarter-deck the sub. found Mr. Greenwood in animated conversation with the commander on the subject of the raid upon the petrol-depôt. Now was Ronald's opportunity.

"Would you care to look over the ship, Doris?" he said. "I can spare half an hour."

"Only half an hour?" asked the girl. "We can't see very much in the time, can we?"

"I suppose not," admitted Tressidar. "But let's make the best of our time. I have to go away in the duty steamboat at a quarter to four. We have to fetch a lighter alongside from Inchbrail—that's three miles up the firth."

"I wish I could go with you," declared Doris. "I simply love little steamboats. They are much more exciting than big cruisers lying at anchor. Couldn't I?"

"Must see what the commander says," replied the sub. "Of course I'd be delighted. Only I'm afraid you'll miss your tea. They're making a scrumptious spread in the wardroom."

"I don't mind," said the girl recklessly. "I generally have tea at least once every day, but not the chance of having a trip in a steamboat."

Doris was certainly a hustler, for in less than the stipulated half-hour they had climbed the lofty navigation-bridge, peeped inside the conning-tower, soiled her gloves in the for'ard turret, and had explored the now deserted mess-decks. It took all the resource at Tressidar's command to persuade her to decline the engineer sub-lieutenant's invitation to descend to the engine-room. Only by hinting that if she did so she would be too late for the proposed run in the duty steamboat did Ronald succeed in "choking off" his super-attentive messmate.

"Miss Greenwood wishes to have a run in the D.S.B., sir," announced the sub., saluting the commander, who was still engaged in conversation with Greenwood, Senior.

"Very good," replied the commander. "Only be as sharp as you can. We want the lighter secured well before dark."

"I suppose, Mr. Greenwood, you wouldn't like a trip, too," asked Tressidar in duty bound, although inwardly hoping that this part of his invitation would be declined.

"No, thanks," was the reply. "To tell the truth, I'm feeling considerably stiff. Bad enough climbing to last me for at least a month. By the bye, do you know if Eric found my umbrella?"

Tressidar delighted his questioner by replying that Eric had recovered the lost property, but he hadn't the courage to continue the story. The A.P. had brought the thing on board. Examination showed that the handle had been "sprung," the silk ripped in three places, the wires bent, and, generally, damaged by salt water. So Eric had handed it over to the carpenter's crew for repairs and renovation. The men did the job not neatly, but too well. The silk they had patched with waxed seaming twine, re-waterproofing it by a liberal application of soft soap and linseed oil This was the outcome of a consultation of the naval recipe book; but since there was no mention of how to waterproof silk, they had adopted the process laid down for waterproofing canvas. The handle they repaired by "parcelling and serving" the fracture and concealing the tarred marline under a long gunmetal tube. The remaining visible portion of the handle they scraped and varnished.

The A.P. could not quite make out whether the "repairs" had been effected as a joke or in real earnest. At all events he quickly settled the matter by dropping the "game" out of a scuttle, intending to lead his parent to believe that the prized umbrella had been lost on that momentous night. And now Tressidar had unwittingly let the cat out of the bag.

The duty boat was fretting alongside the accommodation-ladder. Punctual to a minute Sub-lieutenant Tressidar boarded her and assisted Doris into the stern-sheets. From a manhole in the flat metal engine-room casing a leading-stoker's grimy head and shoulders appeared, his curiosity excited at the appearance of the sub.'s companion. He winked knowingly at the bowman and disappeared to his cramped quarters below.

"Mr. Tressidar!" sang out the commander, leaning over the guard-rails of the quarter-deck.

"Sir?"

"Stand by a minute. I want you to take a packet of correspondence to the 'Velocity.'"

Some minutes elapsed before the article in question was handed down to the boat. Bending and peering into the little cabin, Tressidar noticed that it was already twelve minutes to four.

He nodded to the coxswain. The latter, ordering "Easy ahead," put the helm over and the duty steamboat glided smoothly away from her parent ship.

"You'll be jolly cold," remarked the sub. to the girl. "It's awfully nippy, in spite of the protection afforded by the cabin top. Let me help you into this oil-skin."

Doris accepted the offer, Ronald taking rather an unnecessary time in assisting her into the voluminous yellow coat.

"That's all serene," he explained enthusiastically. "By Jove, Doris, it suits you splendidly."

"It's certainly more useful than ornamental," said the girl, as a shower of spray dashed up from the bows and drifted aft with a hissing sound. "There was once— —"

Her words were suddenly interrupted by a dull crash. Instinctively the sub. and his companion glanced astern. A cloud of smoke partly obscured the fore-part of the cruiser, as she reeled heavily to port with the effect of a mortal blow.

CHAPTER VIII
SPY AND SUPER-SPY

"She's torpedoed, sir!" exclaimed the coxswain as the "Pompey," after slowly recovering herself again, listed until her main for'ard-deck scuttles were awash.

"Hard-a-starboard!" ordered Tressidar. Then under his breath he added, "And those poor little kids on board."

Slowly the pall of smoke dispersed. Outwardly the cruiser showed no signs of her injuries. Swarms of seamen were strenuously engaged in lowering a collision-mat over the hole well beneath the water-line. Others were swinging out the boats.

The "Pompey" was doomed: not by the result of a hostile torpedo, but by an internal explosion. Stoker Jorkler's plot had succeeded, although not to the full extent that he had expected. The detonator had blown a large hole in the wing-plates, but fortunately the explosion had not communicated itself to the forward magazine. Had it done so, the end of the cruiser would have been sudden and complete: not one soul on board would have escaped.

Aft, although the shock of the explosion was distinctly felt, the effect was at first hardly noticeable. Amongst the visitors there was not the slightest trace of panic; in fact, it was with great difficulty that the gunroom officers' could prevail upon their youthful guests to abandon their play and go on deck. Promptly orders had been given to flood the magazines, thus preventing further danger in that direction.

Skilfully the duty boat was brought alongside the stricken cruiser, while almost at the same moment the pulling-boat containing Eric Greenwood and the money-bags rounded the ship's stern.

Assisted by brawny arms, the ladies and children were taken down the accommodation-ladder, the lower platform of which was now three feet under water, and placed in the boats. With full complements the steamboat and the one in which the A.P. was on duty pushed off, slowing down when at a safe distance to await developments.

Other assistance was speedily at hand. Since the cruiser's heavy boats could not be hoisted out in time and those in davits were insufficient for the officers and crew, it was as well that the "Pompey" was within easy reach of other vessels.

A dozen or more badly injured men were the next to be taken off; then, with the utmost precision and discipline, the rest of the crew gained the boats, but not before the collision-mat party for'ard were up to their knees in water.

Clouds of steam issued from the boiler- and engine-rooms, while at intervals muffled explosions of compressed air showed that the water-tight doors, already strained by the explosion, were unable to withstand the terrific pressure of the inflowing sea.

Captain Raxworthy, true to the time-honoured traditions of the service, was the last to quit the doomed ship. Barely had the boat into which he had jumped pushed off a dozen lengths when the huge vessel, shivering like a living creature, turned completely on her beam ends.

For some moments she remained thus, then, heeling still more until her topmasts touched the bed of the harbour, she disappeared from sight, with the exception of one end of her navigation-bridge that still projected a couple of feet above the surface.

As soon as the men landed they were formed up and mustered by divisions. The result of the roll-call showed that nineteen men were missing, and in addition to the dozen seriously injured, thirty men required surgical treatment. Amongst those missing was Stoker James Jorkler.

And when the liberty men returned it was informed that one man had "run." The absentee was reported under the name of Stoker Flanaghan.

In a clump of gaunt pine-trees, halfway up the summit of Ben Craich—the loftiest of the hills in the vicinity of Auldhaig Firth—stood the man hitherto known as Rhino Jorkler.

It is hardly necessary to remark that he was not a Canadian-born British subject. He was a German-American, his real name being Otto Oberfurst. By profession, previous to the outbreak of war, he was a mining-engineer, since then he had been a Secret Service agent in the employ of the German Government.

At first he was engaged in minor activities, under the direction of the notorious Boy Ed, but his zeal so impressed his employer that before long he was entrusted with a desperate mission in the Province of Quebec. Succeeding, he was handsomely rewarded out of the huge sums lavished by the German Government upon the questionable Secret Service and given an opportunity of transferring his activities to Great Britain.

Much as he preferred to work single-handed, he was ordered to report himself to a certain von Schenck, a director of the Teutonic espionage system that prevails in the United Kingdom.

Von Schenck had been, with the exception of periodical visits to Germany, resident in Great Britain for nearly thirty years. At sixty his powers of intellect were undimmed, and since success in espionage depends more upon wits than upon bodily strength and activity, his physical infirmities aided rather than embarrassed his sinister work.

He was of small stature, waxen-featured and grey-haired. He could speak English with a fluency that was faultless enough to take him anywhere without arousing suspicion. From other spies' experiences he knew that a precise regard for the intricate rules of English grammar was frequently a trap. Living unostentatiously in a small house on the outskirts of Edinburgh, he posed as a retired merchant under the assumed name of Andrew McJeames.

With few exceptions von Schenck knew none of his vast army of spies by name, nor did they know of his identity. They were merely numbers—pawns in the great game of espionage played according to the rules and regulations of the degenerate Hun. In a few cases, however, the master spy was personally acquainted with his immediate subordinates, and amongst these was Otto Oberfurst.

It was at von Schenck's instigation that Oberfurst joined the British Navy at Portsmouth. He reckoned on the enormous odds of the newly enlisted stoker being promptly drafted to a vessel in the North Sea. By joining at the Hampshire naval port, less suspicion would be likely to be aroused than if he had entered the service at Rosyth or Cromarty.

Von Schenck was a keen motorist. For miles around the Scottish capital his powerful Mercédès car was known. His kindness in placing himself and his motor at the disposal of a certain military hospital was merely a cloak for a twofold purpose. It gave him an excuse to use the car, in spite of the half-hearted requests from the Government backed by a firm appeal from the Royal Automobile Club; it also enabled him to pick up valuable information from the wounded Tommies, whose pardonable desire to relate their adventures often led them to overrun their discretion. He made a point of never asking a question on service matters of his guests. He relied upon his skill in leading up to any particular subject of which he required information, and sooner or later his wishes were gratified. Within forty-eight hours the information was in the hands of the German Admiralty.

From his place of concealment Otto Oberfurst sat and waited while the lengthening shadows betokened the approach of another night. At frequent intervals he consulted his watch. It was almost identical with the one he had left in the double bottom of the "Pompey."

Occasionally he directed his attention to the dark brown ribbon that marked the position of the main road leading to Auldhaig, but his gaze was chiefly concentrated upon the land-locked harbour. The "Pompey," lying on the extreme west of the line of moorings, was plainly visible. To all outward appearances she looked to be the embodiment of armed security, protected as she was by triple lines of anti-submarine devices that barred the entrance to the firth. In addition to the numerous warships, ranging from large armoured cruisers down to the swift, well-armed craft of the destroyer flotilla, the harbour was protected by four distinct anti-aircraft batteries armed with the very latest type of guns. The positions of these concealed batteries the spy knew with startling accuracy. He also knew that a short distance inland from Auldhaig, and situated in a remote and naturally sheltered valley, was the important munition factory of Sauchieblair. Three times had German aircraft sought to discover the exact position of these immense works. On the last occasion bombs had missed the main cordite factory by two hundred yards; but that was more by good luck than good judgment, for never in the course of their flight over the Scottish coast had they been absolutely certain of their bearings.

Four o'clock. Otto Oberfurst, his hands shaking in spite of his strong nerve, awaited the result of his treacherous handiwork. Ten—twenty—thirty seconds passed, but still no terrific explosion that would rend the cruiser from stem to stern. A wave of horrible uncertainty swept over him. Perhaps suspicion had been aroused and the double bottom had been searched; or a flaw in the intricate mechanism of the timing-gear had prevented the deliberate catastrophe. In either case the failure would be of grave consequences to the German Secret Service plans. The actual proof that an attempt had been made to destroy a warship by internal explosion would make it advisable to discontinue activities in that direction. So long as the British attributed similar disasters to accident, well and good. They could set forth as many theories as they liked, provided that the real reason was known only to von Schenck and his associates.

Suddenly Oberfurst's cogitations were interrupted by the sight of a cloud of smoke leaping skywards from the cruiser. Four seconds later the muffled boom of the explosion was borne to his ears. He could see the vessel listing, but to his intense disappointment she showed no signs of being blown to pieces.

"Himmel!" he muttered. "It is not the magazine this time. I must have miscalculated its position. No matter, another English ship is out of action. Better luck next time!"

He waited until the "Pompey" had disappeared from view beneath the waters of Auldhaig Harbour, then, walking rapidly, he followed a mountain path leading away from the town.

Darkness had fallen when he arrived at a small stone cottage situated in a remote glen. With the ease of a man who was familiar with his surroundings, Oberfurst climbed the stile in the wall enclosing the garden, threaded his way along the winding path, and, avoiding an invisible obstruction in the form of an iron pig-trough, tapped softly upon the window-pane.

"Who's there?" inquired a high-pitched voice.

"All right, mother," replied the spy reassuringly.

Without further delay the door was unbarred and Oberfurst entered the cottage.

"I've run," he declared. "Couldn't stick it any longer."

"Eh?" The old woman eyed him sharply. "What's wrong now?"

"Mother" Taggach, the occupier of the cottage, was a shrivelled-up woman of seventy. She was an illicit distiller of whisky and a receiver of stolen property. The former occupation she plied in this remote cottage; the latter was carried on in a small shop in the outskirts of Edinburgh, where her son kept a marine store. Her minor activities consisted in assisting naval and military deserters, although since the war there was little call for her assistance in that direction. The few "bad hats" of the fleet at Auldhaig soon found out that at Mother Taggach's there were facilities for spending leave with the possibilities of obtaining spirits which, owing to the stringent regulations, were denied them in the town.

Stoker Jorkler was one of her patrons, but Mother Taggach, in spite of her failings, was a strong anti-German. Not for one moment did she suspect the true character of the spy.

"Yes," he continued in answer to her questions. "I've run—deserted. Nerves all gone."

"A pretty sailor you make," remarked the old woman witheringly. "So you want me to fix you up? It's very risky, you know."

"Very," agreed Oberfurst. "But if I'm nabbed I won't peach. Let's have a suit of civilian togs and before morning I'll be miles away."

"Five pounds, then," demanded Mother Taggach.

The spy produced the money. The old woman carefully counted and examined the notes, then from a wooden box she drew a bundle of clothes.

"There you are," she said. "Get along upstairs. You'd best be clear of my house in less than ten minutes."

Quickly Oberfurst effected the change. Beyond wearing civilian garb he made no attempt to disguise himself.

"Here's my old gear," he said, handing the woman a bundle containing his uniform.

"All right, I'll burn them," she remarked. "Though 'tis a waste of good stuff. Where might you be making for, might I ask?"

"Wick," he replied. "I've got a pal there."

He went out into the night and walked quickly until he approached the spot where the mountain path struck the highway running parallel with the east coast. Here he sat down, and from his pocket produced a razor and a piece of soap. In very short time he had shaved the top of his head and his eyebrows, while in place of his smooth chin he sported a greyish beard that would escape detection except under critical inspection. Then, instead of turning northward—for he had deliberately misinformed Mother Taggach—he set his face to the south and tramped briskly in the direction of far-distant Edinburgh.

CHAPTER IX
AN ADVENTURE ON THE HILLS

"I wish to goodness that sister of mine wouldn't do such erratic things," remarked Eric Greenwood.

"Oh!" rejoined Tressidar, with a veiled attempt at inconsequence. "What has she been up to now?"

The conversation occurred two days after the loss of H.M.S. "Pompey." The officers and men of the destroyed cruiser were temporarily berthed in a hulk that had been towed round from Chatham some months previously for use as a depôt-ship.

Mr. Greenwood had returned to Devonshire, declaring that the east coast of Scotland was a little too lively for a man of his mature years and sedentary habits. Doris, of course, remained at the Auldhaig sick-quarters.

"Going for lonely walks when she's off duty," explained the A.P. "Why on earth she doesn't get one of the nursing sisters to go with her I cannot imagine. When I proposed to accompany her, she promptly choked me off. This afternoon, she tells me, she's taking the train as far as Nedderburn, and is going to tramp back over the hills. From all accounts it's a rotten, unfrequented road."

"It is," agreed the sub.

"Yes," added Eric. "And I would insist upon going with her, in spite of her objections, only I am booked for the preliminary inquiry at the Senior's Officer's quarters. That's the penalty for keeping one's shorthand up."

Ronald Tressidar kept his plans to himself, but one of the first things he did was to consult a railway time-table. In it he found that the earliest train the girl could take was at 2.45 p.m. That meant that she would probably set out on her return at a quarter past three, since Nedderburn was only nine miles from Auldhaig and the railway journey took twenty minutes.

His next step, immediately after lunch, was to go ashore and pay a visit to the local garage.

"Sorry, sir," replied the proprietor in answer to the sub.'s request for the hire of a two-seater car. "I've nae ain in the place; but I hae a bonnie leetle motor-cycle and side-car."

"Suppose that will have to do," said Tressidar dubiously. "She'll take the hills all right, I hope?"

Receiving an affirmative reply, the sub. concluded negotiations for the hire of the unaccustomed mount, but before he was clear of the town he found that he had something fairly powerful under his control and also something that was not so very difficult to steer.

For the first two miles the road skirted the northern shore of the firth, then ascending a steep hill by means of a series of well-engineered zig-zags, it swept across a bleak upland. For the most part the country on either side consisted of sheep-pasture, rough stone walls taking the place of the hedges so common in the south. Here and there were thick clusters of gorse, growing to a height of nearly six feet. There were also clumps of gaunt pines that swayed mournfully in the stiff breeze.

After a while the road began to descend with a long, easy gradient. Away on his right he could just discern the galvanised iron roofs and tall brick chimneys of the Sauchieblair Munition Works. It was only from this part of the road that any distant view could be obtained of the magazines without climbing any of the surrounding hills. Just beyond this spot was a fairly extensive wood.

"I'll bring up here and have a pipe," thought the sub. "I am in plenty of time, and it's only a few miles to Nedderburn."

Leaving the cycle and side-car, he paced up and down the road, for the air was much too keen to stand still. Then, having assured himself that there was plenty of petrol in the tank—experience had taught him that there are such things as leaking carburetters and petrol pipes—he restarted.

Less than a mile from the outskirts of the little village of Nedderburn he espied a trim figure walking briskly in his direction. It was Doris Greenwood.

Presently Tressidar's fears gripped him.

"Hang it!" he soliloquised. "What possible excuse can I have for coming out here?"

With a motor-cycle travelling at twenty miles an hour there is little time to decide upon any matter, but by the time the sub. slowed down he had framed some sort of excuse which might or might not hold water.

"Hulloa, Doris!" he exclaimed in well-simulated surprise. "Whatever are you doing in this unfrequented road?"

"Merely walking for exercise," she replied.

"To Auldhaig? It's a long way. Can I give you a lift?"

"Why, you are going in exactly the opposite direction," declared the girl laughingly. "And to find you riding with an empty side-car, Ronald. Now, what does it mean?"

"I'll deal with your question," replied Tressidar, striving to gain time to find a suitable explanation to meet her previous remark. "I couldn't hire a car and I can't ride a motorbike solo, so I had to hire the side-car to keep me balanced. It's quite true that I was going in the wrong direction, but there's no reason why I shouldn't turn the affair round."

"If you are riding with a set purpose," continued Doris remorselessly, "I wouldn't think of detaining you. You evidently are making for somewhere."

"Yes, I am," admitted Tressidar boldly. "I came along here to meet you. It's no use mincing matters. Look here, what do you say to a run out as far as Tuilaburn? It's only seven miles further, and the road across the moors is simply top-hole. We'll be back at Auldhaig well before lighting-up time."

Doris assented. She was not one of those irresponsible young ladies who coyly pretend not to be able to make up their minds. She really admired the tall, bronzed naval officer who had handled the duty steamboat so magnificently in going to the aid of the doomed "Pompey." It was not without ulterior motives, which were now being realised, that she had "choked off" her rather too attentive brother.

Before the girl took her place in the car Ronald assisted her to don his oilskin coat—the same that she had worn on that memorable trip in Auldhaig Harbour. It formed an ideal protection from the biting wind.

Almost before they were aware of it, they ran into Tuilaburn. Here they had tea and talked—of many things. It was close upon lighting-up time when the return journey began.

"By Jove! the little engine does pull well," remarked Tressidar as the motor-cycle ascended the long gradual rise out of Nedderburn. "We'll be in Auldhaig before it's time to light up, you see if we won't."

The words were hardly out of his mouth when, with an ominous succession of bumps, the back tyre punctured.

"The result of boasting," declared Doris cheerfully, as the sub. dismounted and examined the outer cover.

"A nail," he announced. "That's good. It will save me from searching for a small puncture. I'll mend the inner tube in less than ten minutes."

Once again his optimism was at fault, for the cover was an obstinate one to remove. The tube, a butted one, was then patched and replaced. By the time they were ready to resume their journey it was lighting-up time.

For nearly ten minutes Tressidar attempted to get the head-light to burn. It stubbornly refused duty. Examination showed that the carbide was already saturated and useless for illumination.

"We'll risk it," declared the sub. "It's a hundred to one chance that we meet anyone on this unfrequented road, especially a policeman."

"I should not like to see our names figure in a police-court report," remarked Doris.

"No; but they might appear in a very different sort of document," added Tressidar boldly.

Doris made no reply. It was now too dark for her companion to notice the expression on her face. Vaguely he wondered whether he had bungled again.

"What's that glare over there?" asked the girl as they emerged from a little wood on the crest of the hill.

"Only the munition works at Sauchieblair," replied Tressidar. "It's rather strange that a Government factory should show such an amount of light."

"It's out," exclaimed Doris ten seconds later. "What does that mean—a Zepp. warning?"

"Shouldn't wonder," answered her companion. "It's just the sort of night—dark and practically no wind.... Oh, bother!"

The back tyre was again bumping on the ground.

"I vote we abandon ship," suggested Tressidar. "We'll push the thing just off the road and walk the rest of the way. I'll tell the man to send for it in the morning, Hope you don't mind the tramp, Doris?"

They alighted. Tressidar was in the act of urging the heavy motor-cycle upon the slight rise by the roadside when with a rush and subdued roar a powerful motor-car with obscured lights flashed by. Well it was that the cycle was clear, otherwise there was every possibility of its being run down by the reckless road-hogs.

"Three red lights," exclaimed Doris, indicating the rear lights of the disappearing motor. "That's rather unusual."

"There's no law against a fellow having as many red rear lights as he wants so far as I know," said Tressidar. "It's certainly unusual. I say, I believe the car's stopping. Let's get them to give us a lift into Auldhaig."

The motor was now on a slight rise almost four hundred yards from the spot where the motor-cycle had been abandoned. It displayed three red lights vertically.

Before the sub. and his companion had walked more than twenty yards the three lights were increased by three more, so that there was a vertical string of six. At the same time the car was being backed from the side of the road on to the sward.

"Doris," exclaimed Ronald hurriedly, "will you stay here a little while?—do you mind? I'm going to see what those fellows are up to. It looks jolly fishy. You're not nervous?"

"Not a little bit," declared the girl. "Only take care of yourself."

"I'll try," rejoined the sub. "Don't make a sound. If—that is, supposing I don't come back, you had better make your way to Nedderburn and telephone to the senior officer of Auldhaig; but I fancy that there'll be no need for that."

Taking to the grass, Tressidar stole cautiously in the direction of the stationary car. His footsteps made no sound upon the springy turf. As he approached he bent low, taking advantage of the cover afforded by the numerous gorse bushes.

"So that's your little game," he mused. There were two men with the car. One, by the aid of the partly screened head-lamp, was consulting what was evidently a prismatic compass. The other, acting according to the movements of his companion's hand, was slowly shifting the car in its own length.

The mystery of the six red lights was now no longer a mystery. To the sub.'s keen intelligence the whole thing was as clear as daylight. The lid of the tool-box at the rear of the car had been partly raised until it formed an angle of 135 degrees with the back of the body. The lid, being of burnished metal, served as a reflector, so that the three red lights appeared to be six in a straight vertical line.

And that line pointed in the direction of the Sauchieblair Munition Works.

"That will do," said a voice in German—a language of which Tressidar had more than a general knowledge. "We're right on the exact bearing. Call up Pfeiller and inform him that our position is fixed."

The fellow who had been engaged in manoeuvring the car stepped inside the coupé. The faint cackle of a low-powered wireless apparatus was faintly borne to the sub.'s ear.

"Pfeiller reports all right at his position," announced the man after a brief interval.

"Let us hope he is sure on the point," remarked the German with the compass.

"He is a careful man at that sort of work," said the other reassuringly. "Now comes the worst part of the business—the waiting. Himmel! I t is cold on these hills."

"If she picks up the coast lights without difficulty she ought to be here by eight o'clock," said his companion. "These English have already had warning. That is why they have turned out the lights. Can you imagine them, friend Otto, cowering in darkness, waiting for one of our incomparable Zeppelins to blow them to pieces? And there is not even a puny, so-called anti-aircraft gun nearer than Auldhaig."

Ronald Tressidar had heard enough. His first impulse was to retrace his steps quietly and make his way to Nedderburn to procure assistance. But upon further consideration he came to the conclusion that before the spies could be made prisoners the Zeppelin's work might be accomplished. Prompt measures were necessary.

Creeping away to a safe distance, the sub. removed his heavy greatcoat. To have the unencumbered use of his limbs was essential to the work he proposed attempting.

Again he stalked the two Germans. Unheard and unseen he gained the remote side of the car, then working round the front he leapt upon the nearmost of the spies.

Throwing his muscular arms round the fellow's head and applying his knee to the small of his back, Tressidar hurled him heavily to the ground. In falling, the fellow grabbed frantically at the sub.'s ankles. The check was but momentary, but sufficient to put the second Teuton on his guard.

Whipping out a pistol, he fired almost point-blank at the British naval officer.

Whether he was hit or otherwise Tressidar did not pause to consider. Bending low and hunching his shoulders, he charged the armed man, and butting him in the chest sent him flying backwards a good five yards. The pistol was jerked from his grip and fell in the centre of a gorse-bush.

Carried onwards by the momentum of his furious charge, the sub. tripped across the plunging limbs of his opponent and pitched headlong on the ground.

CHAPTER X
THE FOILED RAID

Before Tressidar could recover himself the second German gripped him by the throat, at the same time shouting to his prostrate comrade to bestir himself and find the pistol.

Although his opponent was a heavy, muscular man the British officer, taken at a disadvantage, did not hesitate to attempt to equalise matters. In spite of the pressure of the Hun's fingers on his windpipe, he raised his knees and lashing out literally hurled the German from him.

Agilely turning over, Tressidar sought to regain his feet, but as he did so the fellow he had previously felled leapt upon his back, striking him over and over again with his clenched fists; while the other man, in spite of being temporarily winded, came again to the attack.

In the midst of the desperate struggle Tressidar was most agreeably surprised to hear a voice shouting, "Come on, men. Collar those fellows."

The impending assistance caused the two Germans to take to their heels. Without waiting to ascertain the numbers and strength of the rescue party, they made off, leaving the car and various instruments behind.

Tressidar regained his feet. He could discern the heavy tread of approaching footsteps. He hastened to meet his rescuers, until sheer astonishment brought him up "all standing." The rescue party consisted of one person—Doris Greenwood.

"Are you hurt, Ronald?" she asked in an anxious whisper.

"No, I don't think so," replied Tressidar. "But why——? I thought I told you to sheer off."

"It's not insubordination," said the girl. "You are not my superior officer, you know. I heard the firing and the sound of men scuffling, so I did my level best to imitate a man's voice, and at the same time I stamped hard upon the ground. Have they gone?"

"Yes; but if they find out that you're only a girl—a jolly plucky one, I must say—they may take it into their thick heads to renew the attack. I'll find that pistol and be on the safe side."

While the sub. was searching for the lost weapon, Doris listened intently.

"I cannot hear anything of them," she reported.

"That's rather a pity," said Tressidar, as he groped in the prickly furze. "They may still be hanging round, waiting to stalk us. Hurrah! I've found it."

His hand had come in contact with the barrel of the pistol. He withdrew the firearm, to find that it was a powerful weapon of the automatic type. Examination of the magazine revealed the fact that there were seven unexpended cartridges.

"Where's your great-coat?" asked Doris.

"I left it down there," replied Tressidar, indicating the dim outlines of the gorse-bushes on the other side of the road.

"You'll get a fearful cold without it. Go and get it," continued the girl authoritatively. "We have no sympathy with patients at Auldhaig Sick Quarters who get pneumonia through their own carelessness."

Tressidar laughed.

"I feel inclined to take the risk," he retorted. "But I suppose I'd better obey your orders, even if you won't obey mine."

Holding the pistol in readiness for a surprise attack, the sub. stole cautiously to the place where he had left his great-coat. Without interruption he regained his property and rejoined his companion, then he listened intently. Not a sound broke the stillness of the night.

"Well, we've had to abandon a motor-cycle and side-car and we have a gorgeous motor-car in exchange," said Tressidar. "I say, I hope you are not in a great hurry?"

"Of course not," replied Doris with surprise at the question. "Nursing sisters are not required to be back before nine."

"It may be long after nine," said the sub. seriously. "Stand by while I shift this car. I'll tell you why presently."

The motor-car being on a slight gradient was fairly easy to move even without starting the engine.

"Why, you haven't moved it half a yard," exclaimed Doris

"Precisely. That is all that is necessary just at present. Now let me explain. These fellows were expecting a Zeppelin. It's on its way, I believe, but there's little or no danger for us, I may say. Somewhere—in what direction or how far away I don't know—is another car, showing, I presume, a string of red lights like this beauty. Viewed from an airship, there will be two lines of red lights visible. These, if continued indefinitely, will intersect at a certain spot. There the Zepp. is to drop her bombs; and the desired place is Sauchieblair Munition Factory. Unfortunately I cannot alter both bearings, but by clewing this car round a few feet the point of intersection will be altered at least a couple of hundred yards. I hope it will be four or five hundred, but it won't do to alter the bearing too much in case it doesn't cross the other one."

"And then?"

"We must wait until the Zepp. has come and gone. If we abandon our post our Germans may return and readjust the position of the car. Hulloa! what's that? There's some one coming. Just get into the car, Doris. It's a pretty substantial affair, unless I'm much mistaken."

Doris obeyed without demur. Tressidar, with his pistol ready for instant action, crouched behind the body of the car.

Evidently some harmless individual was approaching. They could hear footsteps crunching on the hard gravel road, but still, the sub. could afford to take no risks of a treacherous onslaught.

"Halt!" shouted Tressidar as the man came within ten paces. "Who are you? What are you doing here?"

The stranger, a big, hulking fellow, halted promptly enough, and in broad Scotch declared that he was only a shepherd on his way home.

"And I'm a naval officer," announced the sub. "I call upon you in the King's name to render assistance. Is your sight good? Can you hear well?"

Receiving a disjointed affirmative reply from the almost dumfounded shepherd, Tressidar continued:

"That's capital. Now, I want you to stand here and keep a bright lookout. There are two suspicious characters knocking about. They are not armed—at least, with firearms, for I've taken the only pistol they possessed. Directly you spot them—that is, if they make up their minds to come back—let me know as quietly as possible. Eh, what's that? You hope they do? Good man! You are a tough customer to tackle with that heavy stick of yours."

The Scotsman, a brawny specimen in spite of his years, for he was nearly sixty, nodded his head with a confidence that assured the sub. of a reliable and energetic ally. Leaving him at his post, Tressidar returned to the car.

"I fancy I heard firing," he remarked.

"Yes," agreed Doris. "I saw flashes. See, there they are again."

She pointed away to the south-east. The crests of the distant hills were silhouetted against a succession of pale flashes and the glare of half a dozen searchlights, while the low rumble of a series of explosions could just be distinguished.

Then the flashes ceased, although the giant beams still searched the sky—and searched in vain. The huge target presented by the Zeppelin had been lost to sight.

"There's something overhead," declared Tressidar. "It's an aerial propeller, but for a Zepp. it's very subdued. You're not nervous, Doris?"

The girl smiled.

"Being nervous wouldn't be of any use, so I must be brave," she replied. "As a matter of fact I am rather enjoying the experience. Do you think——"

A lurid flash and terrific crash, the sound appearing to emanate from a spot within a hundred yards from where they waited, interrupted her words. The flash was followed by two others in quick succession, and then a perfect hail of high-explosive bombs. The Zepp. was hurling down missiles as fast as she could from a height of less than two thousand feet upon what her commander took to be the Sauchieblair Munition Works. In point of actual fact the bombs were dropping, thanks to Tressidar's resourcefulness in altering the position of the leading lights, on the grassland full a mile from the Huns' particular objective.

For nearly twenty minutes the futile operation of bomb-dropping continued. Once or twice the sub. turned to look at the shepherd. The man was gazing stolidly into the darkness with his back turned upon the German firework display. He had been set a particular task and whole-heartedly he was carrying it out.

At length, as if suspecting that they were being tricked, the crew of the Zeppelin ceased hurling explosives. They switched on two powerful searchlights, which, playing in an almost vertically downward direction, swept the ground in order to discover the magazine buildings. To do so the airship had dropped to less than a thousand feet.

"They'll find the place, I'm afraid," thought Tressidar. "If only our people had even a couple of anti-aircraft guns——"

The shepherd touched his arm and pointed down the road in the direction of Auldhaig. Approaching at a furious rate, their presence only apparent by the noise they made, were several motor-cars armed with quick-firers on vertical mountings. Others, with travelling searchlight projectors, accompanied them. The lights were temporarily screened, since the position of the hostile airship could be fixed by the fact that she was playing her searchlights upon the ground.

The mobile quick-firers made no attempt to get into action until the cars were almost abreast of the spot where Tressidar and his companions were. Had they done so, the chances were that the falling shrapnel bullets would do considerable damage to the lightly built roofs of the munition works.

Suddenly six anti-aircraft guns opened fire simultaneously. The air was torn with the shriek of the high-velocity projectiles and the sharp reports of the weapons. The explosion of the shells threw a blaze of light upon the silvery envelope of the gigantic night-raider. It seemed as if it would be impossible for her to escape the wide effect of the bursting projectiles.

Doris clasped her hands and waited, fully expecting that the huge floating fabric would either burst into flame or drop, a crumpled mass of metal, upon the ground.

The Zeppelin lurched. Her bow part tilted sharply downwards. Her searchlights were switched off. At the same time the British searchlights threw their concentrated beams upon their quarry. Smoke was pouring from the hard-pressed airship, until her outlines were hidden by the pall of vapour.

Then, to an accompaniment of a perfect tornado of exploding bombs for the airship had hurriedly thrown out her remaining supply of missiles, the Zeppelin shot vertically upwards with almost incredible velocity. Growing smaller and smaller to the sightseers, it gradually grew more and more indistinct, until the searchlight men were unable to locate its position. The last seen of her was that she was travelling slowly in a south-easterly direction.

"Hulloa! What the deuce have we got here?" inquired a deep, hearty voice. "Car with a blaze of red lights, by Jove!"

Towards the Mercédès car strode a burly, great-coated figure in the uniform of a lieutenant in the R.N. Air Service. Following him were seven or eight men from the crews of the motor batteries.

"You have here a car belonging to a couple of German spies," said Tressidar, advancing to meet the lieutenant.

"Nothing like being candid about the business," rejoined the latter drily. "And who might you be?"

The sub. announced his name and rank.

"You have a lot to explain," said the Air Service officer. "There have been cases of Germans masquerading in British uniforms, you know. You must consider yourself under arrest."

Tressidar raised no objection. It was useless to do so. He realised that, in the circumstances, the lieutenant was perfectly justified in what he did. He only wondered how Doris would take it.

Greatly to his surprise he heard the girl laugh merrily.

"Good evening, Mr. Waynsford," she exclaimed.

The young lieutenant, completely taken aback, did not immediately reply. Striding to the door of the car, he merely returned the compliment and waited for Doris to continue.

"I can answer for Mr. Tressidar's loyalty," she continued. "You see, Mr. Waynsford, we are stranded on the hills. We had to abandon a motor-cycle and we found a motor-car. In fact, Mr. Tressidar captured it. Now I think I'll let you continue the narrative, Ronald."

"By Jove!" ejaculated the lieutenant. "That was quite a 'cute move on the part of the spies, Tressidar, and most smart on your part. I believe we've winged that Zepp. Hulloa!"

A petty officer came up at the double. He was one of the men attached to the portable wireless telegraphy car.

"The Zepp.'s reported flying low over Saltkirk, sir," he announced. "She dropped one bomb on a cottage. Woman and four children blown to bits. The airship was last seen making slowly to the east'ard."

"Very good," commented Waynsford. "We can do no more. Can you pilot the captured car into Auldhaig, Tressidar?"

"Don't think I'd better risk it," replied the sub. "I'm not used to a Mercédès. A British-built car is more my mark."

He had other reasons for declining to be his own prize-master. It would not be fair to Doris to let her risk her life in a strange car and on a rough, hilly road. On the other hand, he did not like the idea of letting Lieutenant Waynsford have the pleasure of the girl's company. Already he was a little jealous of the fellow, he decided. How did Doris get to make his acquaintance during her as yet brief stay at Auldhaig?

"All right, then," rejoined Waynsford. "I'll give you a lift in my car, and get a couple of hands to run the Mercédès to Auldhaig. 'Fraid you'll find rather cramped quarters," he added, as he held open the metal door in the armoured sides. "The shoulder-piece of the quick-firer is awfully in the way."

A moment later the cars were jolting and swaying at forty miles an hour along the road, barely slowing down as they tore through the crowded streets of Auldhaig, for the Zepp. had brought men, women, and children from the houses, all eager to hear of the work done by the anti-aircraft guns.

In this they were disappointed. The gunners, modest when it came to relating their own deeds, were not inclined to give particulars, especially as they were not definitely certain as to whether the Zepp. was crippled.

Having escorted Doris to the gates of the hospital, Tressidar bade her a hasty farewell and hurried towards the harbour. He had already outstayed his leave, and although the extenuating circumstances warranted the breach of discipline, he was anxious to know what was being done afloat. It was now close upon ten o'clock. At ten-thirty he was to go on duty in the guard-boat, which at Auldhaig was the "harbour service" torpedo-boat No. 445, an antiquated craft but quite good enough for the work allotted to her.

Auldhaig Harbour was now comparatively empty. The armoured cruisers had left during the afternoon to rendezvous off the Isle of May; the destroyers had gone to relieve the outer patrol in the Firth of Forth, and the "opposite numbers" had not yet returned to the base. The only vessels left were a couple of light cruisers undergoing refit, four torpedo-boats, and a couple of large fleet auxiliaries.

By this time the steam pinnace had taken the sub. off to the hulk in which the ship's company of the ill-fated "Pompey" were quartered. Tressidar was only just able to snatch a hasty meal before the torpedo-boat was ready to cast off.

Thanking his lucky stars that it was a fine night, although bitterly cold, Tressidar gained the deck of the waiting craft. As he did so the officer of the watch came to the side of the hulk and leant over.

"Message just come through, Mr. Tressidar," he exclaimed. "Zeppelin reported down about fifteen miles south-east of Dunletter Head. All available craft ordered to proceed and investigate. Good luck!"

CHAPTER XI
ONE ZEPPELIN THE LESS

Torpedo-boat No. 445 easily led the procession of small fry. Her speed, a bare twenty knots, was a good two miles an hour more than the rest of the torpedo-boats, while she could give points to the swiftest of the armed trawlers that lumbered in the wake of the rest of the flotilla.

Tressidar stood on a little platform abaft the low conning-tower. He had plenty to do, for the intricate directions as to the course could be adhered to only by a series of careful cross-bearings and observations. A line of hostile mines had been reported off the coast, and already a passage had been cleared by the sweepers. Therein lay a great risk, for although the channel had been reported clear, there was always the possibility of a mine escaping the means employed to rid the sea of these sinister objects, while cases have arisen of a derelict mine being found in a spot that had been reported free only an hour previously.

The officers and crew of No. 445 knew the danger and met it with equanimity. The lightly-built, single-skinned hull of the torpedo-boat would be literally pulverised should she bump against a mine. The concussion would undoubtedly send the frail craft to the bottom like a stone, and those of the crew who survived the explosion would be unable to withstand the piercing coldness of the water. With them, familiarity did not breed contempt; it was merely a matter of indifference. With unseen perils surrounding them, the iron-nerved men were as cool as if the little craft were on a trial run during the piping times of peace.

Ahead the double flash of Dunletter Head lighthouse winked knowingly. It was one of those beacons whose usefulness, nay indispensability, to friendly crafts more than outweighed the service it might render to hostile craft. The absence of those well-known flashes, even for a couple of hours, might result in half a dozen wrecks upon the dangerous Dunletter reefs that thrust their jagged and submerged fangs nearly half a mile seaward from the frowning promontory.

"Starboard your helm," ordered the sub.

"Ay, ay, sir," replied the quartermaster.

Almost on her heel the torpedo-boat swung round. It had reached the limit of a discovered mine-field, and was now free to stand seawards. She, like her consorts, showed no lights. Only a ruddy glare from the funnels of a badly stoked furnace betrayed the presence of one of the flotilla, now a couple of miles on the port quarter. For two tedious hours the boats searched the sea within ten miles of the position in which the Zeppelin was reported. Although searchlights were brought to bear upon the waves, nothing resulted. Apparently the airship had foundered.

Suddenly an idea flashed across Tressidar's mind.

"I'll try it," he thought, and gave an order for the engines to be stopped.

When No. 445 lost way he made tests to ascertain the true direction of the wind. Although it was almost calm when he left Auldhaig, the sub. made the discovery that there was a steady draught from the south-west. He also knew that for the last four hours the tide had been making northwards.

A water-borne Zeppelin, he argued, was to a greater extent under the influence of the wind, and to a lesser extent of that of the tide, although that depended largely upon the area of the submerged portion of the huge fabric. Allowing the airship to have been drifting for four hours, by this time she must be at least sixteen miles from the spot where she dropped, unless in the meanwhile she had sunk.

Accordingly TB 445 made off in a north-easterly direction, the sub. sweeping the sea with his night-glasses with the air of a man who subconsciously feels convinced that his efforts will meet with success.

Shortly after two in the morning a slight mist, accompanied by cold rain and sleet, rendered the searchers' task a most difficult one. Speed was reduced to fifteen knots, and the look-outs doubled, since the little craft was now in the waters frequented by the north-east of Scotland fishing-boats.

"Light on the port-bow, sir," reported one of the crew, as the feeble glimmer of a masthead and port lights loomed through the mirk.

Tressidar telegraphed for "easy ahead," then "stop," at the same time ordering the helm to be starboarded in order to approach the strange craft.

"They're making a deuce of a noise," he soliloquised, as the murmur of a babel of voices was wafted through the night.

Even as he looked the sub. discovered that the beams of the vessel's masthead light were playing upon an immense indistinct mass lying apparently a cable's length to windward. The mass was the envelope of the Zeppelin.

Ordering both searchlights to be unscreened and played upon the airship, Tressidar had the torpedo-boat manoeuvred so that the trawler,— for such she proved to be—bore slightly on the starboard quarter. At the same time the three 3-pounders were trained upon the Zeppelin.

"I wonder if the Huns have collared that craft," thought Tressidar. "It looks jolly fishy."

"Ahoy!" hailed one of the torpedo-boat's men. "What craft is that?"

"Drifter 'Laughing Lassie' of Peterhead," was the reply with an unmistakable Scottish accent.

"Then what are you doing here?" shouted the sub.

"The Zepp.'s right across our nets," announced the master of the drifter. "We aren't going to cut them adrift for a dozen strafed Zepps. They want us to take them aboard, but we just won't."

The fishing-craft was steaming slowly ahead, just sufficient to keep a slight strain upon her nets. The rear gondola of the Zeppelin, dipping beneath the surface, had fouled them, and at the same time the airship was prevented from drifting further to leeward.

Taking care to avoid the nets, for there was a danger of the torpedo-boat's propeller becoming entangled in the meshes of tarred line, Tressidar brought his command slightly to windward of the crippled German airship.

With the exception of the after part she was floating buoyantly, stern to wind. On the platform on the upper side of the envelope were about a dozen of her officers and crew. Others were standing on the light, railed-in gangway connecting the foremost cabin with the midship gondola. Shown up by the glare of the searchlights were several jagged holes in the envelope, caused by fragments of shells from the guns of the anti-aircraft service cars.

[Illustration: "WITH THE QUICK-FIRERS TRAINED UPON THE BULKY TARGET, NO. 445 APPROACHED WITHIN HAILING DISTANCE"]

"Think she'll fight, Bill?" the sub. heard a seaman enquire of his chum.

"Wish to heaven she would," replied the man. "We'd make it hot for them. But they won't, the brutes. They never do when they're cornered."

The speaker was in ordinary circumstances a steady, well-conducted seaman-gunner, who bore testimony to his humanity in the form of a silver medal from the Royal Humane Society for saving life under most hazardous conditions. Yet, without the slightest compunction, he would have sent a shell crashing into the inflammable gases of the Zepp.'s envelope. The mental vision of that ruined cottage with the slaughtered woman and her children had hardened his heart.

It was with almost similar sentiments that Tressidar hoped the Germans would put up a fight. With their superior armament they stood a chance of sending the little torpedo-boat to the bottom, or at any rate sweeping her decks with a murderous fire from her numerous machine guns.

She did neither. Instead, a man exhibited a large white flag, while the rest of the crew stood with folded arms, displaying a complete confidence in the willingness of the British seamen to save them from a lingering death in the wild North Sea.

With the quick-firers still trained upon the bulky target, No. 445 approached within hailing distance.

"Do you surrender?" shouted the sub. through a megaphone.

"Yes," was the reply, given by a tall, burly officer speaking good English. "We are disabled. We give ourselves up as prisoners."

"Very good," rejoined Tressidar. "You're in no immediate danger. Stand by to receive a hawser. We're going to tow you. But remember, any attempt to destroy or cause further injury to the airship will result in the death of every man jack of you. Do you quite understand?"

The German officers conferred amongst themselves. Then one of them gave an order to a member of the crew, who hurried to a hatchway amidships and disappeared from view.

"He's either gone to blow up the gas-bag or else he's been told to countermand a previous order to scuttle her," thought the sub. "Well, the business rests entirely in their hands. They'll have to realise that I won't be fooled with."

"We are ready to be taken in tow," shouted the German officer.

Ordering easy ahead, Tressidar brought his command almost alongside the steam drifter.

"You'll have to cut your nets, skipper," he said, addressing a short, thick-set man whose proportions were grotesquely exaggerated by a stiff oilskin worn over a thick great-coat. "I want you to take that Zepp. in tow and run her into Auldhaig. You will be compensated for the loss of your nets and in addition receive a large sum for salvage."

With the utmost alacrity the master of the drifter gave the necessary orders. The half-mile of nets was cut adrift, and the powerful engines manoeuvred until it was possible to heave a coil of rope into the foremost gondola of the crippled airship.

Meanwhile Tressidar had sent out a flashing message—No. 445 not being equipped with wireless—in the hope of the good news being picked up by the rest of the flotilla. Although there was no response, the sub. gave the signalmen instructions to flash code messages at intervals, in order to impress upon the crew of the Zeppelin that the torpedo-boat was not unsupported.

Slowly the trawler forged ahead, the partly water-logged airship wallowing awkwardly in tow. To guard against treachery—which, Tressidar knew, would be regarded as a smart action on the part of the Huns—No. 445 kept on the starboard quarter of the Zeppelin, ready at the first sign of a suspicious nature to place a shell into the interior of the highly inflammable envelope.

Mile after mile the trawler towed her bulky charge, her course through the mine-infested water being directed by signals from the torpedo-boat, whose searchlights were continually playing upon the prize.

Greatly to Tressidar's satisfaction, he observed that the airship showed no signs of sinking still more. Apparently the air-tight subdivisions enclosing the ballonets were sufficiently strong to resist the pressure of water. The submerged portion, too, acting as a drag in the sea, prevented the Zeppelin from yawing excessively, especially as the wind was now broad on the port beam.

The chances were that at last a practically undamaged and repairable Zeppelin would be brought into a British port.

A red hue in the eastern sky betokened the dawn of another day with the promise of bad weather. Gradually the beams of the searchlights began to pale before the increasing morning light.

Several miles to windward columns of smoke denoted the presence of the rest of the patrolling craft, which, having abandoned their midnight search, were returning to port.

It was now time for the trawler to alter her course eight points to starboard. She had passed the dangerous area, and could now run parallel with the coast until she reached the entrance to Auldhaig Firth.

Of the Zeppelin's crew not a man was visible. Apparently accepting the inevitable, they had taken shelter from the keen air and driving rain until they were ordered ashore by their captors, there to enjoy the comparatively luxurious life of prisoners of war.

Suddenly the whole fabric of the airship burst into sheets of lurid flame. Shafts of dazzling light shot skywards, mingled with flying debris. Almost immediately came the deafening crash of an explosion, followed by a blast of hot air that swept the torpedo-boat like a tornado.

For a few moments Tressidar was unable to grasp the situation. Where the Zeppelin had been was a dense cloud of smoke, that, caught by the wind, was drifted down upon the sub.'s command until the men were literally gasping for breath. Then upon her decks fell fragments of aluminium girders and wisps of burning fabric that, hurled upwards to an immense height, was beginning to fall in all directions.

The trawler, released from her tow, was forging rapidly ahead, the hawser trailing astern with a succession of jerks. Not until later was it ascertained that several of her crew had been hurled to the deck and seriously injured by the blast of the explosion, while the others were so dazed by the concussion that it was some time before the helm could be steadied and orders given to slow down.

"Rough luck!" muttered Tressidar. "Still, those fellows in that Zepp. had some pluck to blow her up with all on board."

But the sub. was wrong in his surmise. Nemesis, in the shape of a drifting German mine, had overtaken the air-raider of the night. In turning, the trawler had fortunately missed the latent weapon by a bare yard, while the airship, having to describe a wide circle, had brought the submerged gondola in contact with the sensitive horns of the mine with disastrous results.

"After all, there's some consolation," thought Tressidar as he went below to write out his report. "There's one Zeppelin the less."

CHAPTER XII
AN OCEAN DUEL

Midway between the coasts of Norway and Iceland and at less than three degrees south of the Arctic Circle the British light cruiser "Heracles" was on patrol duty. She was one of a chain of swift vessels spread out betwixt Iceland and Cape Wrath in order to tighten the net that was being cast about Germany's sea-borne trade.

Germany's mercantile fleet had long since been swept off the five oceans, but her sea-borne trade still continued. Thanks to the incapacity of a certain section of the British Government to grasp the necessity for a stringent blockade, neutrals, bought by Teuton gold, were actively engaged in importing enormous quantities of goods, more than ten times the amount needed for their own consumption, and were waxing rich by means of the inflated prices that the Huns were forced to pay in order to obtain the necessaries for carrying on the war.

But at last, owing to popular clamour rather than to the inclination of the civil authorities, the British Government had been forced to action. The great silent navy, that for months past had had to overhaul ship after ship without being allowed to detain what were obviously supplies intended for Germany, was now unfettered.

"Stop everything," was the order. The "rights" of petty neutral States—parasites upon the belligerent nations—had to be waived if the Great War was to be won by the Entente Powers.

The "Heracles" was a vessel of 4,300 tons, mounting two 6-in. guns and eight 4.7's. Her speed was nineteen knots—sufficient to overhaul any merchant craft likely to be met with in high latitudes. She was manned by the officers and crew of the late cruiser "Pompey."

Six weeks had elapsed since Sub-lieutenant Tressidar was within an ace of bringing a Zeppelin into Auldhaig Firth. It was now late in February. A spell of comparatively fine weather had succeeded a month of continual blizzards. The sea, encumbered by drift-ice, was practically calm. The cold was intense. The vessel's masts and funnels, and in fact every part not readily to be swept clear, were outlined in dazzling white, the snow having frozen into a hard coat. Morning after morning the hoses had to be connected up and hot water played upon the muzzles of the guns in order to remove the ice from the bore. Officers and men, clad in thick woollen and fur garments, were faced with the problem of drawing the line between bodily warmth and activity. If, on the one hand, they wore sufficient to withstand the morning cold, the free use of their limbs was seriously impeded; if, on the other hand, they had to shed their super-coats in order to tackle a job that required agility, they were in danger of being "nipped" by the icy blast.

Yet week after week the monotonous patrol work was maintained. Frequently days passed without a strange sail being sighted, until the monotony became almost appalling.

Nor did the long nights tend to improve matters. Daylight, frequently little more than a pale twilight, lasted only four hours in the twenty-four. The remaining twenty consisted of intense blackness, without even the stars to cheer the men in the long night-watches.

"Sail on the starboard bow."

A wave of subdued interest swept over the ship's company. Anything in the nature of a strange craft was sufficient to break the deadly tediousness. Of course she would only be one of those Norwegian traders outward bound. It was too much to hope otherwise.

The stranger came up rapidly. Upon sighting the "Heracles" she made no attempt to alter her helm, but stood doggedly on her course. She was a large vessel, bordering on 10,000 tons. On her sides were painted the Norwegian colours, while the mercantile ensign of that nation was displayed aft.

A shot fired across her bows had the desired effect. She backed her engines and, gradually losing way, brought up within two cables' lengths of the British cruiser.

"What ship is that?" was the peremptory signal from the "Heracles."

"The 'Frijick' of Bergen," was the reply. "Why are we detained? We are neutrals."

"Must examine your papers," rejoined the British cruiser. "Stand by to receive a boat."

"Away cutter."

The pipes of the bos'n's mates trilled in the keen air as the boat's crew, armed in case of emergency, rushed to their duty. Quickly the falls were manned and the boats swung outboard, Tressidar being in charge.

With a loud splash the boat struck the water. Dexterously the falls were disengaged, the lower blocks swinging with a sharp crack against the cruiser's side.

"Give way, lads!"

As one the double line of blades dipped and the boat drew away from her parent, for the "Heracles" had now circled slightly to starboard and had almost bows on to the Norwegian.

At that moment half a dozen port-lids, cunningly concealed in the stranger's side, were lowered, and a line of flashes leapt from the quick-firers hitherto concealed. Simultaneously two torpedoes shimmered in the dull light on their brief journey through the air before they took to the water and headed at the rate of an express train towards the British cruiser.

Taken completely by surprise, the sub. gave an order to "Back all." The cutter was on the point of entering the direct line of fire. To attempt to return to the "Heracles" was to court disaster, for already shells were bursting against her unarmoured bows.

With the discharge of the torpedoes the disguised German cruiser, for such she was, began to forge ahead. Under a false flag she had attempted to deal a knock-out blow at her more heavily armed antagonist, and she all but succeeded.

Well it was that the British cruiser was pretty well bows on to her antagonist, for the first torpedo, passing almost underneath the cutter's keel, missed the "Heracles'" port quarter by a few yards. The other seemed as if it were making straight for the almost motionless ship when, with a terrific report, a column of water was thrown up a couple of hundred feet in the air at less than half a cable's length from the boat under Tressidar's command.

By sheer good luck as far as the "Heracles" was concerned, the powerful locomotive weapon had struck a huge block of almost submerged drift-ice, sending fragments in all directions. Several of the men in the cutter were slightly injured by pieces of falling ice, while for six minutes the boat rocked violently in the confused water churned up by the explosion.

Meanwhile both ships were rapidly drawing away from the cutter, and were firing furiously. Already the superior gunnery of the "Heracles" was beginning to tell, for several gaping holes were visible in the German cruiser's sides, through which volumes of smoke were pouring. The Hun, unable to score by a coward blow, was showing her heels, and although it was impossible at the present juncture to ascertain which craft had the advantage of speed, she had perceptibly increased her distance before the British cruiser had got into her stride.

Nor had the "Heracles" come off lightly. The first hostile broadside had played havoc with her upper deck. Huge rents appeared in her funnels, thereby decreasing her forced draught, while—which was to be particularly deplored—both her fore and after topmasts had been shot away and with them the wireless aerials.

Keeping slightly out of the wake of the German cruiser lest she should drop a chain of mines in the track of her pursuer, the "Heracles" held grimly in chase, giving and receiving punishment as she did so. Her antagonist's guns were not to be despised, although not equal in calibre to those of the British cruiser; but since the "Heracles" could only bring her bow 6-in. and the two foremost broadside 4.7's to bear against the German's four 5-in. guns mounted aft, the chances were, until the "Heracles" drew broad abaft her foeman's beam, fairly even on both sides.

AN OCEAN DUEL.

[Illustration: AN OCEAN DUEL]

It was modern warfare with the "Nelson touch." Theoretically the naval battle of the present day is fought at long range, but here were two well-armed vessels fighting each other at point-blank distance.

In spite of their underhand tactics, the Germans fought gamely. Undeterred by the accurately placed shells that rained upon her quarter-deck, the Huns stuck to their guns.

Still exchanging shots, the two vessels were lost to sight in the haze of the northern seas, and Tressidar and his eleven men found themselves alone upon the deserted ocean.

CHAPTER XIII
ADRIFT

With the excitement of watching the ocean duel still fresh in their minds, the cutter's crew did not readily realise their predicament. They had sublime faith in the ability of the "Heracles" to give the Huns "a proper hammering" and that in due course the British cruiser would return and pick up her boat.

For some time the sounds of the violent cannonade were borne faintly to their ears; then, save when a man's hearing played tricks upon him, the noise of the firing died utterly away.

Hour after hour passed, but no sign of the returning cruiser. The horrible thought that perhaps the "Heracles" had been sent to the bottom took root and increased in Tressidar's mind. Yet no hint did he give to his men. In order to occupy their minds and to keep their blood circulating—for in the open boat the cold was intense—the sub. ordered them to row, the oarsmen relieving each other every half-hour. Round and round in a vast circle the cutter went. Tressidar was too cautious to take the boat far from the spot where she had parted company with her parent ship, otherwise, should the "Heracles" return and find no sign of the cutter, she would most likely conclude that the boat had either been swamped or blown to atoms by a stray shell.

To add to the discomfort of the cutter's crew, it was now raining the steady downpour accompanied by occasional sleet and drifts of fog. Frequently the extent of vision was limited to less than half a mile. In these circumstances the chances of being picked up by the "Heracles" were greatly diminished.

Presently one of the men caught sight of a grey pointed object forging through the detached pieces of drift ice. At first glance it resembled a destroyer, save for the difference in colour. It was a vessel of some sort, but different from any that the cutter's crew had yet seen. It had a slightly raised fo'c'sle, large superstructure, and two slender masts fitted with wireless gear.

"A German submarine!" exclaimed a seaman hoarsely. "My word, ain't she a whopper!"

It was an unterseeboot of the newest type—resembling a small cruiser rather than the accepted idea of a submarine. Trimmed for surface running, she exposed a freeboard of nearly ten feet. For'ard were two twelve-pounder guns in circular turrets, so arranged that they could be lowered below the deck in a few seconds whenever it became necessary to dive. In the elongated superstructure, which comprised not only the conning-tower but several spacious compartments, were gun-ports fitted with watertight lids. These were now triced up, revealing the muzzles of four seven-pounder quick-firers. From the after end of the superstructure floated the Black Cross of Germany, while abaft were two more "disappearing" guns and the above-water mine-dropping gear.

Already the two for'ard guns were trained upon the luckless cutter. At any moment shells might be dealing death and destruction amongst her crew.

"Stand by with your rifles, lads!" ordered Tressidar. "Keep them out of sight until I give the word."

In silence the men awaited the submarine's approach, ignorant of what was about to take place. The sub. had wisely refrained from making any sign of resistance. He had decided not to give the Germans a chance to justify their opening fire; but should they do so, the cutter's crew would fight to the last.

After a while the submarine slowed down and stopped at a little less than a cable's length to windward of the boat. A couple of heavily clad officers standing on the platform formed by the roof of the superstructure examined the cutter through their binoculars. Then one made a remark to the other and both laughed uproariously.

Meanwhile the bow guns were still trained upon the cutter. Abreast of the superstructure a seaman, acting upon orders from his officers, held up a coil of rope to signify the willingness of the submarine's crew to take the boat in tow.

Tressidar shook his head emphatically. It would be far preferable to remain adrift in the open boat than to trust to the tender mercies of the kultured Hun.

Slowly the submarine forged ahead and circling passed within twenty yards of the cutter. For a few moments Tressidar was under the impression that the U-boat was about to ram the little craft, but he was mistaken.

"No take help from Zhermans?" shouted one of the German officers. "Sorry we have no room for you on board, or we vos take your prisoners to Zhermany."

Twenty or thirty men who formed the submarine's crew laughed boisterously at the plight of the British seamen; but, somewhat to Tressidar's surprise, no attempt was made to molest the cutter. With her crew still jeering, the submarine increased her speed and was soon out of sight.

The short day was drawing to a close. Benumbed by the cold, the men huddled close together for mutual warmth. They were too exhausted to indulge in conversation. Their frozen hands could not retain their grasp upon the looms of the oars, yet uncomplainingly they sat with compressed lips, looking in vain for the return of the "Heracles."

As night came on a lantern was lighted and exhibited from a boathook set upright through one of the thwarts. The rain had now ceased. It was snowing slightly, with the promise of a heavy blizzard before many hours had passed. All around the drift ice floated in compact masses, until there was danger of the boat being nipped between the enormous floes as they ground in the long swell.

Just before midnight the thud of a ship's engines became audible. Gradually the sound drew nearer and nearer. A large vessel, showing no lights, was cautiously making her way through the drift ice.

The ship was not H.M.S. "Heracles." The cutter's crew knew that by the noise of the engines, for it lacked the rhythm of the cruiser's smoothly running machinery.

She was certainly coming in the direction of the boat, but the question was, would she stop. Since she had gone a long way to the northward of the usual trade routes, it was evident that the vessel had good reasons for wishing to avoid examination by the British patrol craft, and would not be likely to stop at the signal of distress.

Accordingly the sub. determined to bluff her. By means of a Morse flashing-lamp, with which the cutter was equipped, a peremptory order to heave-to was sent. For a few moments the men waited in acute suspense. Upon the success of the demand depended their lives, since they had little chance of outliving the rigours of a long winter's night in the ice-infested sea. A steady white light shone through the darkness, followed by the signal "I am heaving-to."

"Give way, lads," exclaimed Tressidar encouragingly. "Another five minutes will do the trick."

Gathering their remaining energies, for the men were almost done up, the rowers urged the boat in the direction of the now motionless steamer, and ranged alongside her towering hull, the rail of which seemed lost in the darkness overhead.

A coil of rope, hurtling from the deck, dropped into the cutter. The bowman, his fingers numbed with the cold, fumbled as he took a turn round the for'ard thwart.

"Lower a ladder," shouted the sub.

"Aye, aye!" replied a voice with a pronounced foreign accent. There was neither cordiality nor resentment in the words; merely an acceptance with a good grace of a situation that could not be avoided.

The cutter was grinding alongside the rust-streaked wall-sides of the steamer. Her exhausted crew had not the strength to fend her off. It was, indeed, doubtful whether some of the men would be able to gain the vessel's deck without assistance.

A wire-rope ladder was lowered from the rail. Owing to the roll of the ship the lowermost rungs were at one moment three feet from the side. At another the ladder slapped vigorously against the iron plating in a manner that promised broken knuckles to the men as they climbed to safety.

Hardly able to move his limbs after his prolonged exposure in the boat, Tressidar gamely ascended. His nerveless fingers could hardly retain a grip upon the wet and slippery rungs. His boots slipped dangerously from the smooth rounded surface of the swaying ladder. Oppressed by the weight of his saturated clothing, he had more than once on the hazardous ascent to pause and regain his breath before he could summon his jaded energies to a renewed effort.

He fancied that the master of the vessel glanced curiously at him as he almost staggered upon the deck. Then, without a word, he drew himself up and waited until the last of his men had gained safety. Then, and only then, did he drop his plan of bluff.

"We were adrift in an open boat belonging to a British cruiser," he explained. "We should be glad of your hospitality until we fall in with another of our warships. Might I ask what ship this is?"

"The 'Freya' of Hammerfest, bound from New York to Gothenborg," replied the master. "We are only too glad to give you assistance; for a few hours, perhaps, since your ships swarm like ants. If you will send your men for'ard they will be attended to. Meanwhile, sir, will you favour me with your company in my cabin?"

"How about our rifles, sir?" asked one of the cutter's crew.

Tressidar hesitated. The men, being armed when they left the ship, ought to be under arms until they returned; but, on the other hand, it was hardly good taste to send them to the "Freya's" fo'c'sle with rifles and ammunition as if they were a prize crew.

The Norwegian skipper noticed his dilemma.

"Perhaps you would like me to take charge of them," he remarked. "Should we be stopped by a German submarine—one passed and was going south-west less than five hours ago—it would go hard with us if they found armed Englishmen on board. I will be responsible that the arms will be returned to you intact when you are transferred to a British ship."

The sub. saw no reason why he should not do as the master of the "Freya" suggested. The chances were that the ship would be examined by a patrol vessel before many hours were passed. There was one problem, however, that he could not exactly solve, nor did he like to ask his host any question on the matter. If the "Freya" were what she was stated to be—a neutral trader from and for neutral ports—why did she go so far out of her course?

The arms were given up and the jaded men sent forward, where they were hospitably entertained by the Norwegian crew, who not only gave them hot food and drink, but lent them clothing while their own was being dried in front of the galley fire. Not until Tressidar was assured that his men were made comfortable did he go aft to the master's cabin.

"You are too tired to converse," remarked the skipper, as the sub. attacked a plain but appetising meal.

"Not at all," replied Tressidar, his anxiety to hear more of his host and the vessel under his command being uppermost in his mind.

The master, after the manner of his race, began by plying the sub. with numerous questions concerning his adventures, to all of which the sub. replied without any attempt at reticence. He knew that mistrust begets mistrust, and that if he "hedged" his own chances of obtaining information would be thrown away.

"So your ship was engaged with a German ship disguised as one of ours," remarked the master of the "Freya." "I hope she sunk her. These arrogant Germans have already torpedoed nearly twenty of our peaceable merchantmen and our Government can but protest If only we were a great nation how we would help to fight them! As it is, we can only expostulate, knowing that expostulation is of no avail so far as a German is concerned."

"Yet the submarine you fell in with this afternoon did not attempt to torpedo you?"

"No; but I think I can explain that," replied the Norwegian skipper. "She passed close under our stern and read our name. These fellows seem to have information of every vessel leaving American ports, and for which port they are bound. Those making for Scandinavia are generally left alone; it is only neutral vessels bound for British ports that are sunk."

"Perhaps that is why you took such a devious course," prompted Tressidar.

"Yes," admitted his host frankly, "and also to lessen the risk of hitting a German mine. Our troubles will commence when we enter the Skager Rack, for the Germans, in defiance of all international law, have mined that too. But before that, I trust, you will have no further need for my hospitality."

The skipper spoke with evident sincerity. His sympathies were wholly pro-British. He quite recognised the necessity for a stringent blockade of Germany and for the restriction of imports into Norway, Sweden, Denmark, and Holland.

"Of course it is a great temptation for our people to enrich themselves," he said, "only it is short-sighted policy. I feel convinced that should Germany win this war—and my opinion is that she won't unless the Allies make a serious and irreparable blunder—the liberty of the smaller States of Europe, even though they have preserved a strict and punctilious neutrality, will be gone for ever. But you have finished your meal: you would like to sleep? There is a bunk at your disposal. Should the slightest occasion arise, I will have you awakened at once."

Thankfully Tressidar accepted the offer. Half asleep, he threw off his clothes and turned in. A minute later he was in a deep slumber.

CHAPTER XIV
A BREACH OF NEUTRALITY

Tressidar awoke with a start to find himself in utter darkness. Accustomed to be aroused at all times and without warning, he was fully awake in an instant.

The "Freya" was rolling considerably. Against her sides the waves slapped viciously. Above his head he could see the seas pouring on deck with that almost indescribable sound that accompanies the rush of green water over the low bulwarks.

The rain had been succeeded by a stiff blow and the tramp was ploughing through a rough sea with the wind broad on her starboard beam.

"Thank goodness no middle watch for me to-night," soliloquised the sub. as he prepared to fall asleep again. "Wonder what the time is? I'll just see to satisfy my curiosity."

He leapt from his bunk and searched for the switch, for the after-cabin of the "Freya" was electrically lighted. Having switched on the light, he consulted his watch. It was twenty minutes to ten.

"By Jove, I've almost slept the clock twice round!" exclaimed Tressidar. "It was nearly two in the morning before I turned in. Seventeen hours at ten knots, if not more. Why, the old tub must be well across the North Sea by this time."

Wondering why the "Freya" had not fallen in with any patrol ships, the sub. dressed and left the cabin. In the saloon he found the Norwegian skipper, who was in the midst of a meal.

"You slept so soundly that we did not like to awaken you," he said as he rose to greet his guest. "There has been nothing to report. We have not sighted a single sail since yesterday. Please sit down and have some food."

"And my men?" asked Tressidar.

"They are all practically recovered except two, who have to keep to their bunks," replied the Norwegian. "They have all turned in again, but if you wish to see them — —"

"No, I won't disturb them," the sub. hastened to declare, lest his desire to communicate with his men might give rise to unfounded suspicion. "To-morrow, perhaps. Where are we now, do you think?"

"About eighty miles due west of Cape Stodt, which is, you may perhaps remember, almost midway between Christiansund and Bergen," was the reply. "In order to avoid meeting German submarines, I have to hug the Norwegian coast. I am afraid we've evaded your cruisers, sir. Believe me, it was not by design, but by accident. Of course there is no reason why you should not return to England by steamer after we land you at Gothenborg, provided you and your men wear civilian clothes and discard your arms and ammunition."

"That is something to be thankful for," remarked Tressidar. "So long as I am back in England and able to rejoin my ship, I am content. Next to being a prisoner of war the lot of an interned man must be fearfully irksome."

"Quite so," agreed the skipper. "Now tell me: when do you think that the war will be over?"

"When we've properly whacked the Germans—not before," replied the sub. firmly.

"Then the sooner the better," added his host. "At the present time it is hardly safe for a neutral ship to be at sea. We neutrals are like a man standing on two rickety stools. At any moment one might collapse and let us down badly. Holland and Denmark are the worst off, I should say. It will indeed be a marvel if they can contrive to avoid being drawn in by the vortex, even as Belgium was."

"We came into the war to help Belgium," remarked Tressidar. "Only—"

The Norwegian smiled blandly.

"My friend," he interrupted, "let me tell you something. The onlookers see most of the game. The cry about violating the neutrality of Belgium that your politicians are so fond of raising is mere clap-trap. It served its purpose to unite the various political factions in England, that was all. You English had a chance that might, perhaps, never occur again. It was a favourable chance to smash German militarism, and, luckily for you, you took it. Even if Belgium had not been involved, Great Britain would have ranged herself on the side of France and Russia. When big Empires wage war, little States do not count."

Tressidar merely inclined his head in assent. He, too, knew that the Norwegian spoke the truth. Long before the German troops set foot in Belgium the British Fleet was "standing fast" in readiness to help in the necessary task of freeing Europe, nay, the world, from the menace of Prussianism as preached by the disciples of kultur.

At daybreak the "Freya" rounded the Naze, the southernmost point of Norway. Ahead lay the broad waters of the Skager Rack. In normal times, following the breaking up of the ice, the sound would be dotted with vessels of all nationalities engaged in trade with the Baltic ports. Now not a sail was visible. The heavily sparred German timber ships, like the rest of the mercantile navy of Prussia, had long since been swept off the seas.

The quaint Russian barques, too, that were familiar in almost every British port of any size, were no longer to be seen. A few Swedish merchantmen, timorously hugging the Norwegian coast, might have been discerned had the weather been clear. Otherwise, save for the spectacular "dashes" of a few German warships—short cruises to cheer up the Huns in the belief that their navy did plough the high-seas—the Skager Rack presented almost as desolate an aspect as the Dead Sea.

The "Freya" hugged the shore closely, keeping well within the three-mile limit. Even at that distance the land was frequently obscured by patches of mist that drove slowly across the sea under the mild southerly wind.

Presently the tramp ran into a thick bank of fog. With a dangerous shore so close under her lee, it was imperative that every precaution should be taken to prevent her being carried out of her course by the strong indraught. Speed was reduced to a minimum necessary to carry steerage way, while the syren was kept going to warn possible approaching vessels of her presence.

Suddenly, like the passing of a compact cloud across the sun, the fog lifted. The ship was still within the three-mile limit, but between her and the Norwegian coast was a fleet of warships steaming rapidly in the same direction and on a parallel course that, if maintained, would bring them within a cable's length of the "Freya."

"By Jove!" exclaimed Tressidar. "They are German vessels."

He was right. There were three light cruisers steaming in line ahead. On either hand were lines of torpedo-boats, while overhead at an altitude of about one thousand feet flew two Zeppelins of the most recent type. The Huns, fearing submarine attack, were taking no unnecessary risks. They were cruising in neutral waters, but the German populace was not to know that.

"Keep your men well out of sight," cautioned the skipper. "Even the Norwegian flag flying in Norwegian waters would not be able to protect you."

As he spoke the leading torpedo-boat of the starboard division sounded her syren imperiously. By all the rules of the road at sea the tramp, being the overtaken vessel, was entitled to hold on her course; but it was evident that the German flotilla was attempting to edge the "Freya" beyond territorial waters, although for what reason none on board her could certainly conjecture.

Nearer and nearer drew the warships, without making the slightest attempt to alter helm. Their syrens were braying frantically. It reminded the sub. of a herd of cattle trying to shift a little dog that impeded their way.

If the "Freya's" skipper held on, he realised that he would give the imperious Huns cause for offence. Reluctantly he gave orders for the helm to be ported in order to yield to the palpably illegal tactics of the German ships.

As the tramp altered her course the starboard column of torpedo-boats did likewise, until they were heading south-east or almost at right angles to the coast-line. The "Freya" was being jockeyed beyond the three-mile limit.

The sub. knew that he and his men were in a tight corner. Should the tramp be compelled to hove-to there was no escape. They could not be passed off as passengers, since their names did not figure on the passenger list. Nor was the ship certified to carry any persons besides her officers and crew.

Tressidar dismissed the proposal that he and his men should hide in the hold. Searched the ship would certainly be, and he was not going to be ignominiously hauled out of the hold by a mob of Germans.

At length, in fact directly the tramp had passed the limit of territorial waters, the peremptory hail to stop instantly came from the nearmost German torpedo-boat, which promptly swung out of station and slowed down.

"I am sorry, but it is not my fault," exclaimed the Norwegian skipper to Tressidar as he telegraphed to the engine-room for half-speed astern.

"You did your best: you had no choice," replied the sub. "We must make the best of the situation."

While the German torpedo-boat was manoeuvring to come alongside (it saved the trouble of sending away a boarding-party), Tressidar sent a couple of seamen to fetch the rifles and ammunition from the cabin. These he dropped overboard. At least they would not be allowed to fall into the hands of the enemy.

Barely had this task been completed when a tall, full-faced, blond unter-leutnant appeared over the side, followed by half a dozen armed men.

Directly he caught sight of Tressidar and the British seamen he half hesitated, fearing a trap. Then, possibly realising that he had thirty German warships to back him up, he waxed bold, and fiercely twirling his fair moustache, haughtily demanded to know what these English swine were doing on board a Norwegian ship?

The skipper of the "Freya," who spoke German as fluently as he did English, explained briefly and to the point, saying that he had acted merely in the dictates of humanity.

"Then so much the worse for you," retorted the German officer.

He walked to the side and reported his find to his superior, the kapitan of the torpedo-boat. Great was the excitement on board, while the news was quickly transmitted by semaphore to the flagship, which happened to be one of the three light cruisers.

Tressidar and the cutter's crew were then ordered over the side and sent on board the torpedo-boat. A thorough search was then made of the "Freya" lest any more British officers and men might still be in hiding, but without result.

"Your vessel is a prize to the German Government," declared the unter-leutnant, addressing the Norwegian skipper.

"A prize?" repeated the master. "For why?"

"You are conveying contraband."

"We are not," protested the "Freya's" captain. "We have not touched at a British port. Our papers prove that. And our cargo is not contraband."

"I did not say contraband cargo," said the German with a leer. "Men can be contraband as well as stores. You had English seamen on board, therefore you are under arrest."

"We were in Norwegian waters when you overhauled us," declared the skipper.

"No," replied the German. "Well beyond the limit. But what is the use of your protesting You are under arrest and the vessel is a prize. If you do not know how to make the best of the business, I will have to show you."

So with a prize crew on board, the luckless "Freya," escorted by a torpedo-boat, was taken into the Elbe, while Tressidar found himself a prisoner of war in the hands of the Huns.

CHAPTER XV
A PRISONER OF WAR

As soon as the Norwegian tramp and her escort were on the way to a German port the torpedo-boat resumed her station at the head of the starboard line.

The British seamen had been sent below as soon as they were transhipped, but Tressidar was told to go aft and await examination.

"You say your ship engaged one of our cruisers?" asked the lieutenant-commander of the torpedo-boat. "What was the result?"

"Your cruiser ran away," replied Tressidar pointedly.

"And then what happened?"

"The 'Heracles' stood in pursuit. An action was taking place. We were left adrift in the cutter."

"And the end of the action?"

"I cannot tell. Both ships were lost in the mist."

"Was the English cruiser torpedoed?"

"That I cannot say," replied the sub.

"It was possible. Were there any signs of one of our incomparable submarines about?"

"We saw one several hours later."

"Then it is certain that your 'Heracles' was sunk," declared the German joyously. Already he had decided to report that a party of English Seamen, the sole survivors of a torpedoed cruiser, had been rescued by a division of the High Seas Fleet. He could imagine the intense enthusiasm in Berlin at the news.

He plied Tressidar with questions to elicit the information as to the exact position where the engagement started, but beyond the vague statement that it was somewhere in the North Sea, the sub. refrained from giving further details.

"The fellow is obstinate," remarked the unter-leutnant to his superior. "Why not lock him up in the fo'c'sle with his men?"

"He is an officer, von Möber," said the lieutenant-commander. "He is entitled to a certain amount of consideration."

"If I had my way I'd make it hot for this Pig of an Englishman, officer or no officer," declared von Möber.

"You are over-zealous," said his superior. "These Englishmen treat our men who fall into their hands in a proper manner."

"Because they fear reprisals," added the unter-leutnant. "Once they began to ill-treat the crew of one of our lost submarines, but we soon frightened them into better manners. That shows how the English fear the German arms."

The young German firmly believed what he said. Like hundreds of his fellow-countrymen, he regarded the considerate treatment of Huns held as prisoners in England as a sign of weakness, while, on the other hand, severity towards British captives was looked upon as a testimony to the certainty of success to the German arms. Leniency to prisoners and to interned Germans in England, instead of raising a spark of gratitude in the minds of the kultured Huns, was accepted as a token of moral weakness on the part of the strafed Englishmen.

German submarines could—and did—torpedo unarmed merchant ships without warning; Zeppelins sailed by night over undefended British towns and villages, raining death and destruction upon them. In both cases these gallant exploits were hailed with wild enthusiasm by the German nation. Yet the humane British, refraining from reprisals of a similar nature, were looked upon by the Huns as a nation afraid to retaliate, so that in the day of reckoning they would be able to make better terms with the All-Highest War-Lord. And this theory, fostered by "inspired" newspapers, was held practically by entire Germany.

The lieutenant-commander of the torpedo-boat was an exception. Practically born and bred a sailor, his outlook was wider than that of the majority of German naval officers, who are first and foremost soldiers, and sailors by the will of their Emperor.

"While Herr Tressidar remains on board he will be treated with proper respect, von Möber," he said firmly, then turning to his prisoner he added,

"I do not ask you for your parole, but let me warn you that a sentry will be posted outside the door, and that any attempt on your part to escape will certainly be discovered and with it your privileges will be withdrawn."

"Thank you," replied Tressidar. "I understand."

He turned and followed a petty officer who had been told off to show him to his place of detention. Just as he reached the small oval hatchway leading below, two heavy explosions in quick succession almost burst the drums of his ears.

So terrific were the detonations that the sub., was for the moment unable to detect their source. It seemed as if the deafening noise came from immediately overhead and from all sides of the torpedo-boat. The frail craft shook like a terrified animal under the rending of the air.

Then, to his unbounded delight, Tressidar saw the leading light cruiser was heeling badly to starboard, her upper works hidden in clouds of smoke mingled with spray.

Following the explosions came a dead silence of nearly a minute, then the remaining ships of the German flotilla opened a rapid fire, the shells hurtling towards a dozen different targets that existed solely in the heated imaginations of the gun-layers. So erratic was the firing that more than once the German ships were in danger of being hit by the projectiles discharged from the guns of their consorts. For full five minutes pandemonium reigned.

Meanwhile the stricken cruiser was still heeling. Already her upper deck on the starboard side was flush with the water. Men were clustering aft or else crowding into the boats that had survived the explosion and were capable of being lowered.

It was a British submarine which had scored a couple of direct hits. In spite of the presence of a double screen of torpedo-boats, notwithstanding the prying eyes of the Zeppelins cruising over the fleet, a plucky lieutenant-commander of one of the "E" class had been able to obtain a periscopic sight of the German flagship. Here was a chance too good to be missed. He immediately gave orders for two torpedoes to be fired. Either was sufficient to strike a mortal blow, for the first struck the target abreast of the foremost gun-turret; the second found its mark fifteen feet for'ard of the stern-post.

Without waiting to observe the result of the explosion, the submarine dived. To turn and speed away from her prey would be courting destruction, for her movements would be distinctly visible to the observers in the Zeppelins, and the torpedo-boats, directed by wireless from the airships, would be rushing to and fro across the submerged path of the British submarine and tear her to pieces with explosive grapnels. So her lieutenant-commander steered her so that she would pass underneath the German flotilla, and then, by compass course, kept in the track that the hostile vessels had previously held. Here the water, disturbed by the propellers of the flotilla, was thick and muddy, and, forming an efficient screen for the Zeppelins, enabled the British submarine to get clean away.

Long before the Teuton flagship had plunged to the bottom and the furious cannonade had died away, the "E Something" was a dozen miles from the scene of her exploit.

The disaster had temporarily unnerved the Germans. Once again, in spite of their cautious cruise in neutral waters, one of the ships had been sent to the bottom. And the irony of the situation lay in the fact that had the ships not altered course to head off the "Freya" beyond the three-mile limit, the opportunity for the British submarine to "bag" a Hun might not have occurred.

Steering a zig-zag course and sheltering between the far-flung lines of torpedo-boats, the remaining German cruisers ran frantically for the Kattegat and thence to the security of Kiel Harbour, while the torpedo-boat in which Tressidar and the luckless cutter's crew found themselves prisoners parted company and steamed rapidly in the direction of the island of Sylt.

It was not long before Sub-lieutenant Tressidar found that his ideas of hospitality differed considerably from the German lieutenant-commander's notions on the subject, for when the tumult on board had begun to subside— and not before—was the young officer sent below.

The "cabin" was little better than a metal compartment below the waterline and immediately underneath the officers' cabins. Although officially designated a torpedo-boat, the craft was almost equal in size to the largest British destroyer, her draught being not less than eleven feet. Built on the "cellular" principal, with double bottoms and numerous transverse and lateral watertight bulk-heads, this type of vessel was considered by the naval architects of the Fatherland to be practically unsinkable, although already several of this particular torpedo-boat's sister ships had failed to come up to expectations when cruel fate brought them within range of British quick-firers.

Save for a solitary electric lamp of low candle-power the sub.'s place of confinement was unlighted. Ventilation, too, was of the most meagre description, for the only air admitted was the already close atmosphere of 'tween decks that filtered in though a small "louvre" over the locked door. Without a sentry had been posted, but the key, instead of being entrusted to him, was kept in the lieutenant-commander's cabin. Thus, in the event of the vessel being sunk, it was fairly reasonable to assume that all chances of the prisoner being rescued depended upon the whim of the commanding officer and the alacrity of the German sentry, even if time permitted for him to risk his life for the sake of an "English swine."

Left to his own devices, Tressidar lost no time in taking minute stock of his surroundings. With the exception of a low bench, the place was devoid of furniture. The inner skin of the hull plating had been newly coated with red lead, and smelt abominably. In addition, some of the seams, working under the strain of the powerful engines, were "weeping" copiously, until the floor was flooded to a depth of two inches.

"Not a dog's chance of seeing what is going on," soliloquised the sub., as he threw himself upon the bench and drew his feet clear of the miniature lake. "I wonder what the game is? I hope, for my sake, and the sake of my men, that this hooker won't be torpedoed or mined while we are on board."

Tressidar was in a bad temper. The fact that he had been made a prisoner through the indefensible and high-handed action of the Huns riled him considerably. If he had had the ill-luck to be captured in fair fight he would, doubtless, have accepted the situation without demur, but to be literally kidnapped without the chance of a blow in self-defence was galling in the extreme.

Several hours passed. Save for a visit from a particularly surly seaman who brought the sub. a very sorry meal, Tressidar was left severely alone, to ruminate over his bad luck.

At length the slowing down of the torpedo-boat's engines told him that she was nearing port, for hitherto she had been racing at top speed and steering a zig-zag course. After twenty minutes, during which the engine-room telegraph bell clanged as many times, the vessel came to a standstill.

Then followed another tedious wait. Apparently the Huns were in no hurry to land their prisoner. But, since there is an end to all things, Tressidar in due course found himself being escorted on deck, preceded and followed by armed seamen.

It was still daylight. The torpedo-boat was berthed, in company with more than twenty others, in a spacious basin. Surrounding the enclosed water was a broad quay, flanked with two-storeyed buildings. The entrance to the basin was, remarkably, on the eastern side or remote from the open sea. Evidently the approach was by a tortuous, intricate channel that skirted the southernmost extremity of the island.

To the westward the outlook was bounded by a range of sand-dunes of varying altitudes. In some places they were about 50 feet in height; in others the grass-grown hummocks slightly exceeded double that dimension. A short distance to the north-west was a lighthouse, a round yellow tower perched upon a tall red cliff, that formed a striking contrast to the white sand-dunes on either side.

In almost every depression between the chain of dunes were heavy gun batteries, while on a broad level road running parallel to the sea and about two hundred yards from the summits of the sand-hills were numerous armoured motor-cars armed with quick-firers of widely differing calibres.

"Ah, I know where I am now," thought Tressidar as he recognised the lighthouse—not from actual acquaintanceship but from an intimate knowledge of the British "North Sea Pilot." "That's Rothe Kliff lighthouse, so they have landed me at Sylt. Next to Heligoland, they couldn't have chosen a stronger place to hold me prisoner. I wonder if they are going to keep me in some wretched prison camp in the centre of the German Empire."

He looked in vain for the cutter's crew. The men had been landed and marched off almost as the torpedo-boat was berthed, and were now on their way to embark in a small steamer for Hamburg.

The exhibition of captured British seamen in that paralysed commercial port was a stroke of diplomacy on the part of the German authorities. It gave colour to the official lie that a portion of the dauntless High Seas Fleet had boldly made a demonstration in force off the Firth of Forth The English had plucked up sufficient courage to leave their fortified harbours and give battle. It was a feeble attempt, and the British fleet broke off the engagement before the Germans could force a decisive action. As it was, a British battleship had been sunk with all hands. A large armoured cruiser had been sent to the bottom, a portion of the crew being rescued by the humane Germans. While engaged in this work of mercy the German cruiser had been torpedoed by a submarine. This was the fairy-tale that was quickly spread--broadcast from Hamburg to Königsberg and from the shores of the Baltic to the Swiss frontier.

Escorted by a file of marines, Tressidar was marched along the quay through throngs of curious and ill-disposed sightseers, of whom nine out of ten were in uniforms. At the end of the quay the escort turned down a narrow lane and finally came to a halt outside a low stone building, almost on the outskirts of the little town. The house stood in its own grounds, which were enclosed by a tall iron fence topped by a complex array of barbed wire. At the gate were two sentries. Two more stood in the portico of the house, while others were much in evidence as they marched to and fro on the raised platforms commanding an uninterrupted view of the grounds.

Inside the fence and separated from it by a distance of twenty feet was another barbed wire entanglement, while in the intervening space were several large and ferocious-looking mastiffs.

This was Sub-lieutenant Tressidar's first introduction to the naval prison of the fortress of Sylt.

CHAPTER XVI
THE FIRST DAY OF CAPTIVITY

Having handed over their prisoner to the charge of a corporal and a couple of men, the marine guard marched off. The sub. was then curtly ordered into a large, almost unfurnished room, the windows of which were heavily barred.

Engaged in conversation at one end of the room were four officers. One was the governor of the prison—a fat German of middle height, whose most striking peculiarities were his bristling, upturned moustache and a shiny, bald pate surrounded by a natural tonsure of raven black hair—another a subaltern who, having been wounded and rendered unfit for active service, was able to "get his own back" by systematically jeering at the prisoners and making their hard lives even yet more unbearable. The remaining officers were doctors.

"Take off all your clothes," ordered the lieutenant, with great emphasis on the word "all."

Tressidar obeyed. As each garment was, discarded it was seized and closely examined by the corporal, who seemed obsessed with the idea that English officers invariably had confidential documents sewn into their clothing. The sub.'s watch, purse, pocket-book, keys, and, in fact, everything in his pockets were handed to the junior German officer, who handled them as if they were contaminated articles, although he took good care to pocket the timepiece and the purse.

Stripped to the buff, Tressidar was subjected to a prolonged and searching verbal examination. Once when he demurred at answering a certain question, the governor reminded him that unless he replied truthfully and unhesitatingly he would have to remain without clothes until he did. And since the temperature was only a few degrees above freezing-point, the threat carried weight.

At the same time his replies were guarded and as inaccurate as they could possibly be without running the risk of betraying the fact. To make a statement that was absolutely inconsistent with details which his inquisitors knew already would be asking for additional trouble.

The interview, having lasted for nearly forty minutes, was followed by a medical examination of a perfunctory nature. So long as the prisoners were not suffering from any disease that might be a source of danger to the garrison, nothing else mattered from the authorities' point of view. The captives might die of starvation without raising a spark of compassion in the minds of the kultured Huns.

"Now," thought the sub., who by this time was shivering with cold, "I suppose they'll let me dress."

They did—but not in the manner he expected, for at an order from the governor, one of the soldiers kicked Tressidar's uniform into a corner of the room, while another emptied a small canvas sack full of dirty and badly worn clothes on the floor at the prisoner's feet.

With feelings of repugnance Tressidar dressed. The trousers were parti-coloured, a half being made from a French soldier's baggy red pair, the other part being of pale blue and indescribably greasy. The coat was a sort of civilian's lounge jacket, of dark grey, with a diamond-shaped patch of scarlet let into the back. It was impossible to cut the distinctive mark away without leaving a corresponding opening in the coat. Wooden-soled shoes with canvas uppers and a flat-topped cap completed his grotesque outfit.

Preceded and followed by his guards, Tressidar was led along a number of stone corridors, separated by metal doors. The cryptic writings on several massive doors opening out of the passages left little doubt in the sub.'s mind as to the uses to which the building was devoted. With typical Teutonic cunning the Germans were using the same roof to shelter explosives and prisoners, regarding the presence of the latter as a shield to guard their warlike stores from the unwelcome attentions of British airmen.

Presently the sub. found himself confronted by a double-locked door provided with a grille. Without stood an armed sentry, while—sinister fact—a couple of machine guns were trained through the lattice upon the occupants of the room. Ponderously the sentry unlocked and threw open the door, and Tressidar found himself urged forward by the effective expedient of having the butt of the rifle jammed into the small of his back.

Then the door clanged-to between himself and his guards. He was in the common room of the Sylt prison for captured British officers.

There were between twenty to thirty grotesquely attired men in the room, all engaged in the difficult task of killing time. Some were talking, others reading the carefully selected and approved literature provided by their captors. Two were playing chess, with knots of critical onlookers crowding round the little table.

At Tressidar's entrance the occupants came forward to greet their latest comrade in misfortune. The reticence generally attributed to Britons both at home and abroad seemed to have vanished.

"You'll have to introduce yourself, old man," exclaimed a pleasant-faced fellow of about the same age as the sub. "How did they bag you?"

In less than a minute conversation was in full swing. Everyone was eager to know the actual facts concerning the war, since it was only by the arrival of new members to the little party that the true state of affairs could be known.

"How about the fleet?" asked one. "Has there been a general engagement?"

"No, worse luck," replied Tressidar. "There has been a decided lack of opportunity."

"And the strafed Huns swore that their High Canal Fleet was out and off the east coast for over a fortnight," added another officer. "Of course we didn't believe it. And is it true that half London is in ashes?"

"Not by any means," said the sub. "Their Zepps. have come and gone. We bagged one the other day. They've done damage in various parts of the country, but not one-tenth of the amount they claim."

"And the Government?" asked an elderly fleet paymaster. "Are they doing anything yet? They were still gassing when I was nabbed, about three months ago."

Tressidar shook his head.

"Sorry I cannot report much progress in that direction," he said. "Until they decide to intern every German in the country things won't get much forrader at home, as far as the Government is concerned."

"The rotters!" exclaimed the fleet paymaster. "And they started with every prospect of doing something great. All factions were united, differences laid aside. The country was solidly behind them. And yet they shilly-shally and mess everything up. If we had had technical men to run the show—naval and military officers of experience—instead of twenty-three (or is it thirty-three by this time?) wobblers, the war would have been over by this time."

The accountant officer had voiced the sentiments of his fellow-captives. Optimism, a sure faith that all's well with the Navy, had evidently gripped their minds, but beyond that there was a vague suspicion that a brake was being applied to the enormous sea-power at the Empire's command.

Conversation proceeded briskly until the clanging of a bell announced that tea—the last meal of the day—was to be served. Into a dining-hall trooped the prisoners—to be counted en route for the third time in sixteen hours.

"Tea" consisted of a nasty beverage made from acorn "coffee" and chicory, with black bread and margarine. This was supplemented by delicacies that had been sent from home, all supplies from that source being placed into a common stock. The quantity received, however, represented but a small proportion of that sent, for although everything entrusted to American societies reached their destination safely—a large camp not far from Berlin—pilfering by the German authorities during the additional journey to Sylt was a most frequent occurrence.

At sunset the prisoners were ordered to bed. No lights were allowed. The dormitory was divided into cubicles, two officers being put in each. Privacy there was none, as the doors were only four feet in height and a couple of sentries continually paced up and down the dividing corridor.

Ronald Tressidar's cubicle was shared with a young flight sub-lieutenant R.N.R., John Fuller by name, who three months previously had fallen into the hands of the enemy on the occasion of a raid upon the fortifications of Borkum. At an altitude of less than a thousand feet a piece of shrapnel had pierced the petrol tank of Fuller's biplane, compelling the machine to alight in the sea within a mile of the coast. With a steady off-shore wind there was a chance of the seaplane drifting to within reach of the waiting destroyers, but for the fact that one of the floats had been perforated on the underside by a fragment of shell. In a waterlogged condition the crippled aeroplane's plight was observed by a German patrol boat, and, half dead with cold and exposure, Fuller was haled into captivity.

Doubtless owing to the fact that the flight-sub. had succeeded in dropping his bombs with disastrous results to the German works, his captors had transferred him to Sylt, where he stood a good chance of forming an integral part of a target for his brother-airmen in an expected raid.

"You'll find it desperately slow work, Tressidar," remarked Fuller "This is my eighty-second night in this hole, and it seems like a dozen years."

"Suppose you haven't tried to get away?"

"There's not a dog's chance, believe me," replied the flight-sub. "Apart from the risk of being plugged by a bullet from the sentry's rifle, the almost certainty of getting brought up all standing on the live wire— —"

"The live wire?" repeated Tressidar.

"Rather. That barbed wire entanglement contains a highly charged electric cable. The current is switched on every night and off again in the morning. The Huns were particularly gleeful in informing us of the cheerful fact. Then there are those mastiffs to take into consideration, so you see there's little chance of success. On the other hand, failure, even if one does escape the dangers I have mentioned, means forty days' solitary confinement. Danvers, of the submarine service, tried it, and he swears it's almost worse than being buried alive. He was a physical and moral wreck when he turned up amongst us again."

"So you think it's no go?"

"My dear fellow," said Fuller, "you have my best wishes, and I believe those of the rest of us here. But that won't help you. Nothing short of an earthquake or a few tins of explosives will clear a way until the Allies beat the strafed Huns absolutely to their knees. That's my opinion, but I may be wrong. In any case, if there's the faintest possible chance, I'm on it."

"Then we'll call it a bargain?"

Without speaking a word Fuller extended his hand. The two men exchanged grips that formed a mutual understanding.

Then Tressidar turned in. For a long time he tossed uneasily on his hard straw mattress. Already captivity was weighing heavily on him, and as yet he had been but a few hours in the hands of the Huns.

CHAPTER XVII
A DASH FOR LIBERTY

Day after day, night after night passed with almost intolerable tediousness. The meagre fare, uncomfortable quarters, their motley clothing, the jeers and taunts of their goalers—all these discomforts, unpleasant though they were, could be borne with fortitude bordering on equanimity. It was the dearth of news and the enforced inactivity that weighed so heavily upon the captive British officers.

The Huns knew this and traded upon it. The prisoners would have welcomed hard labour, provided that it was not of a nature that would directly assist the enemy against their fellow-countrymen. Manual labour they knew to be a tonic to mental inactivity—a means to keep their bodies fit and their muscles in good form. Instead they were permitted but two hours a day in the grounds, and even then football or, in fact, any games were "verboten."

Although the prison buildings fronted on one of the village streets, the rear of the premises overlooked the dunes. In westerly winds the captives could hear the sea thundering upon the outlying sands—a call of freedom to which they could not respond.

When at frequent intervals the dull booming of cannon was borne to their ears, they would look at each other with unspoken words of hope, until they realised that the guns were being fired as practice and not directed upon the long-expected British assault by sea and air.

Sometimes, too, they could see the giant Zeppelins being guided cautiously from the huge collapsible sheds. This took place usually in the late afternoon, at or about the time of the new moon. Away would speed the craven night-raiders in a westerly direction, to return with almost unfailing regularity just after dawn. Once, however, a Zeppelin trailed homewards with its after-part sagging ominously, and before it could be safely housed, it collapsed, a crumpled heap of girders and torn fabric, upon the ground. At another, three airships set out across the North Sea, and only one returned.

Great was the joy of the prisoners on these occasions. Regardless of the threats of their guards, they would give vent to the wildest demonstrations of joy. But they had to pay for these outbursts. A further restriction of their already meagre fare and a complete deprivation of their tobacco and cigarettes was the unfailing penalty. It was worth the punishment, to "let themselves go" over the unquestionable loss of yet another of the Huns' vaunted gas-bags. Amongst the highly organised methods adopted by the Germans for the defence of Sylt was the practice of sending up a couple of observation balloons by day whenever a Zeppelin was not cruising overhead. These strangely shaped balloons were in the form of an egg, with a curved cylinder attached to the end in order to prevent the contrivance from rotating under the influence of air-currents. To the observation car was attached a light but strong flexible wire cable, which was paid out or taken up as required by means of a drum on the ground. At night the balloons were hauled down and partly deflated, but at sunrise they were sent up again with the special object of keeping a look-out for British aeroplanes.

On one occasion a false alarm was given. Promptly the captive balloons were hauled down. The Zeppelins emerged from their sheds and flew—not westwards to meet the threatened attack, but in a south-easterly direction. It was quite apparent that the Germans had little faith in their unwieldy gas-bags as a means of combating the daring British seaplanes in broad daylight; so they sent them inland to a safe distance, rather than risk annihilation at the hands of the intrepid Britishers.

In addition to the artillerymen stationed at Sylt there were several regiments of infantry—men who were supposed to be resting after months in the terrible district of Ypres. From the very first the Huns had a strong suspicion that Great Britain would attempt a landing upon the shores of Schleswig-Holstein, under cover of the guns of the fleet. Consequently a complete army corps had continually been pinned down to this part of the German Empire in order to be in readiness to repel the threatened invasion.

Upon the occasion of the false alarm Tressidar noticed that the infantrymen were promptly sent off to bomb-proof dug-outs, since they could be of little use in defence against aircraft. The gunners, however, stood to the quick-firers, the majority manning the batteries on the dunes, while others were told off to the portable anti-aircraft guns mounted on armoured motor-cars.

With the departure of the Zeppelins the sheds in which they were housed were lowered by means of steel trellis derricks until they lay flat upon the ground. The material of which the sheds were built was light steel, the outside of which had been coated with varnish. While the varnish was still in a viscous state, sand had been liberally sprinkled upon it, with the result that the collapsed sections of the Zeppelin sheds could hardly be distinguished from the surrounding soil.

The false alarm was but one of many. The troops were continually being called to arms, with the result that they were showing unmistakable signs of weariness under the strain. On each occasion the German officers attached to the prison staff took particular pains to inform the British captives that a threatened air-raid had been frustrated by the formidable appearance of the garrison defences.

But one day—it was exactly a month from the time when Tressidar first set foot in the fortress of Sylt—the long-expected attack took place.

Through the brilliant sunlit air six British seaplanes, looking little larger than may-flies, headed straight for the island. Well in the offing lay a parent ship for seaplanes, four light cruisers, and a swarm of destroyers; while still further to the westward the giant battle-cruisers kept in touch with their smaller consorts, ready to swoop down upon the German warships should the latter be tempted to join issue with the audacious British.

Tressidar and Fuller were alone in the common room. Owing to a trumped-up charge of a breach of discipline they had been prevented from joining the rest of their comrades in misfortune for the daily outdoor recreation.

A tremendous outburst of shell from the light quick-firers brought the chums to the barred window. Although they had had plenty of disappointment over the false alarms, they never neglected the opportunity of making for a place of observation when the anti-aircraft guns opened fire. For days they had waited for "something to turn up," and now their optimistic patience was about to be rewarded.

"Five of them, by Jove!" exclaimed Fuller. "No, six. They'll play the deuce with the Huns."

"And possibly with us," thought the sub., but nevertheless his nerves were a-tingle and his hopes centred upon the main idea that the raid would be of brilliant military importance. Personal safety was a negligible quantity.

All around the biplanes were white, mushroomed clouds of smoke from the bursting shrapnel. It seemed as if nothing in the vicinity could escape the concentrated fire from the German guns, yet serenely the seaplanes held on their course, tilting slightly under the violent disturbance of the air.

With their faces pressed against the iron bars of the window the two young officers watched the progress of the aircraft until they were so immediately overhead that the masonry impeded their outlook. The last they saw of the daring raiders was that they were volplaning rapidly.

"Now stand by!" whispered Fuller tersely. "In another few seconds you'll hear the plums drop."

The anti-aircraft guns redoubled their furious fire. The whole building trembled under the reverberation of the deafening reports.

Then, as Fuller had foretold, came the first of a succession of terrific explosions, as a large bomb from the leading seaplane crashed into a shell store.

Although the prisoners could not see the actual damage done to the building, they knew that it no longer existed. A dense black cloud thrown skywards by the detonation threw such a dark shadow that sunlight gave place to a gloom resembling twilight. Thousands of projectiles, hurled far and wide, burst with dire results. Scorched and maimed bodies of victims were projected in unrecognisable masses for nearly two hundred yards from the actual scene of the disaster.

For some moments bombs fell like rain. Several of the gun emplacements in the dunes were utterly wrecked. In others the guns were temporarily disabled by quantities of sand that, hurled right and left by the bombs, choked the bore and clogged the delicate mechanism of the sights and training gear.

The torpedo-boats in the basin also had a rough handling. Several, to escape destruction, put out to sea, but in the confusion many collided in the narrow, intricate channel. Others were sunk alongside the quays. Of the forty naval vessels belonging to the port, twenty-two only escaped.

Expecting every moment to find the building collapse over their heads, Tressidar and his companion stuck to their posts at the window, Presently they saw one of the huge armoured cars proceeding at a furious pace down the military road behind the dunes. As it tore along, its obliquely-pointed quick-firer spat venomously at the British seaplanes until a bomb, falling quite a hundred feet from the car, tore a deep hole in the roadway. At the same time a flying fragment of metal found its way through the narrow slit in the steel plating behind which sat the driver. The man was either killed or seriously wounded, for the powerfully engined vehicle was no longer under control. Gradually, at a speed of approximately forty miles an hour, it described a curve in a right-handed direction, while the gunners, their attention fixed upon the elusive targets a thousand feet or more above their heads, were in ignorance of the danger that threatened them.

"Dash it all!" exclaimed Tressidar excitedly. "That car will barge into something in half a shake."

Already the vehicle had left the broad road and was ploughing with no apparent effort through the sand. It was heading towards the prison buildings.

Through the outer palisade it came, hurtling the steel rods right and left. Then, without checking its headlong career, the car wrenched its way through the double lines of barbed wire, carrying away yards of fencing as it did so.

The anti-aircraft gun had now ceased firing. The gunners, aware of the fact that the car was a derelict, but unable to gain the steering compartment, were helpless.

"Stand by!" exclaimed Tressidar.

The warning was necessary. The motor-battering-ram was charging straight for the window. Promptly the chums backed away from the bars. Judging by the speed and momentum of the petrol-driven vehicle there was great danger of the car charging completely through the stone building.

The next instant there was a violent crash. Stone, mortar, iron bars, woodwork flew in all directions accompanied by clouds of dust, while rearing at an alarming angle upon the mound of debris was the car.

It was totally wrecked. The muzzle of the anti-aircraft gun, having caught in the overhanging masonry, had been wrenched from its mountings, tearing away the steel roof of the car and pinning the two gunners under the heavy metal. The petrol from the burst tanks 'was saturating everything within the limit of its flood, although, fortunately for Tressidar and his companion, the highly volatile spirit had not exploded. To add to the horrors of the scene bombs from the British seaplanes were still falling.

"Come along!" shouted Tressidar, bawling to make himself heard above the din.

"Right-oh," replied Fuller with alacrity.

The sub. had no definite plan. All he knew was that a path had been cleared for them through the formidable barriers. There was a chance—a very slight chance—of liberty, and they seized it.

Crawling over the pile of debris and edging between the upturned side of the car and the jagged wall, they gained the open space between the building and the military road behind the dunes.

Glancing cautiously right and left, the two chums made the discovery that the coast was clear. The gunners of the stationary quick-firers, ensconced in their armoured emplacements, were too busy with their work to look elsewhere. A mile or so down the road and proceeding away from the prison buildings were two armoured cars. Every soldier, not actually engaged in firing at the seaplanes, had returned to the shelter of the dug-outs and bomb-proof casemates. Three distinct and fiercely burning fires showed unmistakable proof that the work of destruction had succeeded.

Through the gap in the shattered fence Tressidar and Fuller made their way. The severed electric wires were spluttering viciously, emitting bright blue flashes as their ends writhed like snakes. The mastiffs were no longer in evidence. Terrified by the crash of the falling bombs, they had scurried for shelter. The sentinels, too, their dread of official punishment outweighed by the fear of death or maiming from the powerful bombs, had deserted their posts, but not before a corporal and two privates had been literally wiped out of existence.

Through drifts of acrid-smelling smoke the two fugitives hastened, until they gained the slight shelter afforded by a dip in the reed-grown dunes.

So far so good, but unfortunately the seaplanes, their mission accomplished, were already on their return journey, their departure greeted by a futile discharge of shrapnel. That meant that before long the Germans would be emerging from their shelters to take stock of the damage before the officials could draft a report to Berlin announcing that yet another raid had been attended by no results of military significance.

"Say, old man," exclaimed Fuller. "What's the next move? We can't hang on here much longer."

"No," replied Tressidar slowly. He was thinking deeply, regretting that he had not previously mapped out a plan should an opportunity like that of the present arise.

Suddenly an idea flashed across his mind.

"By Jove!" he ejaculated, "what's to prevent our nabbing that captive balloon?"

"A great wheeze," rejoined Fuller, kneeling up and peering cautiously in the direction of the observation balloon.

Thank goodness it had contrived to escape attention from the far-flung fragments of the bombs. Partly inflated, and pinned to the earth by a number of cords attached to sandbags, it retained sufficient lifting power to support a couple of men, even if it were unable to rise to a very great altitude.

The balloon was deserted. Imagining that it would be a particular target for the British airmen, and knowing the danger of an explosion in the vicinity of hundreds of thousands of cubic feet of hydrogen, the men in charge had bolted precipitately at the first appearance of the seaplanes.

Unnoticed, the two grotesquely garbed fugitives gained the spot where the giant gas-bag was tethered. Peering over the edge of the car, Tressidar found what he had expected, a box of tools.

"In with you, old man!" he exclaimed.

The chums clambered over the edge of the basket. Each, grasping a chisel, began to sever the cords holding the retaining weights. While six yet remained to be cut the balloon rose slowly from the ground. Its reserve of buoyancy then, in addition to the two passengers, was equal to the weight of half a dozen sandbags.

As the last cord was severed the balloon leapt skywards, until with a perceptible jerk its ascent was stopped. It was held by a flexible steel wire, the bulk of which was wound round the drum of the lowering gear.

"Pliers, quick!" exclaimed Tressidar, swinging himself up into the netting in order to bring himself within arm's length of the span to which the cable was spliced.

Fuller obeyed promptly. As he did so he became aware of something that the sub. in his excitement had not noticed. From their places of concealment numbers of German soldiers were emerging. By the shouts it was apparent that they had discovered the attempt at escape on the part of the two English prisoners.

[Illustration: "'IN WITH YOU, OLD MAN!' HE EXCLAIMED"]

The steel wire was tough and offered stubborn resistance to the pliers. Every moment was precious. Tressidar, too, was now aware of the latest danger that threatened them. In his desperate anxiety to complete his work the pliers slipped from his hand and fell a distance of thirty feet to the ground.

"See if there's anything else to cut this infernal wire," he exclaimed breathlessly, holding out his disengaged hand.

Fuller searched in vain. Amongst the collection of tools there was nothing capable of making a quick job of cutting the wire. The nearest German was within a hundred yards, and, like most of his companions, was armed with a rifle. There seemed every possibility of the luckless fugitives being done in.

Disregarding Tressidar's excitable requests to "Look sharp," the flight sub. snatched up a rifle that was lying in the car. Throwing up the bolt, he discovered, as he expected, that the weapon was already loaded. With a steady hand he held the muzzle within a couple of inches of the wire and pressed the trigger.

The next instant the balloon, captive no longer, was soaring skywards at a dizzy rate, the bullet having accomplished the task that the wire cutters had failed to do.

CHAPTER XVIII
THE DERELICT OBSERVATION BALLOON

"Well done, old man!" exclaimed Tressidar as he climbed back into the basket car. "That was a brilliant idea of yours. Look here, you know something of aeronautical work; I don't, so you had better pilot this contraption."

Fuller shook his head.

"This isn't a clinking little biplane," he said, "It is completely at the mercy of the wind. But we mustn't grumble; we're leaving Sylt a long way beneath us."

Looking over the edge of the car, Tressidar could discern practically the whole of the long, narrow island, which is twenty miles in length and averaging two miles in breadth. Owing to the fact that it was dead low water the island appeared to be a vast peninsula, joined to the Schleswig shore by a broad belt of sand. North and south of the island and running respectively south-east and north-east were two extensive estuaries that almost met at the causeway connecting Sylt with the mainland.

"Which way are we drifting?" asked Tressidar anxiously.

"Hanged if I can make out," replied Fuller. "We've apparently struck a calm patch. The wind was certainly sou'sou'west when we kicked off. See—the smoke from those buildings: it had a decided drift towards the Danish frontier."

"A good easterly gale would be more my mark," said Tressidar. "We would then stand a chance of getting picked up by our patrol craft."

"Unless they started to shell us with the most amiable intention of sending a couple of supposed Huns to blazes," added the flight sub. "So, in the circumstances, Denmark is good enough for me, even if we are lucky enough to fetch it."

For some moments there was silence, broken only by the barking of a dog some thousands of feet below Then Fuller, who had been leaning over the side, shrugged his shoulders.

"We're dropping, I'm afraid," he announced. "It's close on sunset, and with the fall of temperature the buoyancy of the gas-bag suffers. See what you can chuck overboard."

The balloon, being hitherto used as a captive observation machine, was unprovided with an aneroid, or indeed any instrument for measuring the altitude. During the last ten minutes it had drifted steadily in a north-easterly direction, so that, unless the wind changed, the aeronauts were faced with the possibility of "landing" somewhere in the North Sea instead of the shores of Jutland.

Overboard went the rifle, two hundred rounds of ammunition, the telephone, and other miscellaneous articles, all of which stood a good chance of doing a certain amount of damage to the German torpedo-boats at the mouth of Lister Deep. A revolver and fifty small cartridges Tressidar retained, arguing with himself that they might be useful.

"There's a fog coming up," he said, after studying the panoramic view through a pair of binoculars. "A night mist, I suppose. It will make things jolly awkward when we do land."

"It will be a jolly good thing for us very soon," corrected Fuller. "Look, what do you make of that?" And he pointed in the direction of the now distant fortress of Sylt.

"Taubes," exclaimed Tressidar laconically.

"Or Fokkers," added the flight-sub. "Two of the brutes; they'll be hard after us in a brace of shakes. In fact I think they are heading in our direction already."

"Thank heaven it's getting dark," said the sub. fervently, for already the land was shrouded in the gloom of twilight. "And it's getting fairly thick up here. I can hardly discern the aeroplanes."

"They have a bigger object to look for than we have," said Fuller. "We'll have to do one thing or the other—go up or down. Going down means irreparable loss of hydrogen."

"There's nothing left in the way of ballast to sling overboard."

"Yes, in due course," remarked the flight sub. "I see a couple of straps round the basket. We'll have to strap ourselves to the netting and cut the car adrift. It's our only chance."

Tressidar realised the gravity of the situation. The balloon, by no means fully inflated when they boarded her, was appreciably losing lifting power both by the minute yet none the less certain porosity of the envelope and by the fall of temperature. He shuddered, strong-minded though he was, at the idea of having to literally hang in the air with the prospect of a terrific drop to earth should the thin cordage of the netting give way.

Presumably the German airmen were reluctant to plunge into the mist, that was now spreading far and wide and increasing in height. They were still climbing spirally, evidently with the idea of gaining an immense altitude before swooping down upon the derelict balloon.

And every moment's delay meant that their chances decreased and that the odds against the fugitives diminished.

The balloon, still falling, was now swallowed up in the fog. To descend prematurely meant either falling upon the German island of Rom, or else into the German territorial waters. In either case recapture was a foregone conclusion.

The low drone of an air propeller announced the disconcerting fact that one of the Fokkers was approaching. Quickly the noise increased, but in which direction—whether above or below—neither of the British officers could determine.

Then, with a rush of displaced air that caused the balloon to sway violently, the aeroplane swept beneath it at the rate of an express train. Too late had the Huns spotted their quarry. To attempt to rise would result in collision with disastrous results to friend and foe. All the Huns could do was to depress the horizontal steering-rudders and dip sharply underneath the balloon before describing a curve and approaching it at an altitude that would enable them to use their weapons of offence. In this case the Germans hoped to recapture the two officers alive, and with that object in view they were endeavouring to perforate the envelope of the balloon sufficiently to send it with comparative slowness to the ground.

"Now!" exclaimed Fuller.

Both men hacked desperately with their knives they had found in the car. The basket dropped and was lost to sight in the darkness. Tressidar and his companion, clinging to the network, were almost unaware of any change of altitude, although there was a slight downdraught of air, until the balloon emerged from the bank of mist into the gathering darkness.

Tressidar gave a sigh of relief. There were no signs of the second German aeroplane. Evidently it was engaged, as was its consort, in hunting for the balloon in the fog, which was very much like looking for the proverbial needle in a bottle of hay—with the grave risk of an aerial collision thrown in.

By degrees the drone of the propellers died away and complete silence reigned. It was becoming bitterly cold. The two men, ill-clad for a night in the clouds, shivered violently. Their hands lost all sense of touch. Had it not been for the leather straps that encircled their bodies they would have been compelled to drop—to be dashed into unrecognisability upon the ground six thousand feet below.

Half an hour passed. Overhead the stars were shining brightly. Obliquely beneath them a dull blurr of light was visible. It was the searchlights of Sylt. Further away, and in the opposite direction, lights of varying intensity glimmered through the now dispersing fog.

"Hurrah!" exclaimed the flight sub. "The coastwise lights of Denmark. They can't be German, for the bounders are as cautious about showing as much as a candle-light as we are. That patch of luminosity must be the town of Esbjerg."

"We're getting nearer," declared Tressidar after another interval, during which the balloon had revolved half a dozen times on its own axis, for in the absence of the cable connecting it with the earth the supplementary gas-bag failed to serve its purpose of keeping the balloon steady.

"And falling," added Fuller. "We'll have to stand by for a jolly good old bump, I fancy."

They had now good reasons for supposing that they were over Danish territory, for beneath them numerous lights were twinkling. It was as yet only nine o'clock, and the villagers had not yet retired to rest. To the southward—for the aeronauts were now able to determine the cardinal points of the compass by means of the Pole Star—the lights ended abruptly, indicating the frontier line between a nation at peace and a nation at war.

"Rub your hands well," cautioned Fuller. "You'll have to be slippy getting that buckle unfastened. Directly we touch we must cast off simultaneously, or one of us will have another voyage through the air. We are now less than a thousand feet up, I think."

The balloon was again falling, although its descent was by no means rapid. The chums could now hear sounds coming from the country beneath them; even a horse trotting and a man whistling. Yet, with the exception of the lights, nothing was visible. Even the nature of the country, whether flat or hilly, open or wooded, was veiled by the darkness.

"What's that?" asked Tressidar, as a number of dark conical projections seemed to flit past only a few feet beneath them.

"Tree tops," replied Fuller. "We've just missed being left on the top branches of some pines. By Jove, there's quite a steady breeze. If we crash into anything there'll be trouble."

Almost as he spoke Tressidar's feet came in contact with the ground. Then like an indiarubber ball the balloon shot ten feet in the air and again dropped, until the sub. found his boots trailing over a field of grass.

"Stand by!" shouted Fuller warningly. "Mind you don't get entangled in the netting."

Both men unbuckled their straps. They were now clinging with both hands to the network. The bumps became more and more violent, as the balloon lost buoyancy, but at the same time their rate of progress over the ground was too quick to enable them to find a footing.

Suddenly their boots caught in the top rail of a fence.

"Let go!" shouted Fuller.

Tressidar obeyed promptly, to find himself sprawling head downwards in a ditch. Regaining his feet, he found his chum kneeling a few feet from him. There was no sign of the balloon. Relieved of the twenty-four stone weight of the two passengers, it had soared upwards once more and had vanished from their sight.

CHAPTER XIX
THE DESERTED HOUSE

For some moments Tressidar could do nothing but cling to the fence. He was still under the influence of vertigo, caused by his flight through space. Everything seemed to be revolving round and round. But for the support he would have been unable to stand.

"I'm feeling beastly giddy," he gasped.

"Not unusual," replied Fuller briskly. "Sit down and clap your head between your knees. You'll soon feel all right. You are not used to this sort of work."

"And it strikes me I never will be," thought the sub. as he carried out his companion's instructions.

"Better?" asked the flight sub. "Good! I knew you would be. Now, what's the plan of action? I vote we go cautiously, to make sure that we are in neutral territory. We'll have to get decent clothes before daybreak. We're positively not respectable."

"Look here," said Tressidar. "What happens if we are on Danish soil? Do you think we'll be interned if we are discovered? If so, I'm not having any."

"Can't say," replied Fuller. "The Danes are jolly good fellows, but they are sticklers for international propriety. You see, they are in fear of the Huns. They haven't forgotten the loss of Schleswig-Holstein. Is there a British vice-consul at Esbjerg, I wonder?"

"I should imagine so," answered his chum. "But how on earth can we get in touch with him while we are wearing these multicoloured travesties of apparel? We would be run in on sight, and then there would be the deuce of a bother. I don't like the idea of cooling our heels in a Danish internment camp until the end of the war. No, the only thing I can suggest is to turn burglars. In short, sneak some clothes and food, and then make for Esbjerg. We're bound to find a vessel bound for England. As for the stuff we sneak, we must make reparation at the first convenient opportunity."

"I'm on," replied Fuller laconically.

"Then north-east is our course. We'll investigate at the first cottage we come to that doesn't show a light. Suppose I'd better stick to this?" And he held up the revolver in the starlight.

"Might be useful," agreed Fuller. "Especially in this 'dunno where 'e are' district."

Keeping by the side of the fence, the two men stole cautiously along for nearly two hundred yards, till they found their progress barred by a wire railing supported by stout wooden uprights.

"'Ware barbed wire," whispered Fuller.

"It's not barbed," declared Tressidar, running his fingers along a section of the wire. "That's another fairly sound proof that we are somewhere in Denmark, as, I believe, the Danish Government forbids the use of that beastly barbed stuff. I guess the fellow who invented barbed wire has something on his conscience if he's still alive. It must have cost thousands of lives in this war."

Several fields were traversed before the two officers came to an abrupt halt. Not so very far away was a road. They could hear footsteps and then the gradually increasing roar of a motor-cycle.

"A German by the beastly sound of the engine," declared Fuller. "It's almost as guttural with its explosion as a Hun jabbering away in full blast. Look here, this road won't do. Too many people about. Edge away to the right and keep parallel to it."

Within the next hour the chums passed close to half a dozen houses. Lights within showed that the occupants were still up. Caution urged the fugitives to give these buildings a wide berth.

"I'm getting horribly peckish," announced Fuller. "I could swallow a basin full of steerage cocoa without the faintest qualms, and I don't think I would jib at a weevily biscuit. What's that over there?"

He pointed to the faint outlines of a house which, unlike the others they had passed, was unlighted, and also not surrounded by outbuildings. On the side facing them was a row of tall poplars that sighed mournfully in the breeze.

"That's the ticket," agreed Fuller. "Only remember: if you're nabbed I give myself up. We sink or swim together on this trip."

Fortunately the ground was fairly soft, and the sub's wooden-soled foot-gear made no sound. The canvas uppers, too, had no tendency to squeak, but how the soles would behave if they came in contact with a tiled or cobbled pavement was another matter.

On approaching closer to the house, Tressidar made the discovery that it was surrounded by a stone wall of about seven feet in height. This he skirted until he found that the front of the building abutted on a narrow lane that evidently joined the highway at no little distance.

At first the sub. thought that the house was empty, until he noticed drawn curtains over the windows. Possibly there were lights within, for the fabric was heavy and impervious to illumination. There were shutters also, but these had not been drawn-to.

Having completed the circuit of the building, Tressidar paused to consider his next step. One thing he felt fairly certain of there were no dogs on the premises, otherwise even his light footfalls would have aroused them. A strange quietude brooded over the place. Although furnished, it was temporarily without its occupiers.

Thrice he essayed to scale the wall, but owing to his exertions and lack of food the task was beyond him.

"Say, old man," he whispered as he rejoined his chum, "come and give me a leg up. There's a tough bit of wall to tackle. After that it looks simple enough. No need to stop here. Keep close to the wall. If the place is empty, as I think it is, I'll open the door for you."

With Fuller's assistance the sub., having thrown off his boots, found himself astride the wall. On the other side was a rough lean-to shed, which extended to the wall of the house. The roof creaked but held as Tressidar made his way with great care and deliberation over the tarred boards. He was now able to reach a small window without undue exertion.

"Wish to goodness I had a diamond," he soliloquised as he pressed gently and firmly upon the resisting glass. "Hulloa. There's a stack-pipe. I wonder if the guttering will hold?"

Steadying himself by the stack-pipe, Tressidar hauled himself up until he stood upon the window-sill. He was now able to reach the eave of the roof. Testing the spouting with his weight he came to the conclusion that it was fairly sound.

"Now or never," he muttered, and with an agile spring he drew himself up sufficiently to enable him to clamber on the tiled roof. As he expected, there was a dormer-window less than ten feet to his left.

The tiles creaked as he trod. A stork, nesting between one of the chimneys and the roof, flew noisily away, the sudden apparition of the large bird nearly causing the sub. to slide over the edge of the tiles. For some moments he listened intently. No sound from the immediate vicinity reached his ears. Evidently it was safe to proceed.

The dormer-window was diamond-paned. The leads offered little resistance as he pressed against the glass. In a very short space of time he had removed a piece of glass nearest to the fastening; then, inserting his hand, he threw open the casement and drew aside the heavy curtain.

With his head and shoulders thrust into the room the sub. listened again. The noisy ticking of a clock was the only sound that caught his ear.

"Jolly queer sort of house," thought he; "one might imagine it was in good old England. It's the only one that shades the inside lights, and they are mighty particular about doing it. Even this attic window was bunged up."

The open casement was just large enough to allow him to squeeze through. The floor-boards creaked alarmingly as they took his weight. Again he listened. The sound was enough to awaken the soundest sleeper, unless he or she were stone deaf.

"By Jove! A burglar must be a pretty plucky sort of individual," mused Tressidar as he groped his way to the low doorway and commenced to descend the steep, rickety stairs. "Feeling one's way about in a strange house and in total darkness requires some doing, especially with the risk of being bowled over with a poker thrown in."

Systematically the sub. proceeded with his investigations, examining every room as he came to it, until he found himself on the ground floor. Luck was in their favour, for the house was temporarily without its lawful occupants.

The front door was locked. The key had been removed, so the sub. directed his attention to the back entrance.

The massive bolts grated loudly as Tressidar opened the door. There was no necessity to call to Fuller. The flight sub. had heard the unbolting process and was waiting close at hand.

"Stand by," whispered Tressidar. "I'll hand you over a stool."

By the aid of this useful article Fuller had no difficulty in scaling the wall. Together the chums entered the house, and rebolted the door.

"Now we can get a light if we can find matches," said Tressidar. "Every window is curtained. I took the precaution of leaving ajar the window that I tackled first. If we have to beat a retreat, that's our way out."

"I wonder why you rebolted the door."

"Because if we did clear out by that way we would have to scale the wall," replied the sub. "By the window we land at once on the roof of a shed which is almost level with the wall. That's a jolly sight easier. Good! Here are some matches."

His hand had come in contact with a box on the mantelshelf. Close by was a candlestick with a candle in the holder and a short piece in the bowl. Arguing that one of the first things the returning occupiers would look for would be the candlestick, Tressidar took the spare piece of candle and left the other undisturbed.

"Looks like a second-hand-clothes dealer's," remarked Fuller as the two officers entered the back bedroom on the first floor.

The room was long and narrow, extending from front to back. The ceiling was low and heavily beamed. At one end of the room, its canopy screen effectually blocking the window, was an old four-poster bed. On it was laid a suit of clothes. More masculine garments were thrown negligently over chairs and sofa. A medley of coats and trousers hung from pegs in an open wardrobe. A fur-lined great-coat had been thrown upon the floor.

"Take your choice, old man," said Fuller with a grin. "We'll stuff our discarded emblems of servitude up the chimney. It doesn't look as if they had a fire here very often. Wonder who the old josser is?"

Five minutes later the chums were rigged out in worn but serviceable garb. They would easily pass for well-to-do Danish artisans.

"Now for grub," decided Tressidar. "Let's forage in our unknown host's larder."

"Evidently no shortage of food in this establishment," said Fuller, as the two officers ate with a voracity that would have raised a storm of protest in the ward-room of one of H.M. ships. "Dash it all! I feel another man already. Now, what's the plan?"

"Esbjerg, as soon as possible. We'll either have to stow ourselves on board a tramp bound for a British port, or else throw ourselves upon the generosity of her skipper. These Danes are downright good fellows.... It's very quiet down here. I'm curious to know more about the owner of this remarkable place."

"I think your wish will be gratified," rejoined Tressidar grimly, as a motor-car that had driven up at high speed stopped outside the house. "Lights out! Up aloft as sharp as we can."

The two amateur cracksmen had barely gained the bedroom when they heard the key grate in the lock. Then a voice exclaimed in German:

"That will do, Karl. Take this car as far as Rodgrund's farm and await us there. It will not arouse suspicion. Now, Herr Oberfurst, at your service."

CHAPTER XX
TRESSIDAR SOLVES A MYSTERY

Tressidar nudged his companion. German! Their interest was aroused. Although it was no doubt quite a common occurrence for the guttural language of the Hun to be spoken on the Danish frontier, the warning given to the chauffeur of the car to avoid suspicion was in itself a mystery.

The sub. had yet to learn the identity of Herr Oberfurst.

"Yes, I have had a fairly quick journey," said the spy. "Fortunately we did not fall in with any of our incomparable unterseebooten."

"Donnerwetter! I wish I could say the same," retorted the second German crossly. "The frontier is a bore. Why on earth you couldn't arrange to meet me in Hamburg is beyond me."

"A thousand pardons, Count," declared Oberfurst volubly. "Everything depends upon secrecy. It is easy enough to cross the frontier, I admit, but it is returning to Danish soil that is the difficulty. Here am I, an accredited American Red Cross agent, furnished with passports by the owl-eyed British Government. So long as I remain in Denmark there is no cause for suspicion, but should I set foot in the Fatherland, unseen difficulties beset me. My plan is, therefore, I think, an admirable one. Karl Hoeffer is the soul of integrity so far as Germany is concerned. This house of his is well suited for our purpose. Is that not so?"

"I suppose you have good reasons, friend Otto," replied the Count. "But time presses. The 'Nordby' leaves Esbjerg at tide-time tomorrow morning—a matter of seven hours from now. Well, what have you to report? Is the damage done in the latest raid as extensive as the commander of *LZ142* states?"

Otto Oberfurst made a noise that indicated a negative reply.

"Then what?" demanded the count eagerly.

"The airship never got within twenty miles of Manchester, Count; and as for the damage stated to have been done at Newcastle, I have personally visited the town and can find nothing of the kind. Twenty bombs were dropped, all around a small station on a branch line. Doubtless our airmen were deceived by the presence of a mountain lake. It may have looked like an arm of the sea. And how peculiar the English people are! So long as they are not injured or their property destroyed they laugh at our Zeppelins."

"The fools!" ejaculated the count impatiently. Then—

"Now tell us about your work, Herr Oberfurst. Have you a copy of the British Admiralty chart of the shoals of Straits of Dover minefield?"

"It is here," was the reply. "One of von Schenck's men obtained it for me from a compatriot who is actually employed in the British Hydrographic office. Can you imagine an Englishman working in the German Admiralty? Ach! It is playing into our hands."

Tressidar could hear the crackle of the linen-backed paper as the count unrolled and examined the highly important chart.

"Yes," he said slowly. "This is quite genuine. It tallies with reports through other sources. You mentioned Herr von Schenck: how is he?"

The spy hesitated before replying.

"He is well," he replied simply.

"You speak strangely," said the count sharply "What is amiss?"

"A slightly personal matter," explained von Oberfurst. "In short, a pecuniary affair."

"Explain."

"It is following the 'Pompey' business."

Tressidar gave an involuntary start. His hand went to the butt of the revolver in his pocket. He felt sorely tempted to descend and confront the two spies with the muzzle of the weapon until he realised that in a neutral country it is well to be discreet.

"He agreed to pay me twenty thousand dollars," continued von Oberfurst. "I did my work. The cruiser, as you know, was sunk. But von Schenck declared that the destruction was not complete. The ship is capable of being raised and repaired. I doubt it. All the same, he would not give me more than ten thousand dollars, and what is worse he made the draft out in marks, and unfortunately a mark is no longer what it was."

"You have my sympathy; nevertheless I must upbraid you on your lack of duty towards the Fatherland," said the count. "The fall of the mark is but temporary. After the war, when the German arms are victorious——

But let that remain. I will guarantee the difference between the amount von Schenck originally promised and what you actually received. More, I will instruct your New York bank to place to your credit another ten thousand dollars provided you perform another service."

"And what is it?" asked the spy eagerly.

"This torpedoing of neutral vessels is a praiseworthy affair," explained the count. "It will give our mercantile fleet an undoubted advantage after the war, but unfortunately at the present juncture it cuts both ways. Neutrals don't like it, which is natural. Not that we care a pfennig for their likes and dislikes. At the same time they are showing signs of reluctance to supply us with necessary commodities. They plead the rigours of the English blockade, but that is a mere excuse. Now, the Imperial Chancellor has asked me to engineer a scheme to enlist the sympathy of neutrals to a corresponding resentment towards England. Then the desired goods will roll in fast enough."

"I follow you so far," observed von Oberfurst.

"As a man of supreme intelligence you would," rejoined the German flatteringly. "Now, to the point. You are returning in the 'Nordby' tomorrow. A British submarine has been reported off the Vyl Lightship. It is reasonable to conclude that the 'Nordby' will be subject to a scrutiny if not to actual examination. Now, what I want is that you fire a charge of explosive on board the steamer at the psychological moment when the submarine appears."

"I hardly see how," objected von Oberfurst. "There will be no opportunity for me to get below. And the risk to myself — —"

"Ach! You do not think enough," said the count deprecatingly, and contradicting the words he had used a few moments previously. "You are berthed aft? There is no danger to you from an explosion in the hold. You may be certain that in the excitement that follows the appearance of the submarine the attention of all on board except yourself will be directed towards it. It will be an easy matter to slip below. The after-store hatchway will most certainly be uncovered. You will drop the bomb, with a short-time fuse lighted, into the hold, return on deck and await events. All the damage done will be below the water-line, and there are boats. It will not be a long row to the Vyl Lightship. And, just think, ten thousand dollars for a comparatively simple piece of work compared with which the sinking of the 'Pompey' was a colossal task."

"I would prefer to use the clockwork detonating gear. It is infinitely safer," objected Oberfurst.

"Impracticable," decided his companion. "It is no use setting the thing hours ahead. It is a question of minutes. Say three: that will give you ample time to light the fuse and return on deck."

Apparently the spy made a gesture that denoted unwillingness—for the count continued:

"The Americans, as you know well, have a saying 'Money talks.' Here is a sum on account," and the two British officers could distinctly hear the crinkling of crisp paper.

"No gold," said the spy firmly. "The Fatherland has plenty in reserve for use in circumstances such as the present."

"Himmel! You cannot carry ten thousand marks in gold to England."

"I do not intend to do so, Count. I will see that it is placed in the Esbjerg branch of the Danish State Bank."

"Ach! You are perverse," almost shouted the Kaiser's emissary. "Do you think that the car is laden with gold?"

A rupture seemed imminent, until Otto Oberfurst, overcome by his innate greed, exclaimed:

"Well, Count, under protest I will take the notes; but they must be at the local rates of exchange."

"And how is von Arve?" inquired the count.

"Himmel! I have neither seen nor heard of him for weeks," declared the spy. "He was to have gone to Rosyth. I fear the worst, especially as these English have shot three unnamed German agents in the Tower of London. This secrecy is, believe me, very trying to one's nerves. Imagine a man working hard and risking everything for the love of the Fatherland, as many of us are now doing. Then without warning, without even a chance of his name being announced so that all good Germans could honour his heroic sacrifice, he vanishes—and an unnamed corpse occupies an unmarked grave in an English fortress."

"You are getting quite melodramatic, my friend," remarked the count suavely. "A draught of honest Bavarian beer will set you up. I, too, am hungry and thirsty. Within another half-hour we must part company."

The two conspirators rose. Tressidar could hear the shuffling of their feet and the movement of the chair-legs on the oaken floor.

"Come and bear a hand like an old campaigner," said the count, and the twain made their way to the larder.

"We'll have to be moving," whispered Tressidar. "Wait until those fellows make a noise with the plates and bottles, then get to the window."

Creeping with the utmost caution lest the creaking of the floor would betray their presence, the two chums gained the window. The sub., knowing the "lay of the land," went first, dropping noiselessly upon the tarred roof of the outhouse. Then, guiding the flight-sub.'s feet, he waited until Fuller stood beside him.

Having reached terra-firma, the chums retrieved their wooden-soled foot-gear. These they carried with them until they could find a suitable hiding-place.

"We'll make for the high road now," decided Tressidar, when they were at a safe distance from the spies' meeting-place. "We'll pass muster in these togs, and I don't suppose we'll be questioned."

"By Jove! I would like to scrag that fellow," exclaimed Fuller. "The bounder who kippered the 'Pompey,' I mean."

"So would I," agreed Tressidar. "It's a mystery to me how he was able to place the explosives on board. Never mind; we'll lay him by the heels."

Briefly he explained his plan of action.

"Capital, if it works," decided the flight-sub.

Dawn was breaking as the two chums trudged wearily into the little Jutland town of Esbjerg. Guided by a seaman's unerring instinct, they made straight for the harbour.

It was now a little more than half flood. Lying alongside the western pier, that with the mole encloses the outer tidal harbour, were several small tramps with steam raised. They were still aground, and would be for another hour. Amongst them was a wall-sided, grey-hulled steamer, with the Danish colours painted conspicuously on both sides as well as the name "Nordby" in letters six feet in height.

The work of loading was not yet complete, for gangs of stevedores were carrying sacks of smoked bacon and kegs of butter from the quay to the hold. A sleepy young officer was directing operations. He was the only member of the ship's complement visible. The rest of the officers and ship's crew were below.

"Any use trailing in with the crowd?" asked Fuller, indicating the men engaged in loading the vessel.

"I think not," replied Tressidar. "We'll mark time until the skipper puts in an appearance, only I hope he'll come on deck before our man arrives."

Presently a short, rotund man skipped agilely up the gangway. The sub. rightly concluded that he was the pilot, for as he gained the deck the mate sung out an order and the crew emerged from the fore peak. A little later the skipper came on deck and made his way to the bridge, where he remained for some time in animated conversation with the pilot.

Meanwhile the hatches were secured and the last of the stevedores returned to the shore. Half a dozen passengers boarded the ship, but whether the spy was amongst them Tressidar was unable to determine. He wished he had taken the risk of having a look at the fellow while he was conversing with the count.

As each passenger gained the head of the gangway he was addressed by a steward and told which was his cabin, but as every man had to show his ticket it was pretty evident that the two Englishmen could not smuggle themselves on board without an almost certain risk of being challenged.

"The crew look to be pretty hefty chuckers-out," remarked Fuller ruefully, as he looked at the stalwart Danes. "Pity we hadn't knocked up the British vice-consul. I suppose the only thing to be done is to go straight on board and make a clean breast of it to the skipper. These Danes are awfully decent fellows, and their sympathies are almost always pro-British. The trouble is, that neither of us can speak Danish, although perhaps the skipper knows English."

Just then a cab drew up close to the pier and a tall, upright man with a trim torpedo beard alighted. A porter hastened to convey his somewhat scanty belongings. As he did so, a portmanteau slipped from his grasp and, rebounding on the planking of the pier, struck the owner a smart blow on the shin.

"Confound you, you idiot!" he exclaimed.

At the words, uttered in an unmistakably west-country accent, Tressidar walked straight up to the stranger.

"Excuse me," he said. "We're in a regular hole. We are British officers and have escaped from Germany. Can you help us to obtain a passage in the 'Nordby'?"

"You have not broken your parole, I trust?"

"We were never asked to give our parole," replied the sub. "We managed to get away from Sylt."

"Then you must be pretty smart," replied the stranger. "From all accounts it is a pretty tight place to be cooped up in. By the bye, what are your names?"

Tressidar gave the name and rank of his companion and himself

"And mine is Holloway, late navigating lieutenant of the 'Sunderbund.' I'm interned, but the Danish Government have given me ten days' leave on parole. Suppose it won't be infringing any of the conditions if I do give you a hand. Here's some of the necessary. The shipping agent's office is just round the corner. You'll have to look sharp."

With hurried thanks the two chums hastened to purchase their tickets. Directly the lieutenant had mentioned his name they had both recalled the loss of the "Sunderbund," a destroyer that had run aground in Danish waters, and, while helpless, was subjected to the fire of four German light cruisers in defiance of all international regulations. But for the prompt intervention of a Danish torpedo-boat that, regardless of risk, had interposed between the stranded British craft and her unscrupulous assailants, the crew of the "Sunderbund" would have been massacred—there is no other word for it. As it was, the survivors—the officer and twenty-seven men—were rescued and interned.

Without a hitch Tressidar and Fuller found themselves safely on board the "Nordby."

The steward, although guessing from the absence of luggage that the two passengers were British prisoners of war or else men who had been interned and had not been on parole, received them with imperturbable gravity.

"I am anxious to know how you did the trick," said Lieutenant Holloway, as the three Britons paced the deck.

"If you don't mind we'll cut the first part of the yarn," replied Tressidar, making sure that no stranger was within earshot. "We had particular reasons for choosing the 'Nordby.'"

Briefly yet comprehensively he related the incident of the previous night, and that the spy was expected to sail on the "Nordby" with the intention of blowing her up.

"By Jove!" said Lieutenant Holloway fiercely. "Wish to goodness I wasn't bound by my parole. I'd like to have a hand in the business. Unfortunately I cannot. You say the spy isn't on board yet?"

"So far as we can surmise," rejoined Fuller. "You see, we heard him but didn't have a chance of examining the cut of his jib. Hulloa, here's a late bird. Wonder if 'tis he?"

An overcoated man was hurrying to the gangway. Disregarding the solicitations of the porters, he carried his own baggage, which consisted of two large, brass-bound attaché cases.

Nodding familiarly to the steward, the man descended the companion.

"Well?" asked Fuller, turning to his chum, but to his surprise he saw that Tressidar was in the act of straightening himself out, having just completed the task of refastening his boot-lace. "I say, you're a pretty sort of fellow. How on earth could you scrutinise a man if your face is looking at your boots?"

"I saw quite enough of him to satisfy me," replied Tressidar. "What I was afraid of was that he might recognise me."

"Recognise you?" echoed Fuller in amazement and incredulity.

"I said 'recognise me,'" repeated the sub. firmly. "Now I can understand the 'Pompey' affair. That fellow—I knew him in a minute in spite of his beard and moustache—was stoker on board the cruiser."

"Then you must have a wonderful memory," remarked Holloway, "especially as this fellow is one of the engine-room ratings and you are an executive officer."

"I had to speak pretty sharply to him once," said the sub. "He boggled over the steam winch—there was an accident in consequence and a man was killed. Now I come to think of it I don't believe it was altogether an accident, though. At any rate, he's our man. We'll find out which cabin he occupies and how far it is from the after-store-room hatchway. Then we'll have to wait."

"And see?" added Fuller.

"No—act," corrected Tressidar grimly.

CHAPTER XXI
CHECKMATE

The "Nordby" was an hour after her scheduled time in casting off from the quay. Slowly she threaded the tortuous channel until clear of the dangerous sandbanks off the Danish coast. Here the pilot, with ill-concealed relief, handed over the wheel, bade the skipper farewell, and took to the boat that was being towed alongside. Thanking his lucky stars that his duty did not require him to navigate the vessel through the mine-strewn, submarine-infested North Sea, he rowed back to Esbjerg, while the "Nordby," increasing speed, shaped a south-westerly course.

Keeping Otto Oberfurst well under observation, although they took care to render themselves as inconspicuous as possible, Tressidar and Fuller remained on the *qui vive*.

Their compatriot, meanwhile, paced the deck betwixt the mainmast and the taffrail, maintaining a well-assumed indifference to his surroundings. He was aware that the spy had already made himself acquainted with the fact that an interned British officer on parole was amongst the passengers, and Oberfurst was likely to be keeping a stealthy watch on him. So from the moment he had seen the spy board the ship Holloway had kept aloof from Tressidar and his chum.

The "Nordby" was well beyond the three-mile limit when the look-out reported a submarine on the starboard bow. Instantly there was a rush on the part of the passengers and crew to see the strange under-water craft. Speculation ran high as to her nationality and whether she would attempt to destroy the neutral vessel with the ruthlessness peculiar to the Huns.

"She's one of our 'S' class," declared Tressidar to his chum. "That's all right. Now for friend Oberfurst."

The spy was no longer on deck. Down the companion ladder the two British officers hastened and cautiously took up a position just outside the German's cabin. They could hear him fumbling with the locks of his portmanteau.

Then the door was opened, and Oberfurst appeared, with a small leather wallet resembling a camera case slung from his shoulder with a strap.

"Hands up!" ordered Tressidar sternly, the muzzle of his revolver, held by a steady hand, within a foot of the spy's head.

"What for?" demanded the spy in English. "You're talking in your hat, old sport. This is a neutral ship." Then, recognising his former officer he asked, "So you think you've got me, eh? Guess desertion is not an extradictable offence, so you're kippered, Mr. Tressidar."

"We'll see about that, Jorkler," rejoined the sub. "Collar him, old man. We'll see what's in this case."

The spy, still grinning insolently, offered no resistance. Deftly Fuller unbuckled the strap and opened the wallet. Within was a folding camera—nothing more.

While Tressidar still kept his prisoner covered with the revolver, Fuller quickly overhauled the contents of his cabin effects. The search, as far as incriminating objects were concerned, was fruitless. Oberfurst, although he had not previously recognised Tressidar, had seen the two supposed Danish artisans in conversation with Holloway when he had boarded the "Nordby." Quick to act upon the faintest warning, he had thrown overboard the infernal machine, relying upon his forged passports to clear himself from suspicion when the "Nordby" arrived in a British port.

Tressidar and his companion exchanged glances. Both realised that there had been an awkward hitch. Having gone thus far it was impossible to cry halt; while, owing to the lack of direct evidence, there was hardly likely to be sufficient reason for convincing the "Nordby's" skipper of the spy's sinister intentions. Nor could the sub. signal to the British submarine and get her commander forcibly to remove the spy. That in itself would be a gross breach of international neutrality, and as long as Oberfurst remained on board, under the protection of the Danish flag, he was immune from arrest. To do otherwise the British Government would be transgressing its own principles which were stoutly maintained: the historic "Trent" case during the American Civil War. Unless it could be proved up to the hilt that Oberfurst had intended to place a charge of explosive in the hold of the "Nordby," the chances were that the Danish skipper would decline to place the passenger under arrest.

Suddenly a tremendous crash shook the ship from stem to stern. Almost immediately she took a pronounced list to starboard. Tressidar, losing his balance, brushed against his prisoner. Fortunately for the latter, the sub.'s finger was not resting on the trigger of the revolver, otherwise the British Government might have been saved a mountain of trouble.

Taking advantage of the temporary confusion, Otto Oberfurst made a rush for the companion and gained the deck.

Tressidar made no effort to detain him.

"By Jove!" he exclaimed; "that must be a strafed Hun submarine after all. Here's a pretty kettle of fish. If they've had the tip that we're on board it's a moral cert. that they are keen on recapturing us."

"And if we stick here we'll be booked for Davy Jones' locker," declared Fuller. "Let's get on deck."

On gaining the poop they found that the "Nordby" was rapidly settling by the head. She had recovered somewhat from her list to starboard, and as the explosion had occurred for'ard, the boats were intact. These were being lowered without undue haste or confusion. There was no sign of the spy. Lieutenant Holloway, imperturbably smoking a cigar, was standing under the bridge.

"Deuced rum business!" he remarked as Tressidar and Fuller rejoined him. "Thought at first that the spy had succeeded in his attempt, until I saw that the explosion was an *external* one and right for'ard."

"But the submarine?" asked Fuller.

"Had nothing to do with it," declared Holloway with conviction. "She's a British one. I was watching her up to the moment of the explosion. There was no track of a torpedo."

The submarine, with her conning-tower just awash, was lying hove-to at a couple of cable's length on the starboard quarter of the foundering vessel. Two officers and three seamen were visible, the former keeping the "Nordby" under observation with their binoculars.

"She'll give the boats a pluck to the lightship," declared Fuller. "And we can get them to take us on board before we get there. How about you, sir? You'll be rescued by a British craft and consequently your internment——"

Lieutenant Holloway shook his head.

"I'll play the game," he declared. "Any hitch and the Danes won't be so keen on letting our compatriots off for short periods on leave on parole. Hulloa! What's the game now?"

As he spoke the officers and men on the superstructure of the submarine disappeared below, the watertight hatches were closed and secured, and the vessel slid with hardly a ripple beneath the surface.

Shouts of execration arose from some of the passengers and crew of the "Nordby" as they saw what they took to be the cause of the disaster steal away, until the Danish skipper emphatically assured them that the explosion had occurred by the ship coming in contact with a derelict mine, which, in fact, was the case.

By this time only five or six persons remained on board, the skipper being still on the bridge. Two boats had already pushed off. It was merely a question of minutes before the "Nordby" made her final plunge.

"What's that fellow up to, by Jove!" suddenly exclaimed Lieutenant Holloway.

Otto Oberfurst had mounted the main-mast shrouds and was gesticulating violently in the direction of an object broad on the port-beam. The object was a German submarine of the most modern type, running on the surface at a good eighteen or twenty knots.

The Danish skipper saw her too. Whatever his feelings were towards submarines in general, his action showed that he had no love for those sailing under the Black Cross Ensign—the modern counterpart of the "Jolly Roger."

He shouted an order. Three seamen sprang into the rigging and with no little force compelled the spy to descend. Not content with that, they bundled him unceremoniously into the last boat that was rubbing her gunwale against the "Nordby's" starboard side.

They were not feelings of humanity that prompted the German submarine to speed to the vicinity of the sinking ship. Slowing down within hailing distance, her officers and crew came on deck to gloat over the sinking of a helpless neutral merchantman. More than likely they were anxious to ascertain her name so that they could strengthen the claim for the award of Iron Crosses—the highly prized reward for "frightfulness" as practised by the degenerate descendants of Attila.

The Danish skipper enjoined strict silence. He had now jumped into the boat—the last to leave the stricken ship. Otto Oberfurst, lying at full length on the gratings, with two brawny seamen holding him down, was helpless to give another warning. In breathless silence they waited.

"Good!" ejaculated Tressidar as an ever-diverging feather of ripples marked the track of a 24-in. torpedo. Passing within fifty yards of the boat in which he sat, the deadly weapon sped unerringly towards its quarry.

Amidst a tremendous upheaval of water, mingled with smoke and fragments of metal, the unterseeboot vanished for ever; while like a huge whale the British submarine that had dealt the fatal blow shook herself clear of the water.

The appearance was little more than momentary, for without checking her way the vessel dived again and was lost to sight.

"Wonder why?" remarked Fuller.

"I suppose she knows that the lightship isn't so very far off," replied Tressidar, concealing his disappointment at not being picked up by a British craft. "The sea's calm, the boats are by no means overcrowded, and — —"

A warning shout from one of the Danes interrupted the sub.'s words. Looking in the direction indicated by the man's outstretched fingers, the British officers made out the form of a huge Zeppelin. Although five miles away when first sighted by the "Nordby's" crew, it was rapidly approaching. With the wind and driven by five propellers, it was travelling at considerably more than a mile a minute. Nevertheless the alert lieutenant-commander of the British submarine had spotted the airship and had promptly dived.

Attention on the part of the passengers and crew of the "Nordby" was divided between the ship, now on the point of foundering, and the Zeppelin.

The former was now so deep down by the head that the hawse-pipes were submerged, while correspondingly her twin propellers were clear of the water. For a few moments she hung thus; irresolutely, as if loth to make her final plunge. Then, amidst a smother of foam and the gurgling sound of inrushing water, she slid completely from sight, leaving a pall of steam and smoke to mark her ocean grave.

The Zeppelin, finding that the destroyer of the "U" boat had submerged, descended with considerable rapidity until she was within five hundred feet of the level of the sea. Thrice she circled over the spot where the "Nordby" had disappeared, and then, having apparently discovered some signs of the British submarine, she tore away to the north-westward. For nearly an hour she remained in sight, but since she dropped no bombs Tressidar came to the conclusion that her quarry had eluded pursuit.

A little later the "Nordby's" boats parted company. Acting under semaphored instructions from the skipper, two of them made for the lightship, while the third, containing the Danish captain and the German spy, rowed with long, steady strokes towards the Jutland shore.

"The fellow's given us the slip," declared Fuller. "I wonder whether the skipper of the 'Nordby' smells a rat and means to hand him over to the authorities. Pity we didn't make a charge against him."

"What are you fellows going to do?" inquired Lieutenant Holloway. "If I were you I'd lie low and say nothing while you are on Danish soil. If you don't they'll want you to give evidence at a court of inquiry and all that sort of fuss. That can keep till you arrive in England. The sooner the better, as I'll warrant the Huns will make a fine song out of the sinking of the 'Nordby.' That rogue Oberfurst will pitch it in for all he's worth. Yes, I agree with Fuller, in fact, I go farther: it's a pity you didn't settle his hash once and for all."

"Well, there's one thing," rejoined Tressidar. "He won't dare to set foot in Great Britain again."

Wherein the sub. was grievously mistaken, for Otto Oberfurst's activities as a spy within Britannia's gates were by no means at an end.

CHAPTER XXII
THE SHELL-BATTERED HOSPITAL

On returning to Esbjerg, Tressidar and Fuller bade Lieutenant Holloway good-bye and hurried off to the British Consul's office. Acting with the greatest dispatch, that official, having taken down the officers' sworn statements, communicated by telegraph with the British Ambassador at Copenhagen. He, in turn, acquainted the Danish Government with the attempt to destroy the "Nordby" by internal explosion and requested that Otto Oberfurst be arrested.

Already the Danes were too late. The spy, having landed with the skipper of the mined ship, contrived to slip away, and for the present all traces of him were lost.

That same evening Tressidar and his chum sailed for England in a Danish mail-boat, arriving at Grimsby without incident.

Here they separated, Fuller proceeding to the Naval Air Station at Great Yarmouth, while Tressidar made for York in order to catch the Scottish express.

Rumours of naval activity in the North Sea urged him northwards with the least possible delay, but it was not until eight on the following morning that the slow "local" crawled into Auldhaig station.

"You've been remarkably quick, Mr. Tressidar," was the senior officer's greeting, when the sub. reported himself for duty. "It was only an hour ago that we received official news of your escape from Sylt."

"That seems months ago, sir," said the sub.

"No doubt," agreed the rear-admiral. "There's nothing like activity to make the time slip past. Unfortunately we have had little to do here during the last month. By the bye, the 'Heracles' is cruising. She'll be back, I hope, on Thursday."

"What happened when she chased the German cruiser, sir, might I ask? The last we saw of her was when we were adrift in the cutter."

Tressidar had previously made guarded inquiries, but beyond the knowledge of the fact that the British cruiser had come out "top dog," he could gather nothing definite.

"Oh, the usual," replied the senior officer. "The Hun had the advantage of speed. The 'Heracles' had to steer a zig-zag course in order to avoid a submarine. One 'U' boat did, in fact, let loose a couple of torpedoes, but they missed. The German looked like getting clean away when one of our 'Comus' class came up. You know her speed and you can guess the rest. Anyway, the third shot from the light cruiser did the trick, and our two vessels between them managed to rescue about forty of the Germans. The name of the sunken vessel was the 'Dortmunde,' and she was bound for Ireland."

"For Ireland?" echoed the sub. in surprise.

"Yes," continued the rear-admiral. "Unfortunately there's trouble amongst a small section of the extreme Nationalists. The majority of the Irish are loyal to the core. I'm an Irishman myself, born and bred in Leinster, so I can speak with authority. At any rate, the 'Heracles' nipped some awkward little plot in the bud. Once they've tried, the Germans will have another shot at stirring up sedition. These Huns are not deterred by failures, dash 'em! Although they funk the main issue at sea, they still persist in their petty operations, in spite of losses."

"By the bye, sir," said Tressidar, "there's something I wish to report." And he revealed to the astonished rear-admiral the actual cause of the blowing-up of the "Pompey."

"Bless my soul!" ejaculated the senior officer. "D'ye call that 'by the bye'? You haven't said a word to anyone about the business?"

"No, sir, not even to the vice-consul at Esbjerg. Only Mr. Holloway and Mr. Fuller know the secret, and they will take good care not to divulge anything."

"And the spy? Does he know that you are aware of his crime?"

"I think not, sir. He recognised me as one of the 'Pompey's' officers, but I said nothing to lead him to believe I had overheard his conversation with the mysterious count. He admitted that he was a deserter, and braved it out. Before we could get to business—the discovery that he had chucked his bomb overboard rather took the wind out of my sails—the 'Nordby' bumped into a mine."

"Very good. Now, Mr. Tressidar, will you kindly write out a detailed report of what occurred between the count and the spy, and I'll see that it is forwarded to the proper quarter. After that you can stand easy until Thursday. You look as if a good square meal or two will do you good."

The genial Irishman shook hands with his subordinate and did him the honour of asking him to dinner that evening. The sub. could not refuse, although he rather dreaded the ceremonious meal. Also he had made other plans, but he realised that it does not do to refuse a rear-admiral's invitation.

Arrayed in a borrowed mess uniform, since his gear was, as far as he was aware, still on board the "Heracles," Tressidar arrived at the admiral's official residence—a large, old-fashioned mansion standing on the side of a hill overlooking the harbour.

The ponderous repast proceeded slowly and smoothly, course after course was consumed, and by the time the wine was placed upon the table conversation was flowing briskly.

The room was brilliantly lighted with hundreds of candles, imparting an old-world aspect to the uniformed company. The windows, heavily curtained, shut out the light mist that was creeping in from seaward.

"Gentlemen!" exclaimed the senior officer, rapping the table with his mallet. "The King."

According to time-honoured custom, when the height of the deck-beams on board a man-of-war prevented the loyal toasts to be drunk standing, the guests, still sitting, raised their glasses.

Even as they did so a loud crash, quickly followed by another and another, broke the silence.

"Bless my soul!" ejaculated the rear-admiral. "Those infernal Zepps. No, don't draw the curtains, Garboard. If you want to see the fun, go outside."

Then with a "Drake touch" he poised his glass.

"Gentlemen!" he exclaimed. "There is yet time to duly drink His Majesty's health," and the toast was drunk with enthusiasm.

The officers hurriedly prepared to dash off to their various stations, when the door was thrown open and a messenger unceremoniously approached the senior officer.

"Signal just through, sir," he reported. "German cruisers off Auldhaig."

Such indeed was the case. With a recklessness that outrivalled their previous attempts upon the east coast of England, seven large armoured cruisers, taking advantage of hazy weather conditions and being efficiently guarded against surprise by half a dozen Zeppelins, had ventured to the east coast of Scotland. Three small British patrol boats had been sunk before they could give warning, while by that element of luck that had been responsible for many almost incredible happenings of the Great War, the raiders were able to get within effective range of the naval base of Auldhaig without being detected.

On the face of it the attack seemed nothing short of suicidal; yet when the true facts became known it was evident that the Germans were acting upon the principle in which a draught-player deliberately sacrifices one of his pieces to gain two of his opponent's.

The Huns knew that Auldhaig was practically devoid of warships. The nearest British base where any considerable section of the Grand Fleet lay was at Rosyth, and naturally they expected that the giant battle-cruisers under Jellicoe's orders would issue forth to cut off the raiders' retreat.

In that case the German cruisers were to do as much damage as they possibly could to the Scottish north-east coast and turn tail. Although not of the most modern type, they were of a fair turn of speed, and with luck might draw the pursuers within range of a number of submarines, while at the same time Zeppelins would attempt to distract the British by dropping heavy explosives upon the battle-cruisers.

So much for that phase of the operations. The part played by the German warships bombarding Auldhaig was quite subordinate to the main strategy and tactics of the hostile fleet. While the British battle-cruisers were in chase of the raiders, a far more modern and powerful German squadron was to make a dash for the Humber and Tyne ports.

From the terrace of the rear-admiral's house Tressidar watched the flashes of the hostile guns. The Germans had it practically their own way, for, however well protected Auldhaig Harbour was against aerial attack, the place was not armed with heavy gun batteries at all suitable for replying to the ten- and twelve-inch guns of the German cruisers.

Relying implicitly upon her steel-clad battleships and cruisers, Great Britain, neglecting the warning of Scarborough and Whitby, had omitted to provide adequate land defences except at a few of the principal naval ports.

And while enormous shells hurtled upon the town and harbour, Zeppelins, fearing little from the anti-aircraft guns, hovered overhead. Considering the fury of the almost unimpeded fire, the damage done was inconsiderable until a shell burst—at least, so it appeared to Tressidar—fairly on the buildings used as the naval sick-quarters. Long tongues of flame leapt skywards, the glare throwing the surrounding houses into strong relief as the fire quickly gained a strong hold.

Without a moment's hesitation the sub. took to his heels and ran in the direction of the burning building. Here, at least he could be of service. As he ran he thanked Providence that Doris Greenwood was not on duty; but there were other delicately nurtured women exposed to the fury of the hostile shells, as well as perhaps fifty "cot cases," where patients unable to help themselves were in peril of being burnt alive if they had survived the effect of the devastating shell.

Through the gate of the rear-admiral's grounds, where a great-coated seaman sentry with his rifle at the slope paced imperturbably to and fro, Tressidar ran. He could hear the thud of fragments of metal falling from an immense height. The air reeked with the acrid fumes of smokeless powder, mingled with the pungent smell of burning wood.

A shell, falling into soft ground less than thirty yards from the road, burst with an ear-splitting crash. The blast of the explosion hurled the sub. sideways, until he was brought up with his shoulder coming into violent contact with a wooden fence. Fortunately the principal direction of the detonation was directed skywards, and although fragments of the projectile hurtled past him, Tressidar escaped death or at least serious injury by a hairsbreadth.

The sick-quarters were situated on the outskirts of the town and within a hundred yards of the water's edge, whence a pier two hundred feet in length afforded landing facilities for the boats of the fleet.

As Tressidar drew nearer he discovered, to his great relief, that he had been mistaken as to the exact spot where the monster projectile had fallen. Still, the damage done was bad enough, for the shell had dropped in an outhouse close to the main block of buildings. The detached portion had been completely pulverised, while a considerable part of the roof of the hospital had been blown to fragments. Gaping holes were also visible in the walls, while a fierce fire was raging within the building.

It was evident that the ordinary staff was unable to cope with the work of clearing the wards of the patients. Nurses and sick-baymen were working heroically, their efforts assisted by members of the National Guard and a few townsfolk whose dread of the German shells was unable to overcome their energy in rescuing the patients from a terrible death.

Forcing his way through the choking smoke, the sub. toiled like a Trojan, lifting helpless men from beds that were already smouldering and carrying them out into the open air. Six times he plunged into the inferno. The floor-board creaked under his feet. Smoke eddied through the gaping seams. Plaster was continually falling through from the shattered and shaken ceilings, while above the roar of the flames could be heard the crash of hostile projectiles that were falling with terrible rapidity.

"All clear, sir," shouted a blackened and grimy sick-bay steward. "That's the lot of 'em."

As he spoke, a portion of the floor collapsed. The man disappeared from view into a gaping pit of smouldering debris, almost before he had time to utter a cry.

Had Tressidar given a moment's thought he might have hesitated, but in an instant he leapt after the luckless man.

He alighted feet foremost upon a heap of charred wood, from which the smoke poured in thick, eddying clouds. Gasping and vainly endeavouring to check himself from coughing, the sub. stooped and groped. His hands came in contact with the unfortunate man, who in falling must have struck his head against some solid object, for he was unconscious and lying on his back upon the smouldering debris.

Raising the man and hoisting him upon his shoulders, Tressidar looked round for a means of escape. Apparently there was none. Seven feet above his head was an irregularly shaped hole, through which he could discern the flame-tinged smoke. A crash announced that another portion of the roof had collapsed, and with it a part of the outside wall. Even had he been missed, the sub. realised that rescue in that direction was out of the question.

His lack of knowledge of the plan of the buildings, too, was against him. So far as he could make out, he had leapt into a cellar that had been used as a store for hospital goods. Seen through the smoke, the place appeared to have no exit, yet he argued—the thought flashing across his mind—that there must be some means of communication apart from the hole in the floor that had just been caused by the flames.

Choking and spluttering, his eyes streaming with water from the effects of the driving particles of hot ashes, Tressidar plunged into the darkness with his burden lying inertly across his back.

Stumbling between rows of packing-cases the sub: struggled on, until further progress was barred by a solid stone wall. Retreat in that direction was cut off. For a few seconds he stood, still half dazed at the discovery, then, turning, he lurched heavily in the opposite direction.

He was gasping deeply. The lack of pure air and the dead weight upon his shoulders was telling upon his powerful frame. His lungs seemed on the point of bursting. Yet he gamely struggled onwards.

Over the heap of smouldering rubbish on which he had alighted when he had made his voluntary leap into the trap he scrambled, fell on his knees, and with a strenuous effort recovered himself. Beyond was another dark, smoke-enshrouded cavity. Was there an exit in that direction, he wondered?

Again, almost before he became aware of the fact, his head came in contact with a stone wall. Half turning, he propped his burden against the barrier, and with his disengaged hand fumbled helplessly, pawing the rough masonry like a trapped animal.

A comparatively cool current of air wafted in, temporarily dispersing the noxious fumes. Eagerly he took in draughts of the life-giving air. His benumbed brain was just able to realise that not so very far distant was an opening communicating with the outside. But where, and how large?

He edged away to the right. His hand no longer encountered solid wall. There was a aperture torn by a shell. Beyond was comparatively pure air.

Setting the unconscious man upon the ground, Tressidar crept through the narrow opening. Then, gripping his charge by the ankles, he hauled the man, feet foremost, into comparative safety. Utterly exhausted, he dropped to the ground and waited, breathing stertorously as his sorely taxed strength returned.

The bombardment had now ceased, but overhead the roar of the flames and the continual crash of falling masonry and tiles proclaimed the fact that the fire was still maintaining a fierce grip upon the building. The trembling of the walls warned the sub. that his temporary shelter was no longer safe.

Dragging the unconscious man—for he no longer had the strength to lift him—Tressidar backed along a passage and up a short flight of stone steps. Even as he did so, the roof of the cellar in which he had been so nearly trapped collapsed under the weight of hundreds of tons of rubble.

Just aware that people were hastening to his assistance as he emerged into the open air, Tressidar relinquished his burden. But for the support of two stalwart bluejackets the sub. would have fallen.

Then came the anti-climax. He burst into a roar of laughter as he surveyed his borrowed mess uniform, now a collection of scorched rags that would ill-become a scare-crow.

"Dash it all!" he ejaculated. "Poor old Jimmy's mess-kit."

"Never mind," said a low voice. "After what you've done, Ronald, I don't suppose he will."

Tressidar looked up. Through the mist that swain before his smoke-rimmed eyes he saw Doris Greenwood.

CHAPTER XXIII
AT AULDHAIG ONCE MORE

"By Jove, Doris!" he exclaimed. "You here? I say, am I not in a horrible mess?"

"It might have been worse," replied the girl admiringly. "I saw you go, and—and—I thought—oh, I never expected to see you again."

"You never know your luck," said Tressidar. He could think of nothing else to say. The girl's concern on his behalf was more than sufficient compensation for the horrors of that five minutes facing death.

Someone handed him a glass of water. He drank the liquid with avidity and felt the better for it.

"I thought you were on leave, Doris," he remarked. "And you, too, are in a pretty pickle. You weren't hurt?"

The girl's face was grimed with smoke, her uniform soiled with fire and water. On the back of her left hand a rapidly rising white weal was visible.

"No," she replied, "I was on duty. I'm glad I was, although I felt horribly frightened when the shells began to drop. My hand? That is nothing; only a little burn. But I must go. Over there, there are others badly injured."

Left to himself, Tressidar began to realise that he had not come off lightly. Numerous burns, of which in the struggle for existence he had been ignorant, began to assert themselves in a very forcible manner. He stood up and promptly sat down again. The movement racked every limb. His muscles worked like badly oiled machinery. His head was throbbing painfully.

An alert sick-bay man who had been discreetly keeping an eye upon the young officer hurried up.

"Allow me, sir," he said. "I'll get you to bed. They're preparing temporary quarters over yonder," and he pointed in the direction of the rear-admiral's house.

Tressidar submitted without protest. He knew that for the time being he was helpless. Unless he were to miss his ship on the following Thursday, prompt treatment and absolute rest were essential.

Supported by the hospital man, the sub. walked slowly up the hill in the wake of a long procession of cots and stretchers, each bearing a scorched and badly injured patient.

His burns attended to, Tressidar was placed in a bed and given a draught. After that he slept soundly until the following morning, when he awoke to find himself in a temporary ward with four other officers as fellow-patients.

"Thursday?" repeated the fleet surgeon in answer to Tressidar's anxious question. "We'll see. Can't commit myself on that point, you know. A lot depends upon yourself. No, nothing serious. Slight shock to the system, you know. Rest and plenty of food essential."

The whole of that day the sub. saw nothing of Doris. At first he feared that the girl's injuries were more serious than she believed, until enquiries of one of the nurses elicited the information that "Sister Greenwood" was well and was on day duty in another ward.

Meanwhile, news was coming in fast of the progress of the German naval movements. The cruiser that had bombarded Auldhaig, fortunately without so very serious results, had been intercepted in its flight towards the Norwegian coast by a strong squadron of British armoured cruisers. In the burning fight which ensued, the "Heracles" with two consorts had succeeded in heading off two German vessels, and for the time being the two latter were fugitives in the North Atlantic.

For the present they had eluded pursuit but a cordon was being drawn round the isolated hostile ships. On both sides of the Atlantic British warships were lying in wait. Retreat both to Germany and to neutral ports was cut off. Capture or destruction seemed inevitable.

Better still, the attempted raid upon the east coast of England ended in a fiasco. Warned by wireless, the British battle-cruisers issued forth from their bases—not in pursuit of the Auldhaig raiders, as the Germans fondly hoped, but across the North Sea to meet the main hostile warships.

Greatly to the disappointment and disgust of the British tars, the Germans declined battle, and, turning, made off at full speed for the shelter of the guns and minefields of Heligoland.

Early on the second morning of Tressidar's enforced detention in the temporary sick-quarters the sub. was taken into the grounds for an airing. Lying comfortably in a wheeled chair, he was deep in the contents of a newspaper when a bandaged man in hospital clothes and accompanied by a nursing sister and an orderly was wheeled in his direction.

The sister was Doris Greenwood, but the sub. had not the faintest idea of the identity of the patient.

"This man wishes to speak to you, Mr. Tressidar," said Doris demurely.

"You don't remember me, sir?" began the invalid.

"No, I can't say that I do," replied the sub. To tell the truth, he wished both the man and the orderly to Jericho, until he realised that it was solely in an official capacity that Doris was present.

"You pulled me out of that hole the night before last, sir," said the patient, indicating the ruins of the hospital buildings, of which the crumpled masonry and fragments of shattered walls were visible from the grounds. "I'm no hand at a speech, sir, but I want to thank you."

"That's nothing so far as I was concerned," replied Tressidar modestly. He hated a fuss being made merely for doing a plucky action. "You're getting along all right?"

"Middling, sir. By gum!" he exclaimed with intense fervour, "it was touch and go with me."

After a few minutes' conversation Doris gave the word for the orderly to remove the patient, and greatly to the sub.'s disappointment she did not linger.

Doris, however, made amends during the afternoon by spending an hour with him. They talked of many things. Amongst other questions, Tressidar enquired after Mr. Greenwood.

"The pater's simply as skittish as a foal," replied the girl, laughing. "Since his adventure in the cave he's as keen as anything for duty. He's joined the National Guard, and is doing duty at a large reservoir near Plymouth. I wish, for some reasons, I were in Devonshire now," she added wistfully. "Just fancy, it's mid-April and there are hardly any signs of spring in the north. I'm longing for another sight of the red earth and bright green foliage of home There's no place like Devonshire."

"Unless it's Cornwall," rejoined Tressidar, loyal to the county of his birth.

"Practically the same," agreed Doris. "It's all the West Country. Next month, I hope, I'll be able to have a few days there—unless there's a big action out yonder—somewhere in the North Sea, you know."

"I hope there will be," remarked the sub. "Of course it will be a terribly costly affair when it does come off, for the Huns will fight like wild cats rather than let their ships be scuttled in Kiel Harbour. But it will be the climax—an end to months and months of tedious waiting and watching."

He, too, wished for a sight of home—home in the strictest sense. Away from Great Britain, the traveller broadly regards the whole of the United Kingdom as "home"; within its limits he will speak of his own county as "home;" narrowed down, "home" resolves itself, perhaps, into a small house with or without a patch of ground attached.

And now, after nearly two years of war, Britons the wide world over were beginning to realise that home in the broadest and the narrowest sense was in danger. Until Prussian militarism was crushed once and for all time, the freehold of the humblest cottage in Great Britain would not be worth twelve months' purchase.

"You've heard the news of Falkenheim's escape?" asked the girl.

Tressidar had not. The latest he had heard of the German officer who had got clear of the internment camp and had eventually been run to earth in the petrol-depôt, was that he had been sentenced by a General Court-martial to six months' imprisonment.

"He was serving his sentence in Saltport Gaol," explained Doris. "A fortnight ago a portion of the outside wall of the prison was blown in by a charge of gun-cotton. Falkenheim's friends evidently knew exactly in which part of the building he was placed, for in the confusion he was liberated from his cell. Since then all traces of him have vanished. There was a bit of a stir in the papers, but it has quieted down now. I heard Captain Garboard say that the German was a particularly daring submarine officer, and that if he got back to Germany there would be considerable trouble in store for us. People seem to deprecate the spy business, but it shows how active these German agents are."

"It does," agreed Tressidar wholeheartedly, but he was thinking of one spy in particular—the author of the "Pompey" tragedy, Otto Oberfurst.

As a side issue he was wondering whether, by a slice of luck, he might manage to get a few days' leave at the same time as Doris went south. Duty, naturally, came first, but when the West Country beckons, its call cannot lightly be set aside.

Tressidar made rapid progress from his injuries. His indomitable spirit, coupled with a clean, hard-living condition, worked wonders, and by the Thursday morning the fleet surgeon declared him fit for duty.

At noon the "Heracles" entered the harbour and moored in mid-stream. Her smoke-blackened aftermast, blistered and salt-rimmed funnels bore tokens of hard steaming, while several temporarily patched holes in her lofty sides and superstructure showed that German gunnery had taken a toll.

Her orders were brief and hinted at more serious work: she was to land hospital cases, ship ammunition and victualling stores, fill bunkers and replenish oil-fuel, and proceed to Rendezvous K— with the utmost dispatch.

Tressidar's reappearance on board was the subject of considerable surprise, for his messmates were under the erroneous impression that he was still a prisoner of war They had heard that the cutter had been picked up, and that the sub. and the boat's crew had been forcibly removed from the Norwegian tramp in the Kattegat and taken to a German port. Beyond that they were totally unaware of what had befallen the sub. until he turned up, like the proverbial bad halfpenny, upon the quarter-deck of H.M.S. "Heracles."

Assistant Paymaster Greenwood, with his right hand swathed in surgical bandages and his arm in a sling, was one of the first to greet his friend warmly.

"Oh, I've had a great time," he replied in answer to the sub.'s enquiry as to how he sustained his injuries. "In the fire-control platform, you know. Tried to stop a bit of strafed shell. It was luck. I'm off duty in the ship's office for a week at least, and this won't prevent me going aloft when the next scrap takes place."

Eric Greenwood was too modest to relate full details. Tressidar afterwards learnt that the assistant paymaster was assisting a wounded seaman from the fire-control platform to the shrouds when a flying fragment of metal inflicted a nasty gash on the index finger and thumb of the right hand. In spite of the pain, he saw the man safely on deck and returned to his lofty perch. It was not until he was on the point of collapse through loss of blood that the lieutenant noticed his plight and ordered him below.

Night and day the ship's company toiled in order to get the cruiser ready for sea. Eagerly officers and crew awaited the wireless news, hoping for their country's sake that the fugitive German vessels had been captured or destroyed, and for their own that they were still afloat, so that the "Heracles" might have a hand in settling up business. In thirty-six hours the cruiser was ready to proceed, and with the first blush of dawn she slipped quietly out of harbour bound for Rendezvous K— the exact position of which was a jealously guarded secret, known only to the captain and senior navigating officers.

CHAPTER XXIV
A FIGHT TO A FINISH

Twenty-four hours later the "Heracles" arrived at her appointed station, where she relieved her sister-ship the "Proteacius," the latter having to return to replenish her bunkers. Hull down to the nor'ard, her position indicated by a thin haze of smoke upon the skyline, was another British cruiser. Yet another was just visible to the south'ard. These were but a few of the far-flung line that was systematically closing upon the fugitive German ships.

It was realised that the chase might be a prolonged one. In spite of elaborate precautions, it was quite possible for the hostile craft to elude detection for a considerable period. That they were within measurable distance was evident by the fact that the wireless messages between the various British cruisers were continually being "jammed" The Germans, by dint of throwing out wireless "waves," were thus able to interrupt seriously long-distance communication between their pursuers.

Just before midnight a destroyer came within flashlight-signalling distance of the "Heracles." Her message, given in code, was as follows: "'Heracles,' 'Castor,' and 'Pollux' to proceed. Investigate. In event of falling in with enemy, engage until supported by 'Ponderous' and 'Thunderbolt.'"

Due west tore the "Heracles," under forced draught. Morning revealed the presence of the "Castor," seven miles to her starboard beam. The "Pollux" was approximately at the same distance from the "Heracles," but well on her port quarter.

It was a beautiful morning. The sun, rising in a grey sky behind a bank of mist, threw its rays aslant the long rollers of the Atlantic. Ahead the horizon was unbroken. Not a trace could be discerned of the enemy.

At eight bells the wireless jamming suddenly ceased. Did it mean that other units of the squadron were engaging the German cruisers? A far-flung general call received the reply that as yet the enemy had not been sighted.

Half an hour later the "Heracles" picked up a wireless message from one of the fugitives to the other. Most remarkably it was not in code, and was as follows:

"'Lemburg' to 'Stoshfeld': am making my way northward. Endeavouring to fetch Reykiavik. Course presumably clear."

To which the "Stoshfeld" replied: "Concur: will attempt to rejoin you at Reykiavik."

[Illustration: A BATTLE CRUISER SQUADRON]

The message was obviously a "blind," sent out in the vain hope that the British ships would speed northward to prevent the fugitives entering Danish waters and thus claiming internment in Iceland. Accordingly the "Heracles" signalled to her consorts to shape a course to the south-west and to refrain from using wireless until further orders.

Tressidar had just relieved another sub. for duty in the fire-control platform when a strange sail was sighted two points on the starboard bow. Helm was accordingly altered to a course shaped to bring the cruiser close to the recently sighted vessel.

It did not take the "Heracles" long to get within easy telescopic distance. The craft was apparently a large tramp with two stumpy masts and two funnels. She was steaming slowly in an easterly direction, and was consequently almost bows-on to the British cruiser.

She made no attempt to alter her course, and when the "Heracles" hoisted a signal, "What ship is that?" she replied in the International Code making her number, port of departure and destination.

Reference to the code-book proclaimed the tramp to be the s.s. "Scoopcash" of Liverpool, northward bound from Montreal. Almost immediately another hoist of bunting fluttered from her foremast head, quickly followed by others, until the complete signal read:

"Have been chased by large German cruiser. Lat. 45º 17' N., Long. 20º 5' W. Hostile vessels abandoned pursuit and made off to the nor west."

Tressidar had his telescope levelled on the merchantman. The vessel having slightly ported helm was approximately five thousand yards distant.

"Jolly rummy!" he soliloquised. "Is it fancy, or did I see those topsides bulge?" He lowered the glass, rubbed his eyes, then looked again.

"I say, Picklecombe," he remarked, addressing a midshipman, "just bring your telescope and bear upon that vessel's hull. See anything out of the usual? I may be mistaken but——"

The midshipman, quick to act, had already levelled his telescope.

"By Jupiter!" he exclaimed. "If she hasn't dummy bulwarks I'm a lubber."

The sub. promptly telephoned to the bridge, expressing his doubts as to the bona-fides of the s.s. "Scoopcash," with the result that a shot was fired within fifty yards of her bows and the peremptory signal to heave-to for examination hoisted from the "Heracles'" signal yardarm.

With the discharge of the cruiser's gun a sudden change took place on board the supposed tramp. For full a hundred feet aft from her bows a canvas screen dropped, revealing a for'ard turret with two 9.4-in. guns, and smaller turrets, each mounting a 5.9-in. quick-firer.

A succession of vivid flashes leapt from the disguised vessel's decks and half a dozen heavy shells hurtled perilously close to the British cruiser.

Her opponent was the "Stoshfeld." On finding their retreat cut off, the German crew set to work to transform the outward appearance of the ship.

This was effected by raising canvas stretched on poles around the fo'c'sle and poop, thus giving the look of a continuous line of bulwarks level with the permanent superstructure amidships The cruiser's sides were then given a coat of black paint. The next step was to do away with the unmistakable military masts. The fore and main topmast were accordingly struck, the lower masts being demolished by the use of small charges of explosives. The topmasts were then set up, thus giving the appearance of the "sticks" of a merchantman. The centre one of the three funnels was also knocked away, and those remaining were painted red with black tops.

This work having been accomplished, the "Stoshfeld" steamed southward, with the intention of making a South American port. Here, all being well, she could transfer her lighter armament to some of the nominally interned German merchantmen, and the latter could then slip out to sea as armed commerce destroyers.

Unfortunately for her, the "Stoshfeld" sighted a squadron of United States cruisers, and mistaking them for British vessels, doubled back this time on a south-westerly track until she blundered across the "Heracles."

The secret was out. The German cruiser had to fight or surrender; and she chose the former alternative.

For the time being the "Heracles," being unsupported by her consorts, who were far on her quarter, had to engage single-handed her more powerfully armed antagonist. It was an action in which gunnery was the supreme factor. The two vessels were beyond effective torpedo range, while neither had the assistance of bomb-dropping aircraft or the deadly-sneaking submarine.

Almost the first shell from the hostile cruiser struck the "Heracles" twenty feet for'ard of the fore-turret. Her protected belt saved her, but practically the whole of the fo'c'sle was wrecked. Viewed from the fore-top the scene following the tremendous upheaval resembled a ship-breaker's works. The deck was ripped up like cardboard, and the crews of the two 12-pounder quick-firers were literally blown to pieces. Another shell, missing the foremast by a few feet, pulverised the foremast funnel and wrought havoc on the spar deck.

The "Heracles'" reply was a stern one. With one terrific salvo her guns simply swept the German cruiser's decks. Her top hamper disappeared as if by magic. The two remaining funnels crashed over the side, falling across the shields of a couple of 6-inch quick-firers and putting the weapons out of action. The painted canvas burst into flames, and, burning furiously, obscured the German gun-layers' vision, while 'tween decks dense columns of smoke were pouring through jagged holes torn by the British shells.

Evidently the same salvo had put the "Stoshfeld's" for'ard 9.4's out of action, for they did not fire again. The German cruiser then circled to starboard; slowly, for with the loss of her funnels her speed had dropped to a bare seventeen knots. Yet by keeping her stern on to her antagonist she was able to bring her as yet useless after-guns to bear upon the "Heracles."

The latter, also subjected to loss of speed, made no attempt to close. Porting helm, she was able to bring all her broadside guns as well as the bow and stern turret-guns to bear upon the badly crippled "Stoshfeld."

Suddenly shells began to fall with a high trajectory in front and behind the British cruiser. She was, in naval parlance, "straddled" by hostile projectiles fired at long range. The "Lemburg," steaming to her consort's assistance—a deliberate act of self-sacrifice—had commenced to fire salvoes at the "Heracles."

The "Castor" and the "Pollux" were still too far astern to take part in the action. For five minutes the "Heracles" was subjected to fierce fire from the two German cruisers. Shells ricochetted all around her. Only the indifferent gunnery of the "Lemburg" saved her, and since she was outranged by that vessel the British cruiser had perforce to devote her attention to the "Stoshfeld" until the undamaged cruisers could engage.

Quickly the "Castor" passed the "Heracles," steaming two miles to windward, and presently her guns added to the din. Almost immediately the galling fire of the "Lemburg" ceased to annoy the "Stoshfeld's" antagonist, for the second German cruiser had now all her work cut out to engage the other British cruisers.

Giving the "Stoshfeld" a couple of broadsides as she passed, the "Pollux" followed in support of the "Castor," leaving the badly mauled "Heracles" to continue her ocean duel with her seriously damaged opponent.

Between the drifting clouds of vapour, for the cordite was far from smokeless, Tressidar watched the effect of the "Heracles'" projectiles upon the German cruisers, reporting to the conning-tower the result of each direct hit.

Amidships the "Stoshfeld" was little better than a roaring volcano. Her after-guns were still maintaining brisk fire and although she flew no colours, she evidently had no intention of surrendering. In fifteen minutes from the beginning of the action Tressidar was able to report that the German cruiser was listing badly to port. Her steering-gear, too, was much damaged, for she yawed considerably as she vainly sought safety in flight.

Conversely, the "Heracles" was receiving less of a gruelling. The German gunnery, at first most effective, had developed into erratic, desultory firing. In her plight the hostile cruiser swung round and made a determined attempt to ram, but the captain of the British warship promptly countered by turning eight points to starboard and increasing the distance between the two combatants.

"She's going!" almost shouted Tressidar into the telephone.

A bugle note rang out: the order to cease fire. Immediately the British guns were silent, contemptuous of the erratic efforts of a small quick-firer that alone was capable of hurling defiance from the doomed ship.

From below hundreds of British seamen, clad only in trousers and singlets, poured on deck to witness the end of their foe. Boxed in behind armour, unable to see for themselves how events were shaping, almost suffocated by the pungent fumes, they were now able to see the result of their work.

There was no cheering. All signs of elation over the victory were checked by the sight of the shell-torn cruiser about to make her last plunge.

The "Heracles" made no attempt to close until it was evident that the doomed ship was unable to deliver a last, desperate stroke in the shape of a torpedo, then slowly the cruiser steamed towards her opponent to rescue the survivors of her crew.

The British cruiser had only two boats capable of keeping afloat, and these only by means of temporary expedient in the shape of copper sheets and strips of painted canvas tacked over the jagged holes in the planking. But Jack Tar was not to be baulked in his humane efforts. Mess-tables and stools, empty petrol-cans, lifebuoys and lifebelts were pressed into service and carried on deck ready to be cast overboard to support the swimmers.

Suddenly two enormous waterspouts leapt high in the air, one on either side and close to the British cruiser. An ear-splitting detonation followed almost simultaneously, as the "Heracles," trembling violently under the shock, lurched heavily to port.

In the moment of victory she had been mined.

CHAPTER XXV
IN THE MOMENT OF TRIUMPH

Almost stunned by the terrific blast of air, Tressidar, who had been looking down from the fire-control platform, was at first hardly able to realise what had taken place. Not until he was aroused by Midshipman Picklecombe's voice asking faintly for aid did the seriousness of the situation dawn upon him.

The "Heracles" was foundering. The distinct, ever-increasing heel of the platform on which he stood proved that. There was no recovery to the cruiser's list to port.

The "Stoshfeld" during the course of the running fight had thrown overboard a number of mines, each pair connected by a hundred feet length of grass-rope. By sheer good luck her pursuer had missed the lot until she began to steam slowly to the assistance of her foe. Then, her stem engaged in the bight of the rope, two cylinders filled with powerful explosive had been swung against either side, the mines going off on contact with the cruiser's hull.

After the explosion the crew, at first thrown into confusion by the terrific din and the havoc wrought 'tween decks, were hardly able to grip the situation until a bugle sounded the "Still" and the men mustered quietly on the quarter-deck. Orders had been sent to the engine-room to shut off steam and open the safety-valves. The "Heracles," her propellers now motionless—whereby a serious menace to the crew of the foundering vessel was averted—quickly lost way, and making a half-circle to starboard came to a standstill at a distance roughly three thousand yards from her antagonist.

The "Stoshfeld" was now keel uppermost. A couple of hundred of her men had clustered on her bilge-plates, viewing with consternation the result of their own action; for with the mining of the British cruiser all hopes of rescue vanished.

On hearing the midshipman call, Tressidar turned. The two officers were alone, the gunnery lieutenant having left the fire-control platform with some of the instruments that had suffered slight damage from concussion during the bombardment, while the seamen told off to attend to the telephones had followed the lieutenant.

Picklecombe was lying in a corner of the rectangular platform. Blood was oozing from a gash in the midshipman's left shoulder. A sliver of steel, hurled to an immense height, had in falling completely penetrated the light metal canopy and had inflicted a severe wound on the lad who was standing beneath.

The sub. acted promptly. He knew that delay would mean that the helpless midshipman would be trapped within the metal cage and carried down when the ship made her last plunge. The only way of escape was through a small aperture on the floor leading to the uppermost ratlines of the shrouds—and the opening was sufficient only for one man at a time.

Unclasping his knife, Tressidar cut some of the canvas gear into a long strip. The fabric was strong and tough. It formed an admirable sling.

The next step was to lower Picklecombe through the trap-door.

"Can you hang on?" asked the sub

"I think so," replied the midshipman. "I'll try."

The pressure of the canvas slung round the lad's chest gave him great pain, but setting his jaw tightly he allowed no sound to pass his lips. Dexterously the sub. "paid out" until the wounded youngster's feet touched the shrouds and his head and shoulders were below the opening on the floor. Fortunately the list of the ship had brought the shrouds on the starboard side very little short of a horizontal position, and thus Picklecombe was supported almost by his own weight against the wire stays. In a trice Tressidar nipped through and was by the midshipman's side.

"I'm feeling awfully dizzy," exclaimed Picklecombe. "Everything seems turning round."

The sub. gripped him as he spoke, for the lad was on the point of dropping to the deck, a distance of between sixty and seventy feet beneath his precarious perch. To make matters worse, clouds of smoke and steam issuing through the funnels and steam-pipes drifted past and hid the two young officers from the sight of those on deck. Shouting for help was futile, since the hiss of steam deadened all other sounds.

Hanging on tenaciously, Tressidar forced himself between the shrouds and the now almost unconscious midshipman. With his disengaged hand he held the lad tightly to his back.

"Let go!" ordered the sub. peremptorily.

The sense of discipline overcame the midshipman's almost automatic inclination to grip whatever came nearest to hand. He relinquished his hold and his arm fell listlessly over his rescuer's shoulder.

Step by step the sub. descended. The shrouds, stretched almost to breaking-point by the strain of the heavy mast, were so springy under the combined weight that at every moment Tressidar was nearly capsized. The hot steam almost choked him. It also prevented him seeing where he was or whether the ship was actually on the point of foundering.

At length he gained a portion of the shrouds beneath the cloud of vapour. The "Heracles'" fo'c'sle was now awash. Her poop on the portside was dipping. The remaining serviceable boats, which had been lowered and filled with wounded men, were lying-to at a safe distance from the foundering vessel. Officers and men, for the most part stripped, were leaping over the side in knots of half a dozen or so at the time, as if reluctant to leave the good old ship.

The next instant the agitated water seemed to rise up to meet the sub. and his companion. The "Heracles" was capsizing rapidly.

Relaxing his grip upon the shrouds, Tressidar allowed himself and his burden to be floated away by the eddying sea, using his disengaged arm to strike out and avoid as far as possible being entangled in the raffle of gear.

All around him the turmoil of foaming water was emitting steam and compressed air like miniature geysers, while a huge, grotesquely distorted mass seemed to rise out of the sea almost within arm's length. It was the hull of the doomed cruiser, as she turned slowly over until her keel-plates floated bottom uppermost. Various buoyant objects came bobbing to the surface with considerable velocity and added to the danger. A fragment of a shell-shattered cutter missed him by a bare yard. Had it struck, he would have been almost cut in two by the sharp, jagged edges of the woodwork.

Whirled hither and thither by the swirl of the water, Tressidar noticed that the upturned hull showed no signs of disappearing to the bottom of the ocean. The jets of steam, too, had ceased, and the sea in the vicinity of the wreck was becoming comparatively tranquil.

Some distance away the sole serviceable boats were lying off, crowded with men and with scores of less fortunate seamen clinging to the gunwales. A considerable number of the survivors were relying solely upon their swimming-collars; others were clinging, more or less in the water, to barrels, petrol-tins, oars, and mess-gear. In spite of the danger, they were exchanging banter with the utmost zest. The fact that they were a thousand miles from the nearest land never seemed to worry them in the slightest degree.

Numbers of men, finding that the upturned hull still floated, began to scramble up the sides, since the submergence of the two bilge-keels to a depth of about a foot made this a comparatively easy matter. Amongst them were several of the officers, including Assistant Paymaster Greenwood.

Eric happened to see his chum's plight, for, try as he would, the sub. had not strength to haul himself and the now unconscious midshipman into temporary safety. Practically all the ship's company had mustered aft when the "Heracles" turned turtle, and since Tressidar had been thrown out of the foremast shrouds he and young Picklecombe were apart from the rest of the survivors.

Sliding down to the bilge-keel, the A.P., heedless of his injured arm, gripped Tressidar by the shoulders.

"One minute, old bird," gasped the sub. "Give me a hand with the youngster. Be steady. He's been hit—shoulder, pretty badly."

Transferring his grasp to the canvas sling, Greenwood hauled the midshipman into comparative safety, while Tressidar, relieved of the lad's weight, quickly drew himself up the bilge-keel.

"Thanks, old man," he said simply.

"Let's hope we won't have to make another swim for it," remarked the A.P. "We're expecting the destroyers, but they haven't shown up yet. By Jove, the water is cold. Let's shift out of it. The P.M.O. is aft somewhere, I think. I vote we get hold of him and see what's wrong with young Picklecombe."

Carrying the midshipman, the two chums gained the main keel-plates. From there Tressidar surveyed the expanse of sea. The "Stoshfeld" had vanished. The distance was too great to see with the naked eye whether any of her crew were still afloat. All around the horizon was unbroken; sea and sky met in a clear, well-defined line. Of the "Lemburg" and her pursuers nothing could be discerned, but the dull rumble of a distant cannonade showed that the running fight was still in progress.

Greenwood's surmise concerning the surgeon was at fault, the medical staff being in the boats with the wounded and sick cases. Nor was it safe to signal to one of the boats to approach and take the wounded midshipman on board, in case the ship might make a sudden plunge and take the boatload of helpless men down with her.

Having applied first aid to the best of their ability, Tressidar and Greenwood waited, with the rest of the crew, the arrival of the expected destroyers.

Gradually the rest of the swimmers regained the upturned hull until every surviving member of the ship's company was either in one of the boats, on a raft, or on the capsized hull of the "Heracles."

To relieve the tedious wait the men sang the latest music-hall ditties to the accompaniment of a wheezy concertina, which a stoker had contrived to save during the few minutes that elapsed between the mining and the capsizing of the cruiser. Several of the officers had cigarettes in watertight cases; those of the men who were able to keep their supply of "fags" dry in their caps shared them with their less fortunate comrades.

"I don't fancy she's going just at present," remarked Captain Raxworthy to the commander.

"No, sir," replied the officer addressed. "She seems as steady as a rock."

The words were hardly out of his mouth when there was a loud explosion. An under-water valve, under the pressure of air trapped within the hull, had been blown out. An inrush of water followed.

At first the result was imperceptible, but by degrees the hull began to settle by the bows. The stern rose until the tips of the twin propellers showed above the surface.

"All hands aft," ordered Captain Raxworthy, in the hope that the redistribution of weight would keep the hull in a horizontal position.

The precaution was in vain. Shuddering, the huge mass dipped and, gliding, disappeared beneath the surface, leaving four hundred men struggling for dear life in the agitated water.

The end had come so suddenly that there had not been time for the men to leap clear. Numbers of them were sucked down by the vortex caused by the foundering vessel, only to reappear, thirty seconds later, a struggling, wellnigh breathless mass of humanity.

As the "Heracles" made her final plunge, Tressidar and Greenwood grasped the motionless form of Midshipman Picklecombe. They had previously buckled a life-belt, willingly surrendered by a powerfully-built stoker, round the lad; Greenwood had an inflated swimming-collar, while Tressidar had to rely upon his own efforts to keep afloat until he could find something capable of supporting him in the water.

The three officers were in the midst of a crowd of swimmers, all more or less boisterous in their determination to encourage each other. Hard by were the boats, the oarsmen voluntarily taking turns at leaping overboard and surrendering their place to their less hardy comrades. The concertina-player still stuck gamely to his instrument, and, supported by a couple of petrol-tins, was leading the singing of "A Little Grey Home in the West."

Striking out towards one of the boats, Tressidar and Greenwood handed their unconscious charge into the care of the fleet surgeon. Relieved of this anxiety, they floated, exchanging desultory conversation and keeping a longing watch for the expected aid that showed no signs of forthcoming.

Half an hour passed. The singing had died away. Men were realising that every ounce of strength must be jealously guarded. The concertina-player had abandoned his efforts and had allowed the instrument to slip from his benumbed fingers and drift slowly away.

With ever-increasing frequency men would relax their grasp and disappear beneath the surface without a sound. In several instances their comrades would dive and bring the senseless bodies to the surface. Deeds of heroism, the facts of which would never be made public, occurred time after time, but in spite of the efforts of the hardier of the crew many a man "lost the number of his mess."

Overhead the sun shone resplendent in a cloudless sky, as if to mock the feeble struggles of the men in the bitterly cold water. And still no sign of the eagerly expected succour. Hoping against hope, the survivors began to realise that unless almost a miracle took place they would never again see their native shores.

CHAPTER XXVI
THE HOMECOMING OF THE S.S. "MEROPE"

"Evenin' paper. British cruiser sunk."

The shrill cries of a very small youth blessed with a pair of powerful lungs greeted Doris Greenwood as the train in which she was travelling south from Scotland pulled up at Peterborough.

The majority of the passengers heard the announcement with hardly more than passing interest. This was one of the results of the greatest war the world has ever seen. In the early phases of the struggle the loss of a British warship, in spite of the fact that the Press took particular pains to explain that she was a semi-obsolete craft of no great fighting value, was a subject of great concern. On the principle that familiarity breeds contempt, the recurrence of for the most part unavoidable naval disasters was borne by the public with a fatalism bordering upon indifference, save by those whose kith and kin were fighting "somewhere in the North Sea," or were upholding the traditions of the Senior Service in the distant seas within the war zone.

The loss of the "Titanic" in the piping times of peace afforded columns of detailed copy in the Press. The torpedoing or mining of a battleship in the Great War was curtly dismissed in half a dozen lines.

Stepping into the corridor of the carriage, Doris called to the newsboy and bought a paper. An inexplicable kind of presentiment gripped the girl's mind as she unfolded the double sheet of paper, still moist from the printing-press.

The double-leaded headlines gave no information on the particular subject; nor did the rest of the ordinary headings. Sandwiched between reports of local markets and racing was a blurred "Stop Press" announcement:

"The Secretary of the Admiralty regrets to report that the light cruiser 'Heracles' has been sunk. Feared loss of all hands."

How, when, or where was not stated, nor was any mention made of the engagement with the two German cruisers. The uncertainty of the whole business, save for the absolute statement that the "Heracles" was lost, rendered the blow even more stunning. For the rest of the journey to King's Cross Doris sat dry-eyed, hardly able to grasp the dread significance of the terrible news.

The girl had been somewhat unexpectedly given fourteen days' leave. She was on her way to her home in Devonshire, intent upon making the best of every moment of her hard-earned holiday. And now she was going to a house of gloom. Eric and Ronald—her brother and the young officer who day by day seemed more and more to her—were missing and presumably dead.

On arriving in London, Doris found people wildly excited over the destruction of the "Stoshfeld" and "Lemburg." The news had just been published, together with the additional information that the "Heracles" had been engaged with the former hostile vessel, and that after the "Castor" and "Pollux" had sunk the "Lemburg," they had gone in search of their consort and found unmistakable signs that she had been sunk. For the officers and crew of the lost cruiser no hope was now entertained.

It was late in the evening when the girl alighted at the country station of the little Devonshire town. News of the disaster had preceded her. Mr. Greenwood was trying to persuade himself that it was his privilege to be the father of one who had given his life for King and Country, but somehow the attempt was a dismal failure. Mrs. Greenwood was on the verge of collapse and required all the attention that could be given. The horrible uncertainty—the lack of definite evidence—was the hardest for her to bear.

Several days passed. Letters of condolence began to arrive, each missive driving another nail into the coffin of a dead hope. The official notification from the Admiralty of the presumed death of Assistant Paymaster Eric Greenwood, R.N.R., gave the *coup de grâce* to the long-drawn-out suspense.

On the seventh day after her return Doris felt that she must go for a long ramble. The call of the cliffs was irresistible. Accompanied by her dog, she set out in the direction of Prawle Point, a favourite walk in those long-ago pre-war days.

It was misty when the girl gained the edge of the red cliffs. A sea-fog had held for nearly forty-eight hours. The on-shore wind blew cold and clammy, although spring was well advanced and the trees and hedges were acquiring their new garb of verdure. Some distance away the fog signals from Start Point gave out its mournful wail—one blast of seven seconds every two minutes. It seemed in harmony with the times—a dirge over the ocean grave of many a brave seaman, lost in the service of his country. Doris wandered on till she came within a short distance of the signal station. Here she sat, watching the sullen rollers breaking into masses of foam against the jagged ledges of rock that jut out from the wild Prawle Point.

Along the narrow cliff path a sailor was tramping. As he approached, Doris recognised him as one of the coastguards from the neighbouring station. Owing to the importance of the station, the men had not been sent afloat on the outbreak of war, as was the case of hundreds of the detachments scattered around the coast; they did their duty well by remaining for signalling purposes, as several hostile submarines found to their cost.

The man knew Doris. Saluting, he stopped and chatted. Aware of the girl's loss, he tactfully made no reference to the sinking of the "Heracles," but confined his remarks to events in the district.

Presently the sun burst through the bank of mist. As if by magic the sea became visible for several miles. It was not deserted. A long way from shore two large transports escorted by destroyers were proceeding up-Channel. Considerably nearer was a small tramp, steaming in the direction of Prawle Point.

The coastguard paused in the midst of a detailed description of his garden and looked seaward.

"What is that vessel coming straight towards the shore for?" asked Doris.

"Dunno, miss; that is, unless she's been bamboozled by the fog and is coming in to make sure of her position. Maybe the coast appears a bit hazy from where she is. There, I thought so; she's porting her helm. She's off up-Channel."

As he spoke, the tramp hoisted her colours over a red and white pennant—signifying that she wished to communicate with the signal station. Slowing down, she exchanged signals for nearly a quarter of an hour, then proceeded with increased speed in an easterly direction.

"Quite a lot of signalling," remarked Doris.

"Yes, miss," agreed the man. "More'n usual. P'raps she's been chased by a German submarine, though there don't look much wrong with her. You'm curious, miss?"

"A little," admitted the girl. "At these times messages from passing ships may mean a lot."

"True, miss, true," agreed the coastguard as he prepared to resume his way. "I'll enquire, miss, an' if it ain't confidential, I'll nip back and tell 'ee."

The girl sat down again, and, almost unconsciously patting the dog, kept her eyes directed seawards. She had almost forgotten the coastguard's promise when she became aware that he was returning swiftly.

"Miss," he exclaimed excitedly, "'tes good news. Yon vessel is the 'Merope.' She's got on board a hundred an' eleven officers and men from the 'Heracles.' She's landing 'em at Dartmouth."

"Any names?" asked the girl.

"No, miss."

"Thank you," she said quietly, then she set off homewards.

One hundred and eleven survivors. Roughly one in every five of the "Heracles'" original complement. Was it too much to hope that the two in whom she was most concerned were amongst those who had escaped?

Gradually she formed her plans. Until more news was obtainable, she decided not to raise false hopes in her parents' minds. She would keep the tidings to herself until——

The hoot of a motor-car interrupted her train of thought. Bowling along the narrow, sunken lane was a six-seater owned by Dr. Cardyke, a retired practitioner who had been "dug out" of his retreat to act as surgeon to a military hospital.

Recognising the girl, the doctor slowed down.

"A lift, Miss Greenwood? I'm going close to your house?"

Doris accepted the invitation gratefully.

"I'm just off to Dartmouth and back," continued the doctor. "Wonderful things these cars after one has been used to a horse. Get there in no time, to use a common expression."

Dr. Cardyke spoke with all the enthusiasm of a keen motorist, in spite of his sixty-odd years. Had he been any one else but a well-known country practitioner, he might have been "run in" for furious driving times without number, but luck and a "benevolent neutrality" on the part of the police had hitherto steered him clear of the police-courts.

"Dartmouth?" repeated Doris. "Would you mind, doctor, if you—I mean, will you take me to Dartmouth with you?"

"Certainly, my dear young lady," replied the doctor gallantly. "But, pardon my curiosity, for why? It's too late to do any shopping, you know. Early closing day, you know."

"It's not that," said the girl, glad of the chance to confide her secret and her hopes to someone. "There are more than a hundred survivors of the 'Heracles' being landed at Dartmouth, and I — —"

The sentence remained unfinished. Dr. Cardyke gave a grunt that betokened sympathy and encouragement.

"'Pon my word!" he exclaimed as he touched the accelerator. "'Pon my word! How very remarkable!"

The car simply bounded along. The straight level road by Slapton Sands it covered at a good fifty miles an hour; with hardly a perceptible effort, but with many a jolt, it breasted the steep ascent at Stoke Fleming and was soon careering madly down the almost precipitous slope to the valley of the Dart, never halting till it pulled up on the quay of old-world Dartmouth.

"There she is, sir," said a fisherman in answer to the doctor's enquiry. "Just a-comin' round Castle Ledge."

News of the impending arrival of the survivors of the "Heracles," had preceded the "Merope." Already Lloyd's staff at Prawle Point had telegraphed the glad tidings, and the report had been spread far and wide. Hundreds of Dartmouth townsfolk were gathered on the quays and on the high ground by the old castle. Half a dozen steamboats crammed with wildly excited naval cadets had left the College quay and were pelting down the harbour to greet the returning warriors. Dartmouth had not seen such a day since the last pre-war regatta.

Slowly the "Merope" approached the anchorage on the Kingswear side of the harbour. As she drew abreast of the quay Doris could see the comparatively limited expanse of deck crowded with men. Few of them wore naval uniforms. Here and there could be distinguished a seaman wearing a service jumper or a naval cap, but for the most part they were rigged out in canvas clothing. Some were actually wearing garments fashioned out of blankets.

"Hulloa there, Bill," shouted a Dartmouth waterman recognising an old friend on the tramp's deck. "You'm all right, us hopes?"

"Ay," was the reply, "but deuced hungry." The man voiced the sentiments of his comrades. They were in high spirits in spite of short rations.

An outward-bound Scandinavian steamer had effected the rescue of the survivors of the "Heracles," and not being equipped with wireless she was unable to send the reassuring news to any of the British cruisers which were searching fruitlessly over the spot where their consort had foundered five hours previously.

Twenty-four hours later the rescuing ship fell in with the "Merope," homeward bound, and in spite of limited accommodation and provisions her skipper gladly offered to tranship the hundred-odd officers and men of the "Heracles."

Strangely enough, the "Merope" gained the "Chops of the Channel" without getting within signalling distance of any other craft. Then a thick fog swept down, preventing her from communicating with either the Scillies or with the Lizard Station. Food was now running out. The tramp's exact position was unknown, until the sudden dispersal of the fog revealed the fact that she was within signalling distance of Prawle Point. Thus it was that her skipper judiciously decided to put in to Dartmouth, land her supernumeraries and revictual before resuming her voyage to London.

Amidst the scene of excitement Doris Greenwood remained perfectly calm—at least outwardly. Several times Dr. Cardyke glanced furtively at his companion's face.

"Plucky girl," he soliloquised. "Frightfully plucky. If her brother isn't on board, by Jove— —"

A burst of cheering, louder than ever, interrupted his thoughts. The "Merope" had brought up. Her accommodation-ladder was already lowered; a small fleet of boats rubbed alongside her iron-rusted hull.

"They'm landing the whole of 'em at Kingswear side, I'll allow," declared an old salt. "Off to Plymouth 'tes for they—court-martial, or summat o' that sort."

The girl could stand the suspense no longer. Descending from the car, she called to an urchin who was about to put off in a flat-bottomed, leaky punt. It was the only available craft, for almost everything that would float was crowded with sightseers.

"Boy," she called, "will you take me off to that ship?"

The sight of a shilling decided the youngster to break faith with half a dozen of his pals, who were waiting until he had baled out his leaky argosy.

She was only just in time, for the old salt's surmise was correct. Officers and men were to be sent to the Devonport Naval Barracks to await a court of enquiry.

"Hulloa, Doris!"

It was Eric's voice. She hardly recognised in the speaker her brother. A week's growth upon his chin, his alert figure grotesquely hidden in a dungaree boiler-suit, a tarry canvas cap set jauntily on his head, and his arm in a sling.

The A.P. leant over the coaming of the picquet-boat and grasped his sister's outstretched hand.

"Bit of a surprise, eh?" he remarked. "How on earth did you get wind of it? And so jolly near home, too. If ever I felt like breaking ship it's now. Never mind, old girl! This will mean a week's leave very soon."

"And Ronald?" she asked.

"They took him ashore not two minutes ago," replied the A.P. "Cot case, you know— —"

"Not seriously wounded?"

"No. Effects of exhaustion. We all had a pretty rough time, and old Tressidar was a brick... we're off. Push off, boy!"

The picquet-boat began to back away from the ladder, two of her crew using their boat-hooks to fend off the crowd of shore-craft.

"S'long, Doris," was her brother's farewell greeting. "No use coming across. They won't let you into the station. I'll give Tressidar the tip that I've seen you."

As the picquet-boat glided astern, Doris overheard a voice exclaim, "Tressidar's a lucky dog, dash it all!"

It was the engineer-sub-lieutenant who had vainly begged Tressidar for an introduction on the memorable day when the "Pompey" was sunk in Auldhaig Firth.

"Well," was Dr. Cardyke's comment as the girl ran lightly back to the car. "It's good news, I can see. No need to ask that. Now what's the programme?"

"You have business in Dartmouth," she reminded him.

"Done," rejoined the doctor laconically. "Done, while you were risking your life in that cockleshell. Suppose it's home to tell the good news?"

"Yes, if you please," replied the girl, and to her companion's mild astonishment he saw that she was crying. They were tears not of sorrow, but of joy and thankfulness—of relief that the sea had returned to her those she loved.

CHAPTER XXVII
A DAY ON DARTMOOR

"Say, Greenwood, I feel an odd man out with this little crew. Nip in and come along to keep me company. While these young people are roaming over the moors, we'll try our luck with the trout."

The speaker was Dr. Cardyke. A week had elapsed since the "Merope" had put in to Dartmouth. The court of enquiry was a thing of the past, and the surviving officers and men of the "Heracles" had been given leave.

Tressidar had gone home, having first given young Greenwood a ready promise to put in a day or two at the Greenwoods' house, and now the sub. was fulfilling his obligations.

On the morning following Tressidar's arrival the genial doctor had given the Greenwoods and their guest an invitation for a "spin in the car." Cardyke's "spin" meant a whole day on the breezy uplands of Dartmoor. Mrs. Greenwood, still feeling the reaction of her prolonged suspense, was unable to go. Her husband, having to report himself that night for duty with the National Guards, also "cried off," though not without regret. Yet, he argued proudly, work in the service of one's country that does not entail self-sacrifice isn't worth being called patriotism.

Consequently the doctor's guests were Doris and her friend Norah Ward, Eric and Ronald, and, in view of the possibility, nay probability, that he would have to commune with nature while the youthful picnickers roamed the moors, he again threw out an invitation to his old crony with the alluring prospect of trout-fishing thrown in.

"Duty, Cardyke, duty," protested Mr. Greenwood, although the doctor saw that he was wavering. "Must report at Ferncoombe Reservoir at eleven-thirty to-night."

"We'll be back long before then," said the doctor tentatively.

"I know what your motor spins are, my dear fellow," rejoined Mr. Greenwood. "It's a good hour and a half's tramp from here to Ferncoombe, remember."

"Look here, slip into your uniform. A trout won't fight shy of a fly any more for that, you know. We'll have a topping time, and I'll drop you at Ferncoombe on the return journey."

Greenwood senior figuratively hauled down his colours. With great alacrity he donned his uniform of the National Guard, deposited his rifle and fishing-tackle in the car, and took his seat alongside the doctor. The rest of the party were already in occupation of the remaining "crew-space," together with a well-filled hamper and Doris's Irish terrier.

Over the hilly road the car sped, until it gained the outskirts of a little village on the fringe of the wildly majestic Dartmoor.

"She's running badly," remarked the doctor to his companion. "Deucedly strange. I never knew her to act like that before and on a day like this."

He slowed down and pulled up. An examination revealed the fact that the radiator tank was empty.

"Not a serious matter," declared Dr. Cardyke. "I'll ask for a can of water at yonder cottage." A comely, sun-bonneted Devonshire countrywoman willingly complied with his request. While engaged in refilling the tank the doctor casually noticed that two men were passing.

"Joy-riding in war-time," remarked one to his companion in a tone that was obviously intended for the motorists' ears. "Pity those young fellows haven't anything better to do."

Tressidar and the A.P. smiled. They regarded the remark as a joke. Being in mufti, they had been taken for a pair of young slackers.

Not so Dr. Cardyke. Setting the can of water on the ground, he strode resolutely up to the man who had uttered the uncalled-for remark.

"Allow me to inform you," he said cuttingly to the somewhat astonished fellow, "that these gentlemen are naval officers. Both have been in action, and on two occasions their ships have been mined or torpedoed. The young lady [indicating Doris] is a nurse at a naval hospital that has been under hostile fire. Her companion is a voluntary Red Cross worker. My friend here, in spite of his years, is, as you see, a member of the National Guard; while I, a medical man, am engaged in purely voluntary work at three military hospitals in the district. If we choose to take a well-earned holiday, is it any concern of yours? Now, since you have interfered with our business, perhaps you will not object if I meddle with yours. What are you doing for your country?"

"I am engaged on the registration of women workers on the land," replied the man airily.

"Should have thought that the registration part was essentially a woman's work," rejoined Dr. Cardyke drily. "But is that all? Surely you have made an effort to serve in His Majesty's forces?"

"I'm over age," declared the man.

"Then that accounts for it," said the doctor triumphantly. "I noticed that those who are so keen upon urging others to 'do their bit' have good reason, or think they have good reason, for backing out themselves. Yes, sir, I said backing out. Allow me to inform you that no recruiting officer would question your statement if you said you were under forty. Try the experiment or perhaps you haven't the pluck."

The busybody slunk away, and the triumphant doctor returned to complete his task.

The journey was resumed. Up and up climbed the car 'twixt frowning tors and across stretches of wild moor clad in yellow gorse, through which trickled numerous mountain torrents on their way to feed the silvery Dart. Frequently a startled rabbit would rush across the road and dive for safety into the brushwood. Wild birds, alarmed by the purr of the motor, fled with strange cries to seek a more secluded ground. Once a red fox, caught napping, bounded frantically across a stream. These were the only signs of life visible from the car. Of human habitation, not a vestige in the wild expanse.

At length the doctor drove the car very gently on to the side of the road and stopped. This precaution was hardly necessary, since passing vehicles were few and far between.

"Now, you young people," he exclaimed, "it's a couple of hours to lunch time, unless you are ravenous already. Come along, Greenwood. Where's your tackle? A cloudy morning like this ought to make the trout rise. There's a capital stream less than a quarter of a mile away."

By tacit consent the party separated, Tressidar and Doris making their way in one direction, the A.P. and Norah in another. Whence they went and the nature of the conversation was a matter that concerned themselves. At any rate, it was safe to conjecture that they were engrossed in each other's company, since the sub. and his companion returned twenty minutes after the prearranged time and the A.P. and Norah a quarter of an hour later to find that the doctor and Greenwood senior were still lost to time and the call of hunger and were lingering over their rods by the swiftly rushing mountain-stream.

At length, in high spirits, the party assembled for lunch, the fishermen displaying with pardonable pride the successful result of their sport.

"Now, then, Tressidar," sang out the doctor as he prepared to cut a veal and ham pie, "make yourself useful. You might uncork these bottles."

"Shall I dissect the pie, sir?" asked the sub.

"The pie?" repeated Dr. Cardyke. "That's what I'm doing. Why do you ask?"

"We'll have to hoist the S.O.S. signal if you carry on," said Tressidar, laughing. "Already you've dropped a fish-hook into the gravy, and it looks as if there are more to follow."

"A good excuse to remove my coat," rejoined the doctor good-humouredly. "It certainly is hot for this time of year."

According to the custom adopted by freshwater fishermen, Dr. Cardyke had stuck his spare hooks in the sleeve of his coat, and one of them, being insufficiently held by the barb, had fallen into the pie-dish.

After lunch the young officers and their fair companions sauntered off, while Greenwood senior and the doctor had "forty winks," followed by another bout of friendly rivalry by the trout stream.

"By Jove, Doris, isn't this simply great?" exclaimed Tressidar enthusiastically, as the pair gained the top of a rugged tor. "Just look at the expanse of country. Looks a bit misty down in the valleys, though. I hope it won't get too thick. Say, do you mind if I get a pipe under way?"

The rest of the afternoon passed only too quickly. The slanting rays of the sun cast long shadows athwart the gorse as they made their way back to the spot that the sub. had termed the rendezvous. By this time the mist was rising from the low-lying ground and creeping slowly up the hillsides, until the tors looked like islands in a sea of slowly drifting fog.

"It will be pretty thick lower down," declared Eric during the course of tea. "Driving through the mist is jolly tricky."

"Pooh!" exclaimed Dr. Cardyke. "Not with reasonable care. We'll shake it off before we get to Bovey Tracey."

It was not long before the doctor found that very considerable caution was necessary, for the fog was so dense that it was hardly possible to distinguish the narrow road from the rest of the moor.

"Can you see where we're going, Greenwood?" he asked. "Frankly, I can't. It's the worst fog I've ever struck."

"I haven't been able to see anything of the road for the last twenty minutes," confessed Greenwood senior. "I think I'll change places with young Tressidar. He's used to peering through mist, I should imagine."

The car stopped and the change was effected, but Ronald found that he had hopelessly lost his bearings. Everything visible was grotesquely distorted by the fog, and magnified out of all proportion.

"Hold hard!" he exclaimed after another mile or so had been covered at almost crawling pace. "There's something right ahead."

The "something" proved to be a sign-post at the fork of two roads. None of the party had noticed it on the outward journey. Slowly the car was brought alongside. It was the only way to read the directions, if such existed. Unfortunately they didn't. The finger-post, neglected and weather-beaten, was devoid of wording.

"There's a map in that case," observed the doctor. "Would you mind getting it out? We'll soon see where we are."

The map was worse than useless. It was a delusion and a snare, for nowhere within ten miles of where the car was supposed to be was a fork road shown.

"What's wrong?" enquired the A.P. from the rear of the car.

"Out of our bearings. Suppose you don't happen to have brought a compass?" said the sub. "Unless we are going in exactly the opposite direction to the right one, there's not a fork road anywhere about, according to this map."

"Don't forget I'm due at Ferncoombe tonight," sung out Mr. Greenwood jocularly. "Now, Cardyke, get a move on."

Thus rallied, the doctor took the plunge. He restarted the car and followed the right-hand road, arguing with himself that it must lead somewhere, and that the fog wouldn't be so thick when clear of the moors.

An hour passed. The car had covered certainly not more than four miles. The doctor was showing signs of the severe strain it imposed upon his vision and mental powers, but tactfully refusing Tressidar's offer to drive, he stuck gamely to the steering-wheel.

It was now getting dark—and the doctor never drove at night unless it could not be avoided, and then only on roads with which he was well acquainted. With the decline of day the fog lifted slightly, and showed promise of dispersing.

Having stopped to light the lamps—merely a matter of complying with the law, since the obscured glasses gave hardly any illumination, certainly not enough to enable the occupants of the car to avoid an obstruction in time—the tedious journey was resumed, but at a slightly increased speed.

"Now I think I know where we are," declared the doctor; but the next moment he found out his mistake, for the car was on the point of charging a flock of sheep.

A turn of the steering-wheel did the trick. Missing the foremost sheep by inches, the car mounted a slight bank by the roadside and commenced to slide down the steeply shelving slope of a deep valley.

The doctor shoved on the brakes. Although the wheels were locked and the momentum retarded, the car continued its involuntary glide. Then Tressidar had a vague impression that he was flying through the air, and the next thing he knew was that he was sitting in a most aggressive gorse-bush.

CHAPTER XXVIII
AND A NIGHT

Tressidar extricated himself from his uncomfortable position. Although considerably shaken, he was practically unhurt. His first thoughts upon realising that there had been a smash was for the other former occupants of the car. Some distance from and well above him the dimmed light of one of the lamps still flickered. The other had been extinguished, either by the sudden jolt or owing to the glass being fractured. He could distinguish the voices of Doris and Norah and the mild expostulation of Mr. Greenwood to the accompaniment of the bark of the Irish terrier.

He started to ascend the incline. It was so steep that he wondered why the car had not crashed to the bottom of the valley instead of lodging a mere thirty or forty feet below the road.

Before he had taken half a dozen steps his foot came in contact with a human body. It was Dr. Cardyke, still gripping the steering-wheel. The impact had snapped the steering-column like a carrot, and the doctor, describing a parabola over the shattered screen, had carried the wheel with him.

"Hurt?" enquired the sub. anxiously.

"No, only meditating," replied the imperturbable doctor. "I'll be all right in a few minutes. See to the others, please."

The two girls and the A.P. had already alighted, more or less gracefully, while Greenwood senior was wedged in between the seat and the sadly depleted hamper. All had come off lightly, but not so the car.

Its downward career had been stopped by a large boulder. The force of the impact had telescoped the fore part. The front wheels were shattered, the chassis splintered. As a car its days were ended.

"Where's Cardyke?" enquired Mr. Greenwood as he was being extricated from the wreckage.

"Nursing the steering-wheel," replied Tressidar. "He says he isn't hurt."

"Neither am I," added the doctor, who, having regained his feet, was toiling up the slope. "Sorry I landed you all in this pickle. Greenwood, I'm afraid your Ferncoombe Reservoir business is off."

"Not if I know it," resolutely replied the member of the National Guard. "I'll get there, even if I have to tramp it."

"What's the programme, sir?" enquired Tressidar, who, after having found a derelict cushion for the girls, was surveying the wreckage in the dim glimmer of the expiring lamp.

"We'll try to reach the nearest village and find a conveyance," replied the doctor. "It can't be very far. We must be almost on the edge of the moors, although I find I was mistaken just now. I certainly don't remember this place."

"May as well leave everything ship-shape as far as possible," suggested Eric. "My word, what an escape we've had!"

All hands set to work to retrieve the scattered articles. Cushions, portions of the mechanism, fishing-rods, Mr. Greenwood's rifle, the clock and speedometer and a number of other articles were picked up at varying distances from the wrecked car, some having rolled far down the valley. These were placed for safety in the car.

"By Jove, sir!" exclaimed Tressidar. "How many clocks do you carry? I've already found three."

"Three?" echoed the doctor. "Never."

"I'll prove it," continued the sub., leaning over the side door and groping for the floor of the car. This he failed to find, for the simple reason that it no longer existed. Instead was a gaping cavity through which the retrieved articles rolled out as fast as they were stowed away.

Just then the terrier gave a bark.

"Quiet!" ordered Doris. "Quiet, Mike!"

"There's someone coming," declared Eric. "Sounds like a horse and cart."

"Then, thank goodness, we'll be able to find out where we are," added Mr. Greenwood, as the whole party scaled the bank and waited in the road for the approaching vehicle.

It proved to be a pony-trap driven by a very stout farmer. The latter, recovering from his astonishment at being hailed in this out-of-the-way place, informed the doctor that they were four miles from the nearest house, five from the nearest village, and twelve from a railway-station.

"Any motor-cars to be had in the village?" asked Dr. Cardyke. "We've had a bad smash."

"Yes, there be a car o' sorts, zurr," replied the man, laying stress upon the "o' sorts." "Maybe you'll be wantin' oi' tu ax the moty tu fetch you?"

"If you would," said the doctor, "we'll be most obliged. I suppose we can rely upon it being sent?"

"You can rely on oi, zurr, tu giv' the message," was the countryman's non-committal reply, and, overcoming his curiosity to alight and examine the wrecked car, he touched the pony with his whip and drove off.

"Five miles," commented the doctor. "It will take at least an hour before the car arrives. Let's make ourselves as comfortable as possible in the circumstances. Has anyone a match?"

After another twenty minutes the conversation flagged. Everyone was more or less tired, after the day spent in the bracing air.

Presently Mike began to show signs of uneasiness, straining at his collar, through which his mistress had slipped her fingers.

"He smells a rabbit, I think," suggested Tressidar.

"Yes, and if I let him go he may not return for hours. I know him when rabbits are about," replied Doris. "Hold him, Ronald; he's tugging awfully hard."

The sub. did so, at the same time encircling the terrier's muzzle with his left hand. For the time being Mike was silent.

Stealthy footsteps could be heard on the stony road. These were the sounds that had aroused the dog, who had detected them long before the rest of the party.

With a sudden, furious twist Mike broke away from Tressidar's grasp and darted off through the darkness, in spite of insistent calls for him to come to heel.

"Dash it all, Doris!" exclaimed her father. "The brute will frighten the man into fits. If I have to pay for any damage, I'll have the animal dest— —"

His threat regarding Mike's future was interrupted by a yell, followed by an oath—and the oath was uttered in unmistakable German.

"That's good enough for us, old man!" exclaimed Tressidar to the A.P. "Come along. Let's see who the Hun is."

The two officers gained the road and made their way swiftly in the direction of the indiscreet stranger, who was now having a battle royal with the terrier. On hearing footsteps approaching, he bawled,

"Call off your dog, will you? If you don't I'll— —"

The words trailed off into another yell, as Mike nipped a piece out of the fellow's trousers, together with a square inch of adipose tissue.

"By Jove!" exclaimed Tressidar. "It's Jorkler."

The A.P. knew the name perfectly well. He remembered that a Jorkler was reported killed on the occasion of the loss of the "Pompey"; but he was unaware that his real name was Oberfurst and that he was a spy. Tressidar had kept his promise to the rear-admiral in that respect, but now arose the necessity for explanation.

"He's a spy," he said hurriedly. "Take care, he may be armed."

"Not likely," replied the A.P. "If he were, he would have potted the tyke by this time."

Almost before he was aware of it, Tressidar was upon the man. Oberfurst, having ascended a slight bank on the opposite side of the road, was kicking at the terrier, who with canine insistence was striving to get an opening and remove another patch of the German's clothes.

"We've got you, Oberfurst," exclaimed Tressidar. "There are four of us."

The spy recognised the sub.'s voice. Sheer astonishment on being confronted in that remote part of Dartmoor by a man whom he imagined was still interned in Denmark "took the wind out of his sails." Mike, seeing the advantage, leapt forward, only to be hurled backward by a powerful kick of the German's boot.

Simultaneously Tressidar and the A.P. threw themselves upon the spy, but they had not taken into account the slippery state of the ground owing to the heavy mist. Eric, his feet sliding from under him, fell on his face across the body of the still yelping Mike. The sub., adopting Rugby tactics, tackled his man low, but was unable to secure a hold.

In a trice the spy broke away and ran swiftly along the stony road in the direction of the doctor and the rest of the party.

Too late did Oberfurst make the discovery that there were more than two adversaries, for Dr. Cardyke and Greenwood senior gamely sought to bar the German's way.

At the first alarm Mr. Greenwood had seized his rifle. True, he had no cartridges; perhaps for his son's and Tressidar's safety it was as well that he had not.

The doctor, being slightly in advance of his friend, received the brunt of the second phase of the night operations, for the spy, using his feet in the approved Continental style, kicked Cardyke on his left knee, at the same time gripping the doctor's arm.

Then it was that Oberfurst met his Waterloo, for his palm came in contact with the formidable array of fish-hooks that the doctor still kept in his coat-sleeve. Uttering a yell as the barbs lacerated his flesh, the spy again attempted to break away. As he did so, Greenwood senior prodded him in the ribs with the butt-end of his rifle and stretched him out breathless on the road, just as Tressidar and the A.P. again appeared upon the scene.

Otto Oberfurst had been far from inactive since the "Nordby" incident. Having given the Danish skipper the slip, the spy made his way to Aarhuus, whence, having obtained false papers, he posed as a British mercantile seaman whose vessel had been mined in the North Sea.

It was his intention to return to Great Britain with the least possible delay and resume his nefarious operations. For two reasons: firstly, that he thought it unlikely that the British authorities would suspect his presence after what had occurred. The very audacity of his plan would tend to put them off the scent. Secondly, he knew full well that the Head of the German Secret Service would not overlook his blunder unless he promptly outweighed his error by a brilliant coup.

Accordingly he landed at Hull, and before twenty-four hours had elapsed was within an ace of destroying a munitions factory. Foiled, he went south, and, by blowing up two unguarded railway tunnels, delayed important movement of troops on the way to Flanders. Here, again, it was only by a sheer fluke that the troop train was not derailed.

In due course accounts of the demolished tunnels appeared in the Press, with the suggestion that the disasters had been caused by subsidences after the heavy rains, and thus public apprehension was allayed.

Having reported himself to his chief, von Schenck ordered him to the West of England to assist in the escape of three German officers from the detention camp, and to help them to cross to Ireland in readiness for a revolt of the Sinn Feiners. Already the German authorities were in full possession of the knowledge that an armed rising was imminent in Ireland, and in addition to arms being conveyed thither in Hun ships disguised as neutral merchantmen, arrangements had been made for several German officers at present prisoners of war to join the insurgents.

In this West Country detention camp it was a matter of consummate ease to communicate with the imprisoned German officers. Many of the latter were on parole (although it is generally recognised that a Hun regards the breaking of his plighted word as a smart piece of work), and were permitted to go freely into the neighbouring town on two days a week. They were also allowed to purchase English daily papers without the latter being examined when brought into the camp, and thus many a ciphered communication passed between the prisoners and their compatriots without.

Otto Oberfurst's method of getting into touch with the three Huns was simplicity itself. He would buy a daily paper and make a pinprick through those letters required to make up a word or sentence. Only by holding the paper up to the light could the minute holes be detected. Nor was it a difficult matter for the prisoners to obtain maps, pocket compasses, and small but powerful wire-cutters.

The next business was to arrange for the German officers to be taken across to Ireland. In view of the strict regulations governing the departure of British subjects from British ports, it was obviously a matter of almost impossibility to smuggle three young Teutons on board a ship lying in port. Oberfurst had thought of stealing a yacht from some unfrequented harbour, until he realised the risk of being caught by the vigilant patrols in the Bristol Channel and especially in the Irish Sea.

Eventually through an intermediary—he was too wily to negotiate direct—he arranged with the hyphenated American skipper of a Yankee tramp, that was shortly to leave Bristol for New York, to close with the North Devon coast in the vicinity of the unfrequented Hartland Point. The skipper was to heave-to and send a boat ashore at 3 a.m., and pick up the three fugitives.

Oberfurst left little to chance. A powerful motor-car took him from Exeter to a point four miles from the camp. He intended to proceed on foot to a prearranged rendezvous, await the German officers and walk with them for another four miles across the moors, and to pick up another car which was to convey the fugitives to within a short distance of the coast.

Unfortunately for him, on leaving the first car he had followed the road by which Tressidar and his companions were keeping their weary vigil, and now he was a prisoner.

In the event of his plans going awry, he had firmly decided not to be taken alive. At the same time he would make a desperate bid for freedom before proceeding to the last extremity. In this resolve he was thwarted. The intense pain of the laceration of his hand by the fish-hooks, quickly followed by Mr. Greenwood's drastic and effectual action, had completed his discomfiture before he realised that the game was up.

"Now, my fine bird," thought Tressidar as he surveyed his captive, "I'll take good care you don't slip through our fingers this time."

The spy made no movement, nor did he speak a word. Lying on the ground with his legs and arms tied and Mr. Greenwood proudly mounting guard over him, he looked helpless enough; but the sub. knew his man and took no risks. He stood by, ready at the first suspicious movement to act promptly and effectually.

At length the expected motor-car arrived. At the very most it could accommodate five, not including the chauffeur. Here, indeed, was a puzzle. Someone had to be left behind. Mr. Greenwood was on his honour to turn up at the reservoir for guard duties. Tressidar and the A.P. were necessary, being the only active male members of the party, to guard the spy, who could not very well be placed in the seat alongside the chauffeur. Doris and Norah could not be left behind, nor was it desirable for them to be in close proximity to the Hun. Dr. Cardyke was beginning to feel the effects of his tumble, and, taking in consideration his age, it was unwise to leave him exposed to the cold night air longer than could be avoided.

"Then Eric and I will remain with our old pal Oberfurst," said Tressidar. "The rest of you carry on. Don't wait if you find a train at the station. The car can come back for us. How about the wreckage, doctor?"

"Can stop," decided Dr. Cardyke firmly. "I've done with the thing. I'll send a cart in the morning to collect the luggage and things that are of value. Well, good-bye, Tressidar, Wish you luck with your capture."

The car, a wheezy, American-built one, started and was soon lost to sight and hearing in the darkness, while the two naval officers were left with their prisoner.

In an hour and a half the motor returned. Oberfurst, offering no resistance, was placed therein, Tressidar and the A.P. sitting on the seat facing him and keeping a watch on every movement.

Without incident the spy and his escort arrived at the little village. Here Oberfurst was handed over to the care of the local constabulary, the police-sergeant having been cautioned concerning the desperate character of the prisoner. The last train having gone, Tressidar and Eric were obliged to engage the chauffeur to drive home. After a tedious journey they reached the Greenwoods' house to find that the girls had not arrived, and that Mrs Greenwood was in a state of great nervous anxiety.

To make matters worse, two telegrams were awaiting the sub. and the A.P. The former's had been forwarded from his home in Cornwall. Both were of the same nature:

"Report for instant duty at Naval Barracks, Devonport—urgent."

CHAPTER XXIX
WHEN THE TRAWLERS SHOWED FIGHT

"Must be on the move at once," declared the A.P. "Ten precious hours wasted."

"Hardly," corrected the sub. "We've bagged an important prize. But, dash it all! Here I am in mufti, and my kit is at home. Telegraph office is closed for to-night, and there's no train beyond Plymouth even if there were time to make a dash for home."

"And that ramshackle motor has departed," added Eric. "In the words of the great tragedian What's-his-name, 'Alas! sirs, I am undone.' Now, the question is, how are two dog-tired fellows to get to Devonport? It's a serious matter, old man. Who knows? Perhaps the Admiralty have news that 'They' have come out at last. The papers reported signs of German naval activity in the North Sea, you know."

"And therefore I am inclined to doubt whether the Huns have ventured," said Tressidar. "You can bet your bottom dollar when they do come out they won't give the papers time to advertise the fact. But I quite agree with you, old man, this is a serious business. Have you a time-table?"

"Here we are," exclaimed the A.P. triumphantly. "If we pad the hoof to Totnes, we'll just catch the night mail. That will land us in Plymouth at 1 a.m."

He was busy packing his portmanteau, desisting only to hunt up the train. With the sub.'s assistance he contrived to close the bulky leather case.

"Well, good-bye, mother," he exclaimed. "Sorry the governor and Doris aren't here to say good-bye Suppose I can't grouse at having my leave cut down.... May be home again in a few months. So buck up, mother; it's no use being down in the dumps, is it?"

Tressidar had deliberately gone out of the house. The A.P. rejoined him in a few minutes.

"Can't understand why the mater gets in such a stew," he remarked. "She ought to be used to saying good-bye by this time. I do my level best to tell her that there's little danger, certainly less than in the trenches in France, but she won't see it. Now, then; it's six good miles of hilly road. Wonder how old Overfirst, or whatever his tally is, likes being in the cells?"

It was three in the morning when the two chums arrived at the Naval Barracks. Here they received the information that they were both appointed to the brand-new monitor "Anzac," in lieu of two officers who had been sent to hospital. The "Anzac" was leaving the Hamoaze for Portsmouth at 9 a.m.

"Kitted out" by an obliging brother-officer, who also undertook to forward Tressidar's gear as soon as possible, the sub., accompanied by Eric, hurried on board.

Viewed in the waning starlight, for day was on the point of breaking, the "Anzac" appeared to be a vessel of about two hundred feet in length, with a tripod mast surmounted by a large fire-control platform. She had but one funnel, well abaft the mast. For'ard of the conning-tower was a turret mounting a pair of fourteen-inch guns; four six-inch quick-firers thrust their muzzles through casemates in the superstructure; while four twelve-pounder anti-aircraft guns and a pair of searchlight projectors were placed upon the bridge and a raised platform at the after-end of the superstructure.

At first sight the monitor gave the impression that she was top-heavy, until her enormous beam and length beyond each end of the superstructure belied the suggestion. The hull proper was little less than four hundred feet in length, with a maximum beam of one hundred and twenty. Her draught was but five feet six inches, the freeboard being but two feet for'ard and eighteen inches aft. Her maximum speed was a bare seven and a half knots.

The "Anzac" was still in the throes that invariably attend the first commissioning of a new vessel, for she had left the Clyde only three days previously, and had put in to Devonport to ship her fourteen-inch guns. On the run round to Portsmouth she was to undergo gunnery trials, and if no serious defects were revealed, she was to proceed to the North Sea to take part in impending operations.

Dog-tired, Tressidar turned in as soon as the chums had reported themselves to the officer of the watch. It seemed less than five minutes, although it was four bells (6 a.m.), when the sub. was roused and informed that the captain wished to see him.

"A wigging for being late, I suppose," he soliloquised. "A jolly bad beginning."

But he was mistaken. An armed trawler was to be navigated to Portsmouth, and the "Anzac" had to provide an officer and crew for the job. Tressidar, being the most recently joined, was selected by his skipper for this service.

"The 'Gannet' is lying off Wilcove," continued the skipper of the "Anzac." "She's ready for sea with the exception of victualling stores. You will have to demand these from Royal William Yard. She'll do twenty knots easily, without having to drive her, and even if we have a good start you ought to overhaul us before Portland Bill is abeam."

Already the crew told off for the service had fallen in for inspection. They numbered ten hands, including a chief petty officer. The "Gannet's" engine-room staff were already on board, having been shipped when the vessel left Belfast, where she had been re-engined.

The "trawler" was in fact a trawler no longer. A comparatively new boat, with lines that promised a fair turn of speed, she had been taken over by the Admiralty for use as a patrol vessel. Her machinery was removed and turbine engines substituted, giving her a maximum speed of twenty-eight knots. Her armament consisted of two twelve-pounder quick-firers, so woe betide the luckless German submarine that might mistake the "Gannet" for a slow and helpless fishing-craft.

Disquieting reports of the presence of a hostile submarine off St. Catherine's Point, a craft that had hitherto successfully evaded all attempts at capture or destruction, had necessitated the presence of the "Gannet" off the Isle of Wight, and arrangements had been made to "turn over" the R.N.R. crew of another armed trawler directly Tressidar brought his command into Spithead.

By dint of strenuous exertion the "Gannet" was able to leave Plymouth Sound at noon—the "Anzac" having had three hours start—and once outside the Breakwater, the sub. ordered fifteen knots, which were increased to twenty as soon as Bigbury Head was broad on the port beam.

"It would be a rare slice of luck," thought the sub., "if we could bag the strafed 'U' boat in the run up Channel, but that is asking for too much, I'm afraid."

The sea was smooth, with a long, oily roll. The sky was inclined to be misty, although it was possible to discern The Start, now less than ten miles off on the port bow. There were no signs of the "Anzac." The sea appeared to be deserted, except for two large Brixham trawlers, that, with all sail set, were floundering in almost a dead calm at a distance of about three miles on the starboard bow.

"Those luggers seem pretty close together, sir," remarked the helmsman of the "Gannet."

The sub. brought his glasses to bear upon the trawlers. Even allowing for the lack of ability to judge distance when seen through a pair of binoculars, Tressidar was bound to confess that there was something strange about the position of the two vessels. They appeared to be almost side by side. The wind, such as it was, was dead astern. One of the trawlers had her mainsail right out on the port tack, the other on the starboard, so that the outer cloths of each sail were rubbing against each other as the boats rolled sluggishly in the long swell.

"They are showing no signals of distress," said Tressidar. "At least, none are visible. I fancy there's smoke arising from one of them. Deucedly fishy, by Jove! I've a mind to see what the game is. Port your helm, quartermaster. Keep her at that."

With his glasses still bearing upon the Brixham boats, Tressidar puzzled over the situation until the "Gannet" was within a mile of the trawlers.

Suddenly he replaced his binoculars, grasped the handle of the telegraph indicator and called for full speed ahead, at the same time ordering all hands to action stations, for lying between the two fishing luggers was a German submarine.

Almost before the guns' crews could stand to their quick-firers the "Gannet" was within hailing distance. To Tressidar's surprise, he discovered that the unterseeboot was lashed to the fishing-vessels and that four of her crew were standing with their hands held above their heads, while the skipper and deck hands of each trawler were calmly surveying the Germans from the decks of their respective craft.

"You'm too late, maaster," sung out one of the Devon skippers. "Us'n done the trick proper-like. Still, if you'm a mind tu finish the business 'twill save we a mort o' trouble."

"I thought that the Germans were sinking you," replied Tressidar. "Stand by with a line. We are running alongside."

The "Gannet," losing way, made fast to one of the trawlers, and Tressidar, accompanied by half a dozen armed men, gained the fishing-lugger's deck.

The sub. was greeted by a tall, broad-shouldered Devonshire man of about fifty years of age. His heavily bearded face was almost hidden under a sou'wester, in spite of the fact that the sun was shining brightly. On the deck just abaft the windlass was a young German unter-leutnant, bound hand and foot and obviously half dazed with the result of a blow on the left temple. Two German seamen, their clothes saturated with water, were lashed to the mizzen mast.

"ON THE DECK WAS A GERMAN UNTER-LEUTNANT, BOUND HAND AND FOOT"

[Illustration: "ON THE DECK WAS A GERMAN UNTER-LEUTNANT, BOUND HAND AND FOOT"]

The trawler had sustained damage. Her bitts had been carried away, with the result that her bowsprit had run in, and a raffle of head sails and gear littered the fo'c'sle. The other trawler appeared to be undamaged, with the exception of a large rent in her mainsail. The submarine, or as much as was visible above water, looked a wreck. The cover of her conning-tower hatchway was buckled, her twin periscopes had been snapped off close to the deck. Her ensign staff, with the Black Cross flying, was trailing over the side, and one of her disappearing guns had been dismounted.

"She tried her tricks on we, an' we wouldn't have any," declared the skipper proudly. "Them didn't reckon wi' Devon lads, did 'em, Bill?"

His mate, thus appealed to, merely grinned and scratched his head. Nor was the master of the second lugger more communicative.

"Us seed Charlie a-doin' the job properlike, so we gi' a hand. Not as though Charlie wasn't good enough for the job," he explained, "but us thought 'twas a good chance to get our own back, so we chipped in."

Early that morning the luggers "Crown and Sceptre" and "Unity" had left Brixham in company. The weather then was considerably more hazy that it was later in the day. Having made good hauls, the trawlers were beating up towards The Start when a German submarine suddenly poked its ugly snout above water. Making certain that the two craft were really fishing-boats and not armed trawlers, the Hun commander decided to replenish his grub-locker with fish from the English craft and then send the Brixham trawlers to the bottom.

The "Crown and Sceptre," being nearest to the "U" boat, was hailed and ordered to heave-to. Cap'n Charles Hunnable quickly hauled his headsails to windward and took way off the trawler. The "Unity" meanwhile held on, trusting for a breeze to enable her to escape.

"Shall us put up a fight, boys?" asked the Devon skipper. "If us does, there must be no half measures, mark you."

Her crew, consisting of two men and a boy, agreed. The fighting spirit of the shire that boasts of such gallant seamen as Drake and Raleigh still lives, and the Brixham men are worthy upholders of the traditions of the Devon forbears.

"'Tes good," continued Skipper Hunnable. "Long Jarge, do 'ee stand by t' hellum. Jim, you keep along o' me. Peter, slip for'ard an' when I give the word do'ee let jib and fores'l draw."

The submarine had now slowed down and was lying less than twenty yards on the trawler's starboard quarter. It was originally the intention of the German commander to order the Englishmen to launch their boat and bring the fish to their captors, but realising that the boat was a heavy one and that it would take some time to be hoisted out, he ordered the submarine's collapsible boat to be manned.

Into the frail craft stepped an unter-leutnant and three seamen.

"You vos throw us a rope," shouted the young Hun as the boat came alongside. "Your hatches you uncover must and fish ve vos take. Den ve vos you sink in five minutes."

A rope was thrown, the canvas boat was made fast alongside, and the unter-leutnant scrambled up and over the bulwarks, which were about three feet above the deck and seven feet from the waterline.

Directly his legs were astride the rail, Skipper Hunnable's powerful fist shot out like a sledge-hammer.

"You'd take my fish, would you!" he roared. "Take that, you young sausage."

The German officer, stunned by the blow, was grasped by the skipper before he fell overboard. Simultaneously Peter drove a triple-barbed eel spear through the canvas boat and cut the rope that held her.

"Up helm!" ordered the skipper. "Boy, trim your heads'l sheets."

"'Tes no half measures, say I," he continued, and he lifted the unconscious German officer and bore him aft. "Ef 'em shoots, then the'll shoot this gold-braid pup too."

Quick on her helm the "Crown and Sceptre" gathered way and showed her stern to the astonished submarine. The German commander was in a quandary. He dare not shell the trawler for fear of hitting his subordinate, until he drew ahead sufficiently to enable her quick-firer to plank a shell for'ard and between wind and water. He was convinced that the "Crown and Sceptre" was attempting to seek safety in flight, but he was grievously mistaken. Skipper Hunnable's blood was up.

Gybing "all standing," since there was little risk of loss of top-hamper as the wind was light, the Brixham trawler turned and tore straight for her antagonist. Before the submarine could manoeuvre to avoid the blow, the lugger's massive bowsprit struck her on the conning-tower. The hefty spar stood the strain, but not so the bitts. With a rending crash the bowsprit was forced inboard, but the mischief to the "U" boat was already done. The metal hatch was partly torn from its hinges, while in falling off the bowsprit made a clean sweep of the periscopes, wrecked the for'ard gun, and hurled the gun's crew into the sea.

A four-pound hammer hurled by the brawny skipper of the "Crown and Sceptre" hurtled through the air. With unerring aim it struck the Hun commander on the side of the head, killing him instantly.

Held by the raffle of cordage for'ard the lugger swung round broadside on to the submarine.

"Come on, lads!" roared Skipper Hunnable. "The old boat won't hurt where she be."

Seizing axes and crowbars, the crew followed the daring skipper to the deck of the submarine. "Long Jarge," brandishing a formidable hatchet, took his stand by the conning-tower hatchway, ready to deal a smashing blow to the first man that appeared, while the skipper and the rest of his little crew chased the two German seamen who were on deck and drew the watertight slide of the after-hatchway.

The Devon men now had things all their own way. The "U" boat could not dive with her conning-tower hatchway in a damaged condition, or she would fill and sink like a stone. Nor could the trapped Huns use their rifles and revolvers. One foolhardy man attempted to take a chance shot through the after-hatchway, but directly his hand appeared above the coaming, Peter smashed it to a pulp.

The state of affairs now developed into a deadlock. The submarine could not escape, nor could the British fishermen regain their craft without risk of losing the advantage they at present held.

At this juncture the crew of the "Unity," perceiving that Skipper Hunnable was putting up a fight, but ignorant of how matters stood, determined to go to their comrades' aid, and sink or swim in the attempt.

Luffing smartly under the submarine's submerged stern, Skipper Biddlecombe brought the "Unity" up on the "U" boat's starboard side and made fast.

"What be you a-shovin' your five eggs in for, I'd be likin' tu know?" was Skipper Hunnable's greeting to the newcomers.

"No offence, Charlie," replied the fellow-skipper. "Us don't get the chance tu fight the Huns every day."

"True, true," rejoined the master of the "Crown and Sceptre." "You'm handy just now. Bid young Jack bring a shovelful o' coals and a bit o' junk. We'll have to be smokin' them chaps out, I'm thinkin'."

Ignorant of the risk they ran, the fishermen were about to throw smouldering tow down the hatchways into the petrol-laden atmosphere of the interior of the submarine when the Germans, realising the fate that threatened them, began to raise shouts of "kamarade."

"Thought better of it, eh?" said Skipper Hunnable. "Douse them coals, Jack. Now, you rascals, up you come. Four o' you. Drat you! I said four o' you. One, two, dree, four—not a round dozen. That's better. Now, hands up, an' keep 'em up. Rest o' you chaps below there are you a-listenin'?"

"Ja, ja!" was the reply.

"Don't you yah me, you lubbers," shouted the skipper. "Just you stand by, and don't get up to any tricks. If you du, down the lot o' you goes to Davy in double-quick time."

Having secured uninterrupted possession of the prize, the two skippers returned to their respective boats. Then it was that the crew of the collapsible boat that had been stove in, finding that the fishermen did not kill the prisoners in cold blood, swam to the "Crown and Sceptre" and were taken on board and secured.

"Charlie!" bawled the skipper of the "Unity," "wind's fair for home. Shall us try and take this craft in?"

"No need," replied his friend. "Look astern—there's a Government vessel a-comin' up at the rate o' knots."

CHAPTER XXX
A NOVEL DUCK HUNT

Having secured the surviving Germans from the submarine, and made certain that the Huns had not taken steps to destroy their craft on surrendering, Tressidar "wirelessed" the commander-in-chief at Devonport, reporting the capture and requesting that assistance would be sent to tow the prize into port.

The crews of the two Brixham boats cast off and resumed their interrupted run home, as unconcernedly as if bagging "U" boats was an everyday task. At the same time they took good care formally to make a claim for services rendered to the State, and this Tressidar countersigned according to their request.

It was nearly six in the evening before two destroyers arrived from Devonport. One of them took the captured submarine in tow, the other "stood by" in case another "U" boat might be lurking in the track of the prize.

Cracking on full speed to make up for the delay, the "Gannet" came within sight of St. Catherine's light by midnight, and having exchanged secret signals with the patrols in the Outer Examination Ground, she rounded the Nab Lightship and dropped anchor off St. Helen's.

The "Anzac" had already arrived and had gone into Portsmouth Harbour to ship additional ammunition. Barely had the "Gannet" brought up when a Government tug came alongside with her new crew, and took off Tressidar and the men lent from the monitor.

Hardly had the tug backed clear of the trawler when the latter began to heave up anchor. Five minutes later she was under way, bound for the North Sea.

"Something brewing, sir," remarked the master of the tug to the sub. "A whole crowd of them left Poole for the east'ard this afternoon, and seven from Portsmouth. There'll be a hot time out yonder, I'm thinking, before many more days are passed."

The "Anzac" was lying at No. 5 buoy. Her gunnery trials had been postponed by wireless on the run from Plymouth, and orders had been given for her to proceed alongside the Dockyard jetty to allow workmen to make important alterations to the mountings of the 14-in. guns.

Working day and night, the task would be completed in about forty-eight hours, in spite of the fact that the armoured roof of the turret had to be unriveted and removed before the work could be tackled.

"Rotten news, old man," was Eric Greenwood's greeting when the chums met on the following morning. "Seen to-day's paper? No? It concerns that slippery spy, Oberfurst."

"Not escaped?" asked Tressidar eagerly.

"Yes," replied the A.P. "And for once at least the authorities have acted promptly and have enlisted the aid of the Press. Here you are—a quarter of a column, with a detailed description of the wanted man."

The news was unfortunately only too true. The spy had been lodged in a cell in the county police-station, pending a decision as to whether he should be handed over to the civil, naval, or military authorities for trial.

A dull-witted policeman, whose activities hitherto had been restricted to "running in" tramps and vagrants and stopping motorists for exceeding a speed-limit that existed only in his imagination, had been detailed to keep watch on the prisoner. At four in the morning Oberfurst was apparently asleep. At half-past the constable, on looking through the observation hole in the door, saw the spy lying at full length on the floor with a gaping wound in his throat.

Instead of calling for assistance, the overzealous policeman unlocked the door with a view to rendering first aid, instead of which he received a blow over the head with the prisoner's supper-bowl that stretched him senseless across the threshold.

Not until six did the sergeant discover the still unconscious constable, and by that time Oberfurst had received a good hour and a half's start.

A piece of torn red silk handkerchief left in the vacant cell revealed the nature of the spy's ruse. He had tied the crimson fabric round his throat, and in the artificial light the deception was sufficiently realistic to delude the gaoler completely.

The papers, however, were convinced that recapture was the matter of a few hours only, as the district was being thoroughly searched by a strong force of police assisted by the military.

Eric Greenwood, well conversant with the rugged nature of Dartmoor, was of a different opinion, and Tressidar, who had occasion to remember the spy's cunning and daring, was obliged to admit his chum's arguments.

It was recognised, however, that the spy would have great difficulty in getting out of the country, should he wish to do so. Tressidar had previously reported that Oberfurst was in the habit of crossing to the Continent in the rôle of an American Red Cross emissary, and at all the seaports particular watch was kept upon every traveller. Ignorant of the fact that the deception had been discovered—unless the secret leaked out and came to the ears of the numerous German agents still active in Great Britain—Oberfurst might be tempted to risk another trip to Denmark or Holland.

This the authorities hoped he would do, for his capture would then be almost a certainty, while so long as he remained in the country he was a source of danger and anxiety to the realm.

The alterations to the "Anzac's" armament having been completed, the monitor proceeded to the back of the Wight to "calibrate." The gun trials being successful, she proceeded in company with two other monitors up Channel.

It was blowing fairly hard from the south-east'ard, and directly the three ungainly vessels cleared Spithead, they promptly showed what "wet" craft they were. The "Anzac's" low freeboard offered no protection from the "combers" that swept fore and aft, drenching the lofty bridge with blinding showers of spray.

When abreast of the "Royal Sovereign" lightship the wind veered a point or two until it was fairly abeam. The monitor now commenced to roll horribly, at one moment thrusting her bulging sides deeply into the sea, at another rearing until she showed her weather bilge-keel.

Had there been occasion to use her two 14-in. guns, it would have been impossible to train them with any degree of accuracy. Suitable for fair weather and in sheltered waters, the "Anzac," like the rest of her class, proved herself a mean substitute for the super-Dreadnoughts, whose bulk and draught rendered them admirably steady gun-platforms.

"Give me something with plenty of draught," thought Tressidar, as the "Anzac" gave an extra heavy roll. "A craft that will grip the water. If it gets much worse, she'll either have to cut and run for it, or else stand a good chance of going to Davy Jones."

"She'll take it quietly under the lee of the Belgian coast," remarked the navigating lieutenant, who had read his comrade's thoughts. "Especially if the wind veers a few points more."

Early next morning the "Anzac" dropped anchor within the Admiralty breakwater at Dover. Here a flotilla was assembling for the impending operations off the Flanders coast. One of the periodical visits to the German works at Zeebrugge was to be made on an imposing scale.

With the enormous sea-power at their disposal the British Admiralty could with little exertion drive the Huns away from the Belgian coast; but this for strategic reasons was undesirable. The Allied left wing rested on the sea. From the sea it could be fed and supplied with ammunition, and there was no danger of the flank being turned. On the other hand the Germans, not having command of the sea, were under obvious disadvantages. They were constantly open to the fire of British monitors. Thousands of troops had to hold their right flank without being able to fire a shot at the Belgian and British trenches, which terminated thirty or forty miles short of the Dutch frontier. Fears of an invasion under the guns of the British fleet compelled the Huns to hold the useless coast. Zeebrugge, on which they fixed their hopes as a base for their submarines, was no longer tenable. Its mole had been destroyed, its docks and canal basins rendered useless by the British guns. Without attempting to board a single soldier, the British kept a couple of German Army Corps literally on thorns.

At daybreak the monitors, accompanied by a number of destroyers and patrol craft, were within seven miles of the Belgian coast. The British tars made their preparations with grim earnestness and without undue haste.

Amongst the many services to be performed before the huge guns began to hurl their enormous projectiles at the foe, the buoyage of the adjacent neutral waters of Holland had to be made.

For this task a number of picquet-boats were detailed, each under the charge of a sub-lieutenant, who in turn were under the orders of a senior lieutenant. Skill in taking bearings was essential, since there was no desire to err even a cable's length on the neutral side.

Amongst the subs. detailed was Ronald Tressidar, who had to proceed to a point exactly on the three-mile limit, the position being "checked" by independent observations.

Lashed across the bows of the picquet-boat was a nun-buoy roughly three feet in diameter and four betwixt apex and apex. To the lowermost ring of the buoy, which was painted in red, white, and blue horizontal bands, was shackled fifty fathoms of light chain. At the other end of the chain was a "span" of heavier cable, each arm terminating in a fifty-six pound mushroom anchor.

A quarter of a mile to the nor'east'ard a Dutch cruiser was forging slowly through the water, her officers critically interested in the work of the British picquet-boats. The German batteries had refrained from opening fire, possibly on account of the proximity of the neutral cruiser, although it afterwards transpired that there was quite another reason for their passivity.

Keeping his picquet-boat running dead slow, bows on to the tide, so that the little craft was practically stationary over the ground, Tressidar determined his position.

"That's about it, sir, I think," he called out, addressing the senior officer, who was in another steamboat a short distance away.

"Near enough," replied the lieutenant. "At all events, I don't suppose the Dutchmen will quibble over it."

"Stand by to let go!" ordered the sub., speaking to the seamen for'ard. "Lower away roundly."

Mushroom anchor No. 1 disappeared with a splash, and having made sure that it was holding, Tressidar ordered easy ahead so as to drop the second anchor well clear of the former.

"Let go!"

The second anchor clattered overboard, taking with it the length of chain and the nun-buoy. Then, to the sub.'s surprise, the buoy, instead of floating sedately upon the surface, began to move rapidly through the water, impelled by some unseen force. So great was the rate of progress that the buoy frequently dragged beneath the surface, leaving a tell-tale swirl in its wake. Its direction was roughly south-west, which meant that it was being dragged *away* from neutral waters.

In a trice Tressidar grasped the situation.

"Full speed ahead, both engines!" he shouted, at the same time bidding the coxswain put the helm hard over and keep the picquet-boat dead on the buoy.

The lieutenant in the other steam-boat, having seen the nun-buoy dropped, was proceeding to another position when he, too, noticed that something was amiss, and promptly turned his craft and followed.

"Submarine foul of the bridle, sir, I think," shouted Tressidar through a megaphone.

The lieutenant had no doubt on that score, for being well astern, his steamboat was in the "wash" of the submerged craft, while the sub., being almost immediately above the submarine, was well in front of the disturbed water.

"Collar that buoy," sung out the sub., addressing the two bowmen. The latter, armed with long boathooks, poised themselves on the lurching foredeck, like harpooners waiting for a whale to appear.

"Got her, sir," shouted one of the seamen, as he deftly engaged the head of the boathook in the metal rung of the nun-buoy. "She's carrying too much way; I can't get her aboard."

"Hold her, both of you!" exclaimed Tressidar, fearful lest the ring would carry away and the chain disappear from sight.

The picquet-boat was certainly gaining upon the submerged craft, for in a little while the seamen reported that the strain on the cable was diminishing. At length, by dint of the united efforts of the two men, the nun-buoy and about two fathoms of chain were lifted on the deck of the boat, and a couple of turns taken round the pedestal of the for'ard gun.

"Got her, by Jove!" exclaimed the sub. triumphantly as he ordered the engines to be stopped and allowed the picquet-boat to be towed by the submerged craft.

The trapped submarine had attempted to steal towards the British monitors, and having taken her bearing through her periscope, had submerged in Dutch waters. This was obvious, since the buoy, actually on the line of demarkation, had been swept away from the neutral zone.

At first her commander had been ignorant of the unpleasant fact that he was towing a British picquet-boat in addition to dragging two mushroom anchors over the sandy bottom; but when he made the disconcerting discovery he altered his course and attempted to make for Zeebrugge. This he did blindly, since he dare not rise to show her periscope above the surface. By dint of careful helmsmanship the picquet-boat also turned and kept dead in the wake of her invisible tug. By this time a dozen steamboats belonging to the flotilla arrived upon the scene.

Presently the drag of the anchor made itself felt, for the bottom of the sea had changed from sand to stiff mud. Still ignorant of the nature of the obstruction, the German lieutenant-commander was under the erroneous impression that he had fouled the moorings of a mine. He therefore reversed engines and attempted to back clear of the entanglement.

The easing-off of the strain on the chain gave Tressidar warning. Promptly he ordered "easy astern," at the same time megaphoning his suspicions to the nearest steamboats.

Unprovided with explosive grapnels, the boats were unable to make an end of the submarine by detonating a charge of gun-cotton against her hull. The *coup de grâce* would have to be administered by a destroyer, and up to the present no attempt had been made by the boats to summon one to their assistance. Officers and men were thoroughly enjoying their novel duck hunt, and were in no hurry to finish the sport.

But when the submarine commenced to back astern the possibility of her disengaging herself from the toils became apparent. Quickly two picquet-boats dashed in opposite directions across her supposed track, each craft towing a stout grass-line astern, to which were attached lumps of metal in order to sink the otherwise buoyant fibre.

The operation was successful, for the rope, caught by the revolving propellers, wound round the shafting like coils of steel, until the electric motors were brought to a dead stop.

"That's done the trick," exclaimed the lieutenant gleefully. "We've collared the tin of sardines and now we'll have to wait for the tin-opener. What water have we?"

A cast of the lead gave eleven and a half fathoms with a bottom of mud mingled with shells and coarse sand. The submarine, finding herself disabled, had "sounded" and was resting on the bed of the sea.

"Suppose we couldn't hike her clear and tow her alongside the 'Anzac?'" hazarded Stephens, one of the subs. "A strain of the old ship's steam capstan would heave her to the surface in a brace of shakes. Pity to rip up the strafed hooker when we have a chance of collaring her intact, isn't it?"

"May as well try," replied the lieutenant, who was loth to destroy the craft that had given him a "run for his money." "Tide's rising. We'll lower a couple of bights of chain and see if we can shift her. I don't suppose she has a deadweight of more than a couple of tons—if that. Hulloa! The ball's opening."

The German batteries had hitherto deferred opening fire for fear of damaging the submarine, which had left Zeebrugge and had made a circuitous course through Dutch waters. Having allowed her ample time to get clear of the danger zone, the Huns had begun to fire.

"Hang it all!" ejaculated Tressidar. "We'll have to send for the destroyers after all to finish the job."

But there was yet a respite, for the "Anzac" and two of her consorts were standing in and interposing themselves between the shore and the boats. In a few minutes the action became general, the 14-in. guns hurling their shells with terrific precision upon the hostile batteries.

Slowly the tide rose, and with it the strain of the hawsers began to take up. Deeper sunk the hulls of the steamboats, but the submarine showed no signs of leaving her muddy bed.

Unconcernedly the boats' crews "stood by," though not without risk, for, although the monitors successfully drew the enemy's fire, ricochets from the German guns came perilously close.

Suddenly bubbles appeared on the surface alongside the "Anzac's" picquet-boat's quarter, and with them a metal cylinder shot up from beneath the water. To it was attached a light line and a canvas tally on which was roughly scrawled the word "Communication."

"Steady, there," cautioned Tressidar, as one of the seamen prepared to fish up the object with his boat-hook. "Pass the bight of the line under it."

Ordering easy ahead, the sub. allowed the picquet-boat to travel as far as the scope of chain permitted, at the same time taking a steady strain with the bight of the rope until the cylinder broke away from the line that led to the submarine. Nothing happened so far as an explosion was concerned, for the sub. had his suspicions that there might have been a ruse on the part of the trapped Huns.

The cylinder was roughly twelve inches in diameter and two feet in height. It was one of a regular pattern supplied to German submarines for sending communications to the surface in the event of the vessel meeting with an accident that prevented her from rising. The diameter, being exactly the same as that of the torpedo-tubes, enabled the canisters to be discharged through them by means of compressed air.

"What sort of a haul have you got there, Mr. Tressidar?" enquired the lieutenant. "H'm, communication, eh? Suppose it's all right. There's no detonating mechanism inside, I hope?"

"I'll see sir," replied the sub., and ordering his men to the other end of the boat, so as to be out of harm's way in the event of an explosion, he unscrewed a disc in one of the ends of the cylinder. Within was a sheet of paper on which was written, "We surrender. Spare our lives. We will ascend in ten minutes from now—6.15 a.m., mid-continental time. Max Falkenheim, Kapitan-leutnant."

"By Jove, sir, we've made a capture!" announced Tressidar, handing the document to his superior officer. "It's signed by that fellow Falkenheim, the man who tried to escape from Auldhaig."

"And was afterwards rescued by some of his precious compatriots when they blew in the wall of his prison. I remember," added the lieutenant grimly. "One of the foxiest rascals that ever sailed under the Black Cross ensign. Yes, by smoke, *dulce et decorum est* to lay that chap by the heels. Pity you cut that rope, though."

"Why, sir?" asked the sub.

"Because we cannot now reply to the strafed Huns. See, there's a telephonic receiver inside the cylinder, and the wires are led inside the rope. Writing that note was to make sure that we should know of their willingness to surrender in case we didn't notice the telephone. Confound that brute! That was a near one."

The lieutenant's remark was addressed to a huge shell that, having already ricochetted once, struck the water within twenty yards of the nearest steamboat, and rebounding again, finally disappeared in a column of spray a mile away. The displacement of water caused by the impinging of the projectile made the little flotilla rock violently, while officers and men were drenched by the deluge of foam.

"Hurry up! Hurry up!" muttered the lieutenant impatiently, by way of invoking the submerged "U" boat. "You've had a good ten minutes and we want to make your acquaintance."

A reply came in the form of a slight disturbance of the water. The submarine was "blowing" her water-ballast tanks.

Then slowly—so gradually that the picquet-boats had ample time to back clear—the surrendered craft rose to the surface, as if dubious of the fate that awaited her.

The conning-tower hatch was thrown open, and Kapitan Falkenheim appeared, followed by his unter-leutnant. Still in doubt as to their reception, they saluted their conquerors, who punctiliously returned the compliment. At the same time the crew issued from the after-hatch and formed up, holding their hands above their heads.

"Ve vos surrender—so," shouted Falkenheim.

"All right," replied the British lieutenant. "We accept your surrender, provided you do no damage to your craft."

"Dot is so," agreed the kapitan. "Nodings done is to der unterseeboot."

Skilfully two of the picquet-boats were manoeuvred and brought alongside the prize and the German officers and crew were taken off. The bridle of the moorings that had been the cause of the submarine's misfortune was cast off—it had simply caught to the for'ard horizontal rudders—and the vessel taken in tow.

A signal was made for a destroyer to take charge of the prize, since the steamboats were too small for the task. Their share of the business was over. The kudos was theirs; they were content to shift the burden upon their comrades of the destroyer-flotilla.

Suddenly a bomb hurtled through the smoke-laden air and exploded with a terrific detonation close to the leading picquet-boat. The frail craft literally crumpled up and disappeared in a cloud of smoke, leaving a sub-lieutenant and two badly wounded seamen struggling for dear life.

Overhead was a German double-fuselaged biplane, intent upon the destruction of the captured submarine so that she might not fall into the hands of the British.

Another bomb dropped, without effect beyond sending a fragment of metal through the funnel of the "Anzac's" steamboat. Regardless of the danger, other picquet-boats dashed up to rescue the survivors of the sunken craft, while from the approaching destroyer a steady stream of shells was directed upon the hostile battleplane.

Unconcernedly the German aviators hovered overhead, circling and dropping their lethal missiles with a set purpose, until a bomb alighted fairly upon the fore-part of the submarine.

When the cloud of smoke had drifted away, the chagrined British sailors saw their prize had been snatched from their grasp. She was sinking.

Slowly her bows dipped. Her stern rose until the tips of her twin propellers were visible, then with the violent inrush of water she disappeared from sight and narrowly missed taking with her the "Anzac's" picquet-boat that was engaged in towing her.

But retribution was at hand. Heading swiftly towards the German aircraft was a British seaplane. So intent were the Hun airmen upon their task of scattering the little flotilla that they failed to notice the danger until the seaplane opened fire with her automatic gun.

Vainly the German aviators attempted to circle and bring their fixed gun to bear upon their attackers. The British seaplane had the equivalent to the weather-gauge of the old days of sailing—the advantage of superior altitude.

Struck in a vital part, the enemy battleplane appeared to crumple up in mid-air. Falling like a stone, the machine struck the water a tangled mass of struts and canvas. Quickly a picquet-boat hurried to the aid of the foe, but she was too late.

The wreckage, upside-down, was kept from sinking by the only undamaged float. Strapped to their seats, the Hun pilot and observer, even if they had escaped the hail of bullets, were drowned like rats in a trap.

"It's not been so dusty," commented the lieutenant in charge of the steamboat flotilla as he gave the signal for the various boats to return to their respective ships. "Sorry we didn't get that 'U' boat into port. Still, there's one the less."

CHAPTER XXXI
MONITORS IN ACTION

Under a screen of smoke from a far-flung line of destroyers the "Anzac" picked up her steamboat's crew. Being under fire, she could not hoist in the picquet-boat. Wind and tide being favourable, the boat was cut adrift. Unless sunk by a chance shot, she could be recovered when the monitors withdrew at the conclusion of the bombardment.

"Fire-control platform, Mr. Tressidar," ordered the captain when the sub. reported himself in the conning-tower. "Mr. McTulloch has just been sent down—badly wounded. Look alive—we want the range of Battery 45 pretty quickly."

The monitor had ceased firing, owing to the smoke from the intervening destroyers. It also gave the guns a chance to cool, for they had been firing continuously for the last two hours.

Through the acrid-smelling smoke that wafted from below the sub. made his way to one of the oblique legs of the tripod mast. One glance showed that it was no longer possible to gain the lofty platform by that means, for the metal tube was torn half-way through by a shell, a dozen or more of the metal rungs of the ladder had been shorn away, and the steel was still unbearable to the hand owing to the heat generated by the terrible impact.

Fifteen feet above the sub.'s head dangled the frayed end of the rope by which the officer he was about to relieve was lowered from the fire-control platform. McTulloch, seriously wounded by a fragment of shell, had hardly gained the deck ere another sliver of steel had cut away his means of descent.

Crossing to the second inclined leg of the tripod mast, Tressidar found that the steel ladder was comparatively intact. The metal tubing of the mast had been dented in several places and perforated more than once. The metal, too, was hot, but not to the same extent as was the damaged leg.

Up through the drifting smoke the sub. made his way, the whole fabric of the mast trembling under the continuous discharge of the heavy ordnance.

When half-way up he felt a terrific jar, accompanied by a roar that outvoiced the noise of the guns. The smoke was torn by lurid flashes; fragments of metal hurtled past him or struck the mast with a sound like that of a heavy hammer clanging on an anvil.

Temporarily blinded by the glare and partly stunned by the concussion, Tressidar hung on like grim death. It was the triumph of muscles over mind, for the action was purely automatic. Out swung the tripod mast till the leg by which he was ascending was perpendicular, although normally inclined thirty degrees to the vertical line. From beneath him dense clouds of black and yellow smoke vomited from the superstructure, to the accompaniment of the crackling of flames and the groans of the wounded.

A hostile shell had scored a direct hit, partially wrecking the after-end of the superstructure, making a clean sweep of the gear, including the two anti-aircraft guns.

Tressidar was yet to know this. He was merely aware that the Huns had "got one home." He wondered whether he was still alive, until the mist cleared before his eyes and he found himself still clinging to the slippery rungs.

At last he reached the small platform at the head of the two sloping legs where they joined the higher and vertical "stick" of the tripod. Ten feet above him was the oval aperture leading to the fire-control platform. Hitherto the metal tube had formed a defence between him and the direct line of fire—a moral protection rather than a real one, since the metal was not proof against heavy shell-fire. But now, owing to the vertical rungs being on the fore-side of the mast, he was directly exposed to the fire of the shore batteries, and the Hun had a nasty habit of using shrapnel in conjunction with the high-explosive shells.

Another crash this time high above his head. For the moment he thought that the fire-control platform had been swept out of existence, for a raffle of spars, wire-rigging, and splinters of metal tumbled past him, some of the debris so close that he felt the "windage" on his cheeks.

Instinctively he ducked. When he raised his head again, he saw, to his relief, that his appointed post still remained—at least the "deck" of the fire-control platform was intact. The shell had struck the topmast, cutting it in twain and bringing the wireless aerials with the severed portions as it fell to augment the debris already lumbering the deck.

The destroyers had now forged ahead. Their smoke no longer screened the "Anzac" from the enemy. The monitor's guns, elevated to an angle of thirty degrees, were pointed shoreways, but neither sent forth its fifteen hundred pounds of death-dealing shell.

"Good heavens!" ejaculated Tressidar. "They're waiting for someone to register."

Spurred by the thought, he redoubled his energies, swarmed up the remaining rungs of the ladder, and squeezed through the narrow aperture on the deck of the fire-control station.

The sight which met his gaze was a terrible one. The metal roof had been ripped through as easily as if it had been made of cardboard; a dozen jagged holes were visible in the sides. The delicate instruments were shattered almost out of recognition.

Huddled in one corner was the gunnery lieutenant. At his feet lay a seaman; another was lying inertly across the body of the first. Seated on the floor was Eric Greenwood with his head resting on his drawn-up knees. The A.P. had been struck by a fragment of shell that had inflicted a nasty scalp-wound. Partly stunned by the concussion and blinded by the blood that streamed from the wound, he was just able to recognise his chum.

"A clean wipe out," he muttered weakly. "Everything blown to blazes. No use hanging on here, old man."

It was not a time for Tressidar to attend to his chum. Seizing the voice-tube communicating with the conning-tower, he reported the destruction of the registering gear. There was no response. He was talking to empty air, for both voice-tubes and telephone-wires had been severed; and since the target was invisible, the "Anzac's" huge guns were practically useless without the directing force in the fire-control station.

Risking death, Tressidar looked out over the side of his precarious perch. The monitor was circling slowly to port. The fire that had broken out in the superstructure was practically under control, thanks to the copious stream of water played upon it by the "Downton" pumps; but the deck looked a veritable shambles. Owing to her low, armoured freeboard the "Anzac" had escaped injury 'twixt wind and water, but almost everything on deck that was not protected had disappeared in a veritable holocaust. The single funnel, partly shot through, had buckled about fifteen feet close to the deck, the bent portion resting against the after-leg of the tripod mast and swaying dangerously with each roll of the ship.

The turret, scarred by several glancing hits, was still intact, although hardly a vestige of grey paint remained; while the two guns had shed their coats through the tremendous heat generated by the sustained firing. The bridge had been swept clean away; only a few bent and twisted stanchions remained. With its disappearance the top of the conning-tower was revealed, the massive steel plating showing signs of a complete fracture that extended from the edge about to the centre of the elongated, domed roof.

The sight was not an encouraging one. It was evident that the "Anzac" had received a terrible hammering and was no longer able to keep her station.

Tressidar next devoted his attention to the rest of the flotilla. The remaining monitors had fared considerably better. One, however, had lost her tripod mast, while damage to topmasts and wireless masts seemed pretty general. They had succeeded in breaking down most of the resistance on the part of the enemy, for with few exceptions the shore batteries were silent. Aided by wireless from the seaplanes that serenely hovered over the German defence, the monitors' guns had wrought terrific destruction upon the fixed positions amongst the sand-dunes. Most of the hostile shells came from mobile batteries, which were more difficult to locate; but as their guns were limited in weight and calibre, these were puny when compared with the monster weapons that the monitors had succeeded in silencing.

All this Tressidar took in almost at a glance. He had two tasks to perform: to rescue the A.P. from his perilous position and to inform the conning-tower of the state of the registering apparatus.

Mentally he compared the present situation with that on board the "Heracles," when he had to take Midshipman Picklecombe down from the fore-top. Eric Greenwood was a hefty man, whereas the midshipman was a mere slip of a youth. The "Anzac" was still under fire—a desultory one, but none the less nerveracking—while the "Heracles" was not subjected to the attentions of hostile shells when she was on the point of turning turtle. Again, there was a vast difference between the ratlines of the cruiser and the slippery steel rungs of the monitor's tripod mast.

"It's more than a one-man job," decided Tressidar reluctantly. "There isn't enough rope to lower him down. I'll nip below and get assistance."

The A.P. was now unconscious. He had fallen sideways, his head resting on his arm Even as Tressidar bent over him he became aware that the whole fabric of the fire-control platform was collapsing. The tripods, already damaged, had given way under the strain and were toppling overboard.

Throwing his left arm round Greenwood's inert body and hanging on like grim death to a steel handrail, Tressidar braced himself to meet his impending fate. The platform was inclining slowly but surely. Already his feet were wedged against the now almost horizontal side. Through the shattered roof he could see the water.

"There'll be a deuce of a smash," he thought. "Wonder if I can jump clear before we're trapped?"

The triple mast had buckled, but its fall was retarded by the strain upon the metal tubing. Instead of snapping off like a carrot, it was as though the tripod was held by a stiff and rusty hinge.

For perhaps five seconds the fall was retarded, then with a quick movement the bulky top-hamper lurched with a sickening movement until it brought up across the broad deck, with the metal box in which the sub. and his chum were penned hanging seven or eight feet over the side.

Bruised and shaken, Tressidar retained his alertness of mind and body. Without relaxing his grip upon his chum he scrambled through the partly demolished roof. It was the only way, since the aperture in the floor was too small for a hurried exit, especially when burdened with a helpless comrade.

Not knowing how he did it, the sub. found himself perched on the mast with the A.P. clasped tightly to his back. Now it was that his gymnastic training proved of service, for, in spite of his burden, he walked the outboard part of the now almost horizontal mast and dropped lightly to the "Anzac's" deck—the only unwounded executive officer of the crippled monitor.

CHAPTER XXXII
THE "ANZAC'S" DAY

On deck a few smoke-begrimed seamen were engaged in directing hoses upon the still smouldering wreckage of the superstructure; others were unbattening the armoured hatches and clearing away some of the debris.

Handing Greenwood to the care of two of the men, Tressidar made his way to the conning-tower, with the intention of reporting himself to the captain.

The entrance, protected by a section of armoured plate set vertically, was blocked with wreckage. The sub. put out his hand to steady himself as he surmounted the obstruction. To his surprise the metal wall was hot, almost unbearably so. The impact of the shell that had cracked the dome of the conning-tower had generated intense heat to the rest of the structure.

Within lay the bodies of the captain, first lieutenant, and three seamen. One of the latter had been struck on the temple with a sliver of steel that had entered the narrow slit in the armoured walls. The rest of the occupants were stunned, as effectually as if each had been hit on the head with a club, for blood was trickling from their mouths and nostrils.

It was no time to render assistance. A glance ahead showed that the "Anzac" was still describing a vast curve. Already she had turned more than nine points and was again drawing within range of the invisible shore-batteries.

Grasping the wheel of the steam steering-gear, the sub. attempted to steady the vessel on her helm. There was no response. The mechanism was no longer in order.

The voice-tube communicating with the engine-room was fortunately intact, although the telegraph-indicator had been shattered by the tremendous concussion. On enquiry, Tressidar learnt that the main steam-pipe of the port engine had been fractured by a shell that had entered the engine-room, although the main force of the explosion had been directed against the coal in the wing bunkers. Down below, the artificer engineers and engine-room ratings were toiling desperately, placing copper sheathing on the fractured pipe and making it secure by means of "lagging" and rope.

Only the starboard engine was running, with the result that, in the absence of control of the helm, the monitor was circling aimlessly.

The sub. tried another voice-tube. To his satisfaction he was answered by the chief quartermaster.

"Hand wheel party present?" enquired Tressidar.

"All present, sir," was the reply.

"Then connect up and stand by."

Quickly the change was made, and once more the battered monitor was under control.

By this time Tressidar had discovered that he was actually in command. Reports from the carpenter's crew revealed the satisfactory news that the "Anzac" was still sound below the water-line, while the engine-room staff expressed their belief that the defects in their department could be temporarily made good within half an hour.

Men were busily engaged in ridding the deck of the wreckage of the tripod mast, which they did by the simple yet drastic expedient of completely severing the legs by means of gun-cotton charges.

Although the training-gear of the turret was undamaged, a glancing shell had snapped six feet off the chase of one of the 14-inch guns, rendering it useless for further service. The other gun was intact, but so furious had been the firing that only three rounds remained.

With the destruction of the aerials and the dislocation of the delicate apparatus, communication by wireless was no longer possible; nor was there any spar from which a signal might be flown. Sound signals, too, were useless, since the deafening cannonade between the other monitors and the shore outvoiced all other noises.

A patrol-boat presently dashed up and drew close alongside the damaged monitor, and asked if any assistance were required.

"You might take our wounded," replied Tressidar. "We've a number of casualties And we should like instructions from the flagship. No; we are still under control and capable of making five knots. There is no necessity for a ship to be detached to tow us."

As quickly as possible the wounded officers and men were transhipped, the patrol-vessel meanwhile wirelessing the senior officer and requesting instructions for the "Anzac," stating that she was no longer able to resume her station in action.

The reply was: "Proceed to Harwich under own steam." There was no mention of a destroyer being sent as escort.

When, at length, the engine-room repairs were effected, the sorely battered monitor, looking little better than a mass of scrap-iron above the low deck, forged slowly ahead on her homeward voyage. The survivors, having washed and changed, were piped to dinner, the principal item of the menu being "Zeppelins in the clouds," namely, sausages served with gravy.

"Rather ominous," thought Tressidar amusedly, as he overheard the men discussing the food "Ominous for the Huns, though."

Two hours later the rest of the flotilla was out of sight, although the dull rumble of gunfire proclaimed that the bombardment was still maintained. At four in the afternoon the North Hinder Lightship was sighted. From that point westwards there were no sea-marks, the Galloper and other light vessels off the Suffolk coast having been withdrawn.

Slowly the "Anzac" steamed, her rate being considerably less than Tressidar had anticipated. With the loss of the major portion of the funnel and the weak spot in her main steam-pipe her horse-power had fallen appreciably.

Night came on and with it a mist. Stellar observations were no longer possible. Navigation depended solely upon dead reckoning on a compass course and the constant use of the lead.

At midnight Tressidar, having previously instructed the quartermaster of the watch to awaken him should anything occur, lay down on the deck in the wake of the conning-tower. In less than a minute he was sleeping fitfully, the drums of his ears throbbing with the reaction after the deafening cannonade.

It seemed to him that he had been asleep but a few seconds when he was awakened by a dull, grinding noise and the quartermaster shouting to the engine-room for "hard astern."

The "Anzac" was aground.

"The men in the chains reported fourteen fathoms not a minute ago, sir," said the quartermaster. "The water must have shoaled like the roof of a house."

The hull was throbbing under the pulsations of the engines as the twin screws lashed cascades of phosphorescent water past the monitor's bulging sides. The ship showed no tendency to slide off. She had struck hard.

The sub. ordered the engines to stop. He knew that it wanted two hours to low water. Further attempts to get the monitor off must be deferred until after quarter flood, which would be at four forty-five in the morning.

Fortunately the sea was calm. There was little wind. At some distance away the sullen rollers were breaking heavily on the shoal. Since the monitor was not making water and lay on the lee side of the submerged bank, there was little danger. Provided the wind did not spring up, she would float without damage with the rising tide.

But the unpleasant fact was apparent that Tressidar had run his ship ashore—a far more serious case in the eyes of My Lords than if the monitor had been lost in action.

With dawn the mist dispersed. By observations the sub. discovered that the "Anzac" had bumped on the Galloper Shoal. He had not made sufficient allowance for the cross set of the tide, and instead of passing between the Outer Gabbard and the Galloper, the monitor had "smelt out" the latter, with ignominious if not serious results.

No other vessel was in sight. With her boats destroyed, the "Anzac" had no means of laying out an anchor astern. Even if she had, the steam capstans were useless, having suffered with the rest of the deck gear during the bombardment. The monitor would have to get off under her own steam.

Tressidar was still searching the horizon with his telescope when one of the seamen raised a warning shout:

"Zepp. dead ahead, sir."

There was no mistaking the form of the immense rigid airship. Flying at a height of two thousand feet, she was heading in a direction that would bring her almost immediately above the stranded monitor. The belated night-raider, returning from a visit to the Midlands, had allowed dawn to overtake her before she was more than a few miles from the Suffolk coast.

There was little time to be lost, for the hostile airship was moving through the air at a rate of nearly fifty miles an hour. Without doubt she would do her best to destroy by means of bombs or aerial torpedoes the stranded British monitor.

At the word of command the gun's crew manned the sole workable weapon—the 14-inch turret-gun. Up from the magazine by means of the hydraulic loading-tray a huge shell was hoisted. It was one of the remaining three—a new type of gigantic shrapnel, similar to those fired with disastrous results on the Turks by the super-Dreadnought "Queen Elizabeth." For once, at least, a 14-inch gun was to be used as an anti-aircraft weapon.

Under the sighting hood the captain of the turret directed the training of the huge but docile piece of ordnance. The target was an easy one as regards bulk, for the gun-layer could plank shell after shell with unerring accuracy into an invisible target fifteen miles away; but, on the other hand, there was the speed and great elevation of the Zeppelin to be taken into consideration.

Anxiously Tressidar watched the chase of the sixty odd tons of metal, as the muzzle of the weapon, moving as smoothly as a billiard cue, reared itself into the air. For an instant it seemed to hesitate, then with a flash and a deafening roar the gun spoke. A mushroom of black smoke, 'twixt which the course of the projectile could be followed, leapt from the recoiling weapon.

"Too high," muttered the sub. disappointedly, as the trail of smoke from the tracer of the shell mounted higher and higher, until it looked to be far above the flimsy target.

The next instant he felt like cheering madly and doing an impromptu hornpipe, for the shell had exploded above and within a very short distance of the doomed Zeppelin. Had it done so at ten times the distance the result would have been much the same.

Literally riddled with fragments of metal and smitten with the full force of the blast from the explosion, the airship began to drop with fearful rapidity, her ends curling upwards like a writhing worm. Then, like a flash of lightning, the whole of the buckled fabric burst into flames, the disintegrated fragments falling with a series of splashes into the sea.

For quite a minute after the collapse of the air-raider there was silence on board the monitor. The dramatic suddenness of the whole affair could at first hardly be realised. Then a rousing cheer burst from the throats of the depleted ship's company. The "Anzac" had created a war-record—bringing down a Zeppelin with a 14-inch gun.

CHAPTER XXXIII
A SPLINTER OF SHELL

Almost before the cheering died away an alert seaman raised the warning cry of "Submarine on the starboard quarter."

He had just caught a glimpse of the pole-like periscopes of a submarine ere they vanished beneath the surface of the placid sea.

Of her nationality there could be no doubt. A British one would have had no occasion to submerge, since the stranded monitor flew the White Ensign from a spar temporarily set on end and lashed to a stanchion in lieu of her demolished ensign-staff.

The "U" boat was evidently standing by to cover the flight of the Zeppelin should any cruiser stand in pursuit, for the airship was flying comparatively low, instead of the usual altitude of ten thousand feet, when annihilated by the "Anzac's" fire. Having witnessed the destruction of the Zepp., the "U" boat had approached the monitor with the intention of avenging the loss of the air-raider. She had no idea that the "Anzac" was aground, for by this time she was almost waterborne and lay on practically an even keel; while, since the whole of the sandbank was submerged, there was no indication of shallow water.

Nevertheless it seemed as if the monitor would fall an easy prey to the German torpedo, for there was not a single gun that could be brought to bear in the direction of the submarine.

Tressidar was not kept long in suspense. The feather-like wake of the approaching weapon was clearly visible as the torpedo made unerringly towards the immovable target.

"Stand clear there, aft!" shouted the sub.

Those of the crew who had been watching the approach of the submerged weapon promptly scurried across the deck so as to be as far from the point of impact as possible. Of serious damage to the monitor there was little fear, owing to the complex nature of her bulging sides. The loss of twenty feet of side plating would matter but little, since the buoyancy of the monitor would not be appreciably altered.

But the expected explosion did not occur. Set to run at a depth of twelve feet, the torpedo struck the sandy bottom at a distance of between eighty and a hundred yards short of the target.

For another twenty yards it ploughed through the sand, until its delicate rudders were damaged by tearing through the comparatively hard substance. Then with an erraticity that torpedoes have been known to display, the weapon made a sharp curve, and rising to the surface continued its undecided way like a hydroplane, its course being marked by a line of spray in its wake.

Again the monitor's crew cheered—this time ironically. The shoal that had proved a stumbling-block was now guarding the stranded craft in no uncertain manner.

After a lapse of a quarter of an hour the submarine cautiously poked her periscopes above the surface, although quite half a mile from the spot where she had previously dived. Once more she fired a torpedo, with almost the same result, for instead of turning on impact with the shoal, the weapon struck nose first into the sand and remained there.

The commander of the "U" boat was evidently puzzled. He could not understand why the two torpedoes should have missed the mark; he was also at a loss to account for the fact that the British vessel had not attempted to open fire.

Nevertheless he was wary. With the idea of drawing the monitor's fire, he released one of the communication buoys, towing it a hundred yards astern of the submerged craft. The resistance of the buoy caused a decided feather of foam that could not escape the eyes of the crew of the monitor. At the end of five minutes the buoy was drawn under the surface and taken on board the "U" boat again, by means of an automatic winding machine and a system of "air lock" doors. Examination showed that the relatively easy target was untouched.

Hence the commander of the German submarine came to the correct conclusion that the monitor was not capable of defence. Again the periscopes appeared above the surface and a prolonged examination of the British vessel was made. The German officers soon came to the decision that it was safe to rise and attack the monitor by shell fire, provided the "U" boat kept on the starboard quarter of her enemy.

"There she is, sir!" reported a petty officer to Tressidar, as the "U" boat rose to the surface at a distance of nearly two miles off.

Glasses were brought to bear upon the submarine, and it was then seen that the Germans were preparing to use their two "disappearing" guns. To reply was impracticable, for the submarine was well beyond effective rifle-range, and the sole serviceable turret gun could not be trained sufficiently abaft the beam to bear upon the enemy.

"Action stations!" was the order. Since the crew were without present means of offence or defence, all they could do was to take cover behind the armoured parts of the ship and "take their gruelling "; but every moment the tide was rising, and before long it would be possible to back off the shoal, turn and bring the gun to bear upon the Hun.

With little delay the "U" boat opened fire. The first half-dozen shells flew either above or wide of the monitor, but presently the small but relatively powerful missiles began to find a mark.

From his post in the conning-tower, which, in spite of the fractured dome, was proof against the small-calibre shells, Tressidar watched his opportunity. He made no effort to get the "Anzac" off the shoal until he felt certain that she would glide off without difficulty. Then, he hoped, there would be time to train the 14-inch gun on the submarine before she had a chance to trim for diving—and only two rounds for that particular weapon remained.

The gun, already loaded, was trained as far aft as possible, so that the moment the monitor swung round it could be brought to bear.

A leadsman, risking the flying fragments of shell, ran forward and, throwing himself at full length upon the low fo'c'sle, took soundings.

"By the mark two less a quarter," he announced.

"Good," muttered the sub. "That's what we want."

An order to the engine-room and the twin propeller began to churn up water and sand. With hardly a jar the monitor glided astern—and struck again, this time by the heel.

"Full speed ahead port engine; starboard, easy astern," shouted the sub. through the voice-tube; then, in his eagerness to see whether the vessel would answer to her helm, he left the shelter of the conning-tower.

The next instant he felt as if he had hit his head violently against a door-post. Thousands of lights danced before his eyes. Vainly he clutched for support. His fingers closed upon empty air. He was dimly conscious of falling on the deck and of someone throwing his arms around his waist, and then everything became a blank.

When Tressidar recovered consciousness he found himself lying on a cot that had been brought upon deck and lashed down on the aft-side of the shell-torn superstructure.

Standing by were two sick-bay stewards, who, in the absence of a doctor, had been attending to their youthful "skipper."

Almost the first thing of which the sub. became aware was the fact that the monitor was again under way. The steady roll combined with the subdued thud of the engines proclaimed the pleasing news. Also the firing had ceased, which tended to prove that the "U" boat had either been sunk or had taken herself off.

"Have we settled her?" were Tressidar's first words.

"She's done for, sir," replied the second quartermaster. "Only——"

"Only what?" asked the sub. anxiously, for the face of his informant had disappointment written on every feature.

"We were just out of it, sir. Turret gun was about to bear when the 'U' boat went bang. One of our seaplanes did the trick, sir; only we were within a brace of shakes of plugging her with a 14-inch shell at the same time. Didn't spot her at that distance until she planked a bomb fairly on the strafed Hun's conning-tower—and she was only about a hundred and fifty feet up when she let rip. That's the worst of those seaplanes, sir; always nosing in where they ain't wanted, if you don't mind my saying so," he added apologetically and at the same time with a tinge of professional jealousy.

Tressidar smiled. By so doing he became aware of a pain shooting through his head.

"Well, what have I got?" he asked, addressing one of the sick-bay staff.

"Steel splinter embedded in right femur——"

"Right what?" repeated the sub. anxiously. "That's the right thigh, I believe? But my head?"

"All right, sir, as far as we know," reported the man. "No doubt it is the sudden shock to the system, sir; I've known it like that before to-day. We've had to leave the splinter in the wound, sir, but we'll soon have a surgeon on board. We're just approaching Harwich. We've exchanged signals and asked for medical assistance."

"There's a steamboat making for us now, sir, added the quartermaster.

"Any casualties?" enquired Tressidar.

"Five men down, sir. The last half a dozen shells from that submarine tickled us up a lot."

"Very good; see that the doctor attends to them first," said the sub. "Don't say a word about me until they have been dealt with."

"But we have already reported that you've been hit, sir."

"Then annul that part of the signal," ordered Tressidar firmly. "I'm quite comfortable. Now, remember, the men are to be seen first."

By the time the busy fleet-surgeon was free to attend to the sub.'s injuries, Tressidar was far from comfortable. Hot, throbbing pains shot through the wounded thigh. From the waist upwards he felt cold and shivery. More than once he felt as if he were on the point of losing consciousness again.

"It's no use disguising the fact, Mr. Tressidar," said the doctor in answer to the sub.'s point-blank question. "You have had a narrow escape. But for the prompt attention of these men in checking the flow of blood from the femoral artery you would have bled to death."

"Shall I lose my leg?" asked Tressidar, his mind filled with apprehension at the possibility—not so much of being a cripple, as of having to sever his connection with the Service.

"I think not.... No, no operation until we get him ashore.... Yes, up to our eyes in work... quite a big action... we had them this time... Our casualties heavy.... Shotley full up... had to send for additional staff."

These disjointed sentences were what Tressidar overheard in a conversation between the fleet-surgeon and his assistants. "Quite a big action." Not, of course, The Day, but a fairly decent scrap somewhere in the North Sea.

"Hurrah!" exclaimed the sub.

"Here, this won't do," remonstrated the doctor. But the reproof fell upon deaf ears. The sub. had relapsed into unconsciousness.

CHAPTER XXXIV
EXIT OBERFURST

Von Oberfurst awaited the dawn of day with considerable trepidation. For the present he was a free man, but his position was far from enviable. He was hunted, that he knew. Already a hue-and-cry had been raised and the desolate moors were being searched with the utmost diligence and precision.

Having broken out of the prison cell, he had gained the outskirts of the little village and had made his way in a north-easterly direction with the intention of falling-in with the escaped German officers. Soon he was lost in the mist that still hung heavily around the tors. He had neither map nor compass. Both had been taken from him when taken into custody. Without them he was like a ship without a rudder, and having implicitly relied upon them in his previous adventures, he realised his helplessness.

He was hungry and thirsty. The meagre fare provided at the police-station overnight was already forgotten. Food was not to be had, but for drink there were the many moorland rivulets that trickled down to join the waters of the silvery Dart and other rivers that drain the heights of Dartmoor.

At length he was forced to come to the conclusion that he must hide until nightfall—sixteen hours of mental and physical strain. To attempt to proceed in daylight was to court disaster.

Looking around, the spy discovered a number of irregularly shaped rocks partly hidden by bracken. Towards this spot he made, treading warily on stony ground so that his footsteps might not leave traces on the dew-sodden grass. Then carefully, without breaking so much as a solitary stem of bracken, he crept into his place of concealment.

He found himself in a narrow space enclosed by four masses of rock, and sheltered from the sun by the tall bracken. There were hundreds, thousands even, of similar clusters of rocks scattered about this part of the country, where a man provided with food and water could hide for days with little fear of discovery. From his place of concealment he could command an extensive stretch of moorland without showing his head above the skyline. So far as he could see—for the mists were now dispersing—there were no signs of human habitation.

He still retained his automatic pistol. Taken from him at the same time as were his other belongings, it had been carelessly left on the kitchen table in the constable's cottage, and Oberfurst had taken particular pains to repossess himself of the weapon ere he shook the dust of his cell from off his feet.

Having taken stock of his surroundings, the spy stretched himself on the ground, lying on his right side with his face pillowed on his arm. His ear almost touching the ground enabled him to detect sounds quicker than he might otherwise have done. He was badly in need of a rest and sleep, especially as he was contemplating another all-night tramp; but he knew that he was a noisy sleeper, and on that account he feared to run the risk.

Presently a dog barked. The sound came from a long distance. It was a long-drawn, deep bark, that boded no good to the fugitive.

"Those English have brought bloodhounds to track me," he muttered. "Well, I can hold out until I have only one cartridge left. They will never again take me alive."

At almost the next moment he felt himself seized by an almost uncontrollable panic. He started to crawl from his lair and run blunderingly and aimlessly across the open moors, if only to put a greater distance between him and the deep-baying hounds.

On second thoughts he decided to remain and hold his own. Nearer and nearer came the unpleasant sounds, until the spy was able to see the animals.

There were two enormous bloodhounds, unmuzzled, but held in leashes by two powerfully built men, whose heated faces and laboured breathing bore testimony to the strength and speed of the powerful brutes. Behind them rode a sub-inspector and three policemen, neither of whom was armed so far as the spy could see.

Unerringly the bloodhounds followed the invisible track taken by the fugitive until they reached a spot at less than eighty yards from his place of concealment. Here the animals began circling, sniffing the while and almost dragging the arms of their custodians from their sockets.

Breathlessly Oberfurst kept watch. He remembered that he had crossed a small stream close to the place where the hounds were held up. By so doing he had unwittingly destroyed the scent.

"The first stream we've had to cross, worse luck," said the inspector. "I had my doubts concerning the brutes, and now we're baulked."

"They'll pick up the scent on the other side, sir, never fear," rejoined one of the keepers confidently. "It will be a hundred pounds easily earned."

"The fellow's no fool," declared the inspector. "He struck this stream on purpose. I'll warrant he's waded a hundred yards or more up the brook on purpose to do us."

"I wish I had," thought the spy, regarding the dogs with returning apprehension, for he could distinctly see the bloodshot eyes, their heaving, overhung, foam-flecked jaws, and the ivory whiteness of their massive teeth.

"Down stream I should think, sir," said another policeman. "He'll be making for the coast. Ten to one that's the reason why a German submarine was seen hanging about off Bolt Tail."

"Perhaps," admitted the inspector. "In any case it's no use wasting time. Lift one of the brutes over, Tomlins; don't let his feet touch the water. Keep the other this side and see if either picks up the scent afresh."

In his excitement Oberfurst fingered the sensitive trigger of his automatic pistol, remembering only just in time that even the slightest touch was sufficient to fire the weapon. Then, placing the pistol on the ground within easy reach, he waited.

At first the hound that had been taken across the stream showed signs of retrieving the scent. Down went his head, up went his tail he tugged furiously at the leash.

"Good old boy!" exclaimed the inspector encouragingly; but he was doomed to disappointment, for the animal, after making two or three circles, came to a standstill with his nose in the air.

"Thought so," continued the inspector. "The fellow's waded along the stream. Hard lines!—we stood a good chance before the military step in. I hear that nearly five hundred men are being sent from Okehampton and a whole mob of Boy Scouts."

The police, accompanied by the hounds, moved away, disappearing from sight in a southerly direction. Oberfurst had obtained yet another respite.

During the heat of the day he lay close, at times dosing fitfully. Tormented by the extreme warmth of the atmosphere, for there was not a breath of wind and the sun beat pitilessly down upon the rock, famished and parched, he endured and waited for dusk.

During the afternoon numbers of soldiers in extended order passed by. Two of them came within ten paces of the spy's lair, keeping their eyes fixed, not upon their immediate surroundings, but on the distant expanse, as if they expected to get a glimpse of the fugitive as he ran across the gorse-covered moor.

Towards seven o'clock the air echoed and re-echoed with the shrill blast of whistles. The troops, or at any rate the bulk of them, were being recalled. To his intense satisfaction, Oberfurst saw hundreds of rabbits emerging from their burrows and frisking in the slanting rays of the sun. That was almost an infallible sign that they had little to fear from human beings.

Cautiously the fugitive emerged from his place of concealment. His limbs were stiff with remaining for hours in a confined space. Deftly he massaged the muscles of his arms and legs, until he felt their suppleness returning; then, crouching on all-fours, he stole towards the brook that had already done him good service.

Soon he was lapping the clear, running water, taking in copious draughts that cooled his parched throat and gave renewed vitality to his exhausted frame.

"Hands up!"

The words, rapped out peremptorily and unexpectedly, took Oberfurst by surprise. Starting to his feet, he obeyed the order, fully expecting to find himself surrounded by a cordon of khaki-clad men.

Instead, he was confronted by a solitary figure clad in the uniform of a scoutmaster. His challenger was a man of more than middle age, bordering, perhaps, on his sixtieth year. He was tall, sparely built, but well knit and erect. His tanned features formed a striking contrast to his light grey hair.

"You are, I presume, the wanted spy, Otto Oberfurst," continued his captor. "You are, indeed, wise not to attempt to give trouble, for there is plenty of assistance at hand."

As he spoke the scoutmaster produced a whistle. Before he could place it to his lips the spy's arm dropped. Like a flash he had his captor covered with his pistol.

"It is now your turn to 'hands up,'" sneered the German. "Obey instantly, or you are a dead man."

"Perhaps," rejoined the other coolly. "Meanwhile I will do my utmost to raise an alarm. If I fail, your pistol-shot will complete the work."

Looking the spy straight in the face the scoutmaster again raised his whistle. In a flash Oberfurst realised the truth of his opponent's remarks. After all, he was not "out" with the intention of committing unnecessary murder. His sole anxiety was to break through the cordon and put a safe distance between him and the bleak heights of Dartmoor.

Throwing away the pistol, Oberfurst folded his arms.

"You have won," he remarked simply.

"To avoid further trouble, I will take possession of this little toy," said the scoutmaster.

He stepped forward a couple of paces and bent to pick up the weapon. As he did so, the spy suddenly lashed out with his left foot. Skilled in the Continental style of boxing, he knew exactly how to gauge his distance and kick with the greatest effect.

Taken completely by surprise, the luckless Englishman, who in all good faith had accepted the spy's surrender, dropped like a log, before he had time to utter a sound.

Coolly Oberfurst regained possession of his pistol, fully expecting to find himself assailed on all sides. Agreeably disappointed, he proceeded to strip his unconscious victim of his coat, gaiters, and hat. This done, he dragged the scoutmaster to the spot where the spy had lain in concealment.

"He will not recover consciousness for several hours—if he does at all," soliloquised the spy, with a shrug of his shoulders. "That is his affair, not mine. Now I must assume the character of officer of Boy Scouts. I wish I were more certain of my new duties."

For a couple of hundred yards Oberfurst proceeded cautiously, then, drawing himself erect, he set off at a swinging pace across the moors. Bluff, not concealment, was to be his watchword.

It was now dusk fast emerging into night. Once more the evening mists were rising from the swamps in the valleys. Overhead the stars were beginning to show against the declining after-glow in the north-western sky.

For nearly a couple of miles Oberfurst proceeded without interruption. Everything seemed absolutely still, save for the swish of his boots and gaiters through the bracken. It was as if his pursuers had finally abandoned their quest in the belief that the fugitive had contrived to get clear of the district.

Suddenly a whistle resembling the call of the peewit sounded from a spot almost in front, and out of the gorse rose half a dozen youthful forms clad in the well-known Boy Scout "war-paint."

The spy's first inclination was to take to his heels, but, remembering his resolve and noting the diminutive size of the lads, he stopped.

"What troop do you belong to?" he asked.

"The Endscoombe First, sir," replied the patrol leader. "We're the Peewits."

"Thank goodness I've fallen in with some scouts," rejoined the spy. "I have lost touch with my troop—the Third Oakendene. I suppose you have seen nothing of them?"

The patrol-leader, a sharp-witted Devon lad of about fifteen, "smelt a rat." For one thing, he had never heard of the Oakendene Troop; for another, he was fairly conversant with the disposition of all the scout troops engaged in assisting the military and police to scour the moors.

"I think we can help you, sir," he replied, almost without hesitation. "At any rate, we'll put you on the right path. Will you take charge of the patrol?"

The question was a "feeler." It had the desired effect, for in giving words of command the spy gave himself away. His knowledge of British army drill was comprehensive, but of scouting he knew practically nothing.

The rest of the boys "tumbled" to their patrol-leader's ruse. Without showing suspicion at the unusual orders, they set off in Indian file.

"It's a strange thing that we should lose our scoutmaster and find another who has lost his troop," remarked the patrol-leader. "Of course we may find him a little further on. We're nearly at the Three Bridges road now."

"So I believe," rejoined Oberfurst, whose keen ear had detected the steady tramp of armed men. "In that case you've taken me out of my way. No, I don't blame you, but I'll say 'Good night.'"

He stopped abruptly, determined to give his attentive companions the slip—in a seemingly casual manner if possible, failing that to make a dash for safety.

The patrol-leader waited no longer. A warning succession of blasts upon his whistle rent the night air. Oberfurst found himself confronted by a ring of staves.

His hand flew to his pocket. The patrol-leader caught the dull glint of metal. Like a flash his staff descended upon the spy's wrist. The pistol fell to the ground, while like a pack of hounds the boys threw themselves upon the German.

Of what happened during the next few seconds none of the scouts had a decided opinion. All they knew was that while they were attempting to secure the man as he lay kicking and struggling on the ground there was a muffled report. One of the lads, uttering an involuntary cry of pain, clapped his left hand to his right arm. The spy, after writhing convulsively for a brief instant, ceased to struggle.

Alarmed by the whistle and the pistol-shot, a number of soldiers and police hurried up to find their "man" lying insensible on the ground and the scouts rendering first aid to their wounded comrade.

"Here's the spy, sir," declared the patrol-leader, addressing an army officer. "He shot one of us, so we had to stun him."

The lieutenant bent over the prostrate Hun and flashed a torch-light in his face.

"You're right, sonny," he said. "It means a hundred pounds to you scouts. Hulloa, though! You need not have troubled to belabour him with your poles. He's as dead as a doornail."

Otto Oberfurst had kept his vow not to be taken alive. In the mêlée he had regained possession of his pistol and had sent a shot clean through his brain. The bullet in passing out had lodged in the arm of one of the scouts.

A police inspector joined in the examination.

"Yes," he agreed; "he's saved a file of soldiers a job."

"And has done a pack of lawyers out of a fat sum," added the lieutenant grimly.

CHAPTER XXXV
TRESSIDAR'S REWARD

In the well-kept grounds of a naval hospital, far removed from the danger-zone, where Zepp. alarms were unknown and the angry buzz of raiding Taubes did not disturb the peaceful atmosphere, two bronzed but obviously "crocked" officers were sunning themselves in comfortable camp-chairs.

Ronald Tressidar had only just been able to dispense with the aid of crutches, and with the assistance of a stout stick and the shoulder of a fellow-patient he could get about the grounds without much difficulty.

Eric Greenwood, although outwardly the "fitter" of the twain, was still suffering from the effect of the injuries sustained in the monitor's fire-control platform. His fate was literally in the balance, for he was about to undergo another "medical board," upon the finding of which his retention in His Majesty's Navy depended.

Tressidar, too, was chafing under the enforced delay. Complete rest after strenuous activity afloat is all very well, but in time it palls horribly. The call of the sea, strong even in the far-remote times of peace, was now irresistible. Rumours of activity on the part of the German fleet had grown persistent until the sub. realised the possibility of The Day being pulled off while he was still cooling his heels in the grounds of the naval hospital.

"Yes," declared the A.P., throwing the morning paper on the grass beside his chair, "I'm bored stiff. We want something to cheer us up. Solid good news, and no more silly tosh in the shape of purely hypothetical statements of what may happen if something else doesn't."

"What's upset your apple-cart now, old man?"

"Look at the news. Another hostile cruiser raid, followed, presumably, by a letter from an amateur Lord of the Admiralty expressing regret for the damage done to the bombarded town and a promise that if the enemy try it again they'll feel sorry for themselves. Ten days ago, too, the Press was deriding an official Turkish communiqué. Now, as in previous cases, the report proves to be absolutely correct. It makes a fellow feel particularly savage, doesn't it?"

Tressidar shrugged his shoulders.

"Because we are out of it," he replied. "Out there, when we are doing our individual bit, we had the satisfaction of knowing that whenever a chance occurred we were too many for the Huns. We don't advertise; we are not allowed to let others advertise for us, still the work goes on. Out of touch with events afloat, we are apt to be influenced by the opinion of the great and uninformed British Public. Still, I admit, a little good news would be welcome. Here's Fuller to cheer you up," he continued, as the flight-sub. came limping up over the grass. "Well, my festive bird, how goes it?"

The flight-sub. had not been long in following his former companion in captivity. It was he who had bombed the submarine just as the refloated monitor was about to bring her remaining 14-inch gun to bear upon the "U" boat. Having accomplished this feat, Fuller flew back to Harwich to summon assistance to the badly damaged "Anzac," and, by the irony of fate, had slipped from the second rung of a ladder on board the parent ship and had fractured his ankle.

"What's that?" demanded the newcomer as he tendered his cigarette-case. Our A.P. requires cheering up?"

"Yes; he's developed a bad grousing attack," replied Tressidar. "Got it badly, don't you know."

"Fact," agreed Greenwood. "I never was like it on board, was I, Tress.? It must be this rotten inaction."

"No, you haven't time to have the blues out there," agreed the sub. "Afloat we're fed on actions; but here we eke out a miserable existence on words. Yes, Fuller, I think we want cheering up."

"Let me begin," said the flight-sub. "Now, this is official. Message just come through. Listen: Yesterday morning in thick weather one of our destroyer flotillas came in touch with some hostile cruisers. The latter broke off action, but not before H.M.T.B.D. 'Ypres,' Lieutenant-commander Terence Aubyn, D.S.O., succeeded in torpedoing a large cruiser supposed to be the 'Opelm.'"

"Lucky blighter, Aubyn!" remarked Tressidar enviously. "I've met him once or twice. Wish to goodness I had been shipmates with him in that scrap."

"And now for a personal matter," continued Fuller. "For the simple reason that I merely did what I am paid to do, they've slung a little decoration at me. I've been given the Distinguished Service Cross for busting up a 'U' boat that was trying to strafe you, but couldn't."

In the midst of the blunt and hearty congratulations of his chums, Fuller suddenly noticed a nursing sister approaching.

"I'm off," he exclaimed hurriedly. "There'll be a deuce of a breeze if she finds that I'm out here without that fakealorum caboodle of a wheeled chair. Come along, Greenwood; bear a hand. S'long, Tress.; don't give the show away."

The A.P. obligingly did as the flight-sub. had requested and Tressidar was left alone.

A light footfall caused him to look up. Standing a few feet away was Doris Greenwood, who, of course by a pure coincidence, had been transferred from Auldhaig to the south-west coast hospital a few weeks previously.

"Have you seen Eric?" asked the girl, who was holding three or four envelopes in her hand. At the risk of losing his balance, Tressidar leant sideways and peeped under his camp chair.

"I cannot see him anywhere here, Sister," he replied, loyalty to the retreating Fuller compelling him to avoid a direct reply. "At all events, I was left here in solitude to meditate upon the fraility of human friendship, when like a guiding star——"

"Please don't be idiotic," said Doris with mock severity. "Here is a telegram for you."

"Thank you," said the sub. promptly. "Now, won't you accept this vacant chair (believe me, it's very comfortable) and open the wretched thing for me? You know telegrams always give me a bad time. For instance, this flimsy, orange-coloured envelope might contain the information that my great-great-aunt has died and left a cool million to be divided equally between her one and only great-great-nephew and the Home for Lost and Anaemic Cats. So please open the fateful missive and read me the momentous news."

"You want a lot of humouring, Ronald," said the girl as she seated herself and began to rip open the envelope. "If all the other patients were like you——"

"Heaven forbid!" ejaculated Tressidar piously.

The wire was a "private tip" sent by a friend "up-topsides" at the Admiralty.

"*Your promotion dated from the twenty-ninth,*" read Doris.

"Hurrah!" exclaimed Tressidar joyously, sub. no longer but a full-fledged lieutenant. "This must be my birthday."

"*Also awarded D.S.O. for 'Anzac' affair,*" continued the girl. "Ronald, you are a lucky fellow. I congratulate you heartily. You seem to get everything you want."

Like a flash came the sailor's instinct to act promptly. Tressidar's powerful, bronzed hand closed over the girl's firm wrist.

"Ay," he rejoined. "And, best of all, you, Doris."